PRAISE

"*The Sea Lanterns* is a poignant and uncompromising novel. With gritty and luminous prose, Nickol demands the reader's attention on every page as he explores the price of ambition at all costs."

SOON WILEY, AUTHOR OF *WHEN WE FELL APART*

ABOUT THE AUTHOR

Ben Nickol is the author of two collections of short stories (*Where the Wind Can Find It* and *Sun River*) one novella (*Adherence*). His fiction and essays have appeared widely, in *Alaska Quarterly Review, Boulevard, Fourth Genre, Crab Orchard Review, Tin House Online*, and elsewhere. After teaching for several years in the MFA program at Wichita State University, he returned to the Inland Northwest to pursue a career in law. You can find him in the hills with his wife, Amy, and two young sons.

For more about Ben and his work, visit *www.bennickol.com*.

THE SEA LANTERNS

BEN NICKOL

www.vineleavespress.com

Print Edition
ISBN: 978-0-6454365-5-6
Published by Vine Leaves Press 2023

This is a work of fiction. Any similarity between the characters and situations within its pages and places or persons, living or dead, is unintentional and coincidental.

"Mission in Carmel" Copyright © 1961 by Richard Hugo, from *Making Certain It Goes On: Collected Poems of Richard Hugo* by Richard Hugo. Used by permission of W. W. Norton & Company, Inc.

Cover design by Jessica Bell
Interior design by Amie McCracken

 A catalogue record for this book is available from the National Library of Australia

For Joe—
Let's jump as high as we can, then land
on two feet

I believe the bones in any tomb
have moving parts, and something runs
unnamed across the altar
when candles dwindle and the church is dark.
Richard Hugo

PART 1

PART 1.

1.

MY BOSS IN PULLMAN, where I worked before Fog Harbor, always asked why I wanted to be an A.D. Clark was his name—Dale Clark. Maybe you've heard of him. He was an A.D. himself—he'd run four athletic departments, two of them at Power Five schools—but still he couldn't grasp the appeal. "Do you have eyes?" he'd ask me. I'd be sitting across the desk from him, expressionless, hands composed in my lap. Consequential figures, I'd noticed, always displayed composed hands, expressionless expressions; I'd drilled this into my tissue.

"I mean," Clark'd say, his DALE CLARK, DIRECTOR OF ATHLETICS nameplate taunting me like a middle finger, "do you see what you see when you see me?"

He meant that he was a chump. Yeah, he was paid. Yeah, he stood atop the heap. But his job was to hire glamorous coaches—celebrities, really—who made ten times what he did, and who did as they pleased for a year or two before fucking him however they chose. The missionary of fucking an A.D. was a recruiting violation: pay a kid cash. But coaches were lusty, and all the time invented new positions and angles. Get a DUI, grope an employee, punch an employee, say "colored players" into a microphone. Punch a wife, falsify a degree, *scream* "colored players" into a microphone. Choke a kid at practice. It got to where you hoped they'd simply lose games, which was a gentle, sweet way to be fucked. Though now and again, if an A.D. lived clean and said nightly prayers, a coach'd win titles and avoid scandal … and fuck his boss just once, with the crisp, clean pump of leaving for a better job. At which point, you smeared on lipstick and started over again.

"Be a surgeon," Clark told me. "You're a bright guy. Or a veterinarian. That's better than sports, nobody cares about animals."

Which was classic Clark. Talented man, but what he didn't get—or what he'd gotten once, decades ago, then forgotten—was you didn't select a life after weighing it on a scale. You didn't compare paths, ponder terrain. You *went*, and afterward that was you. And if you looked back? Well, if you look back, if you're that sort of person, then I don't have anything for you.

———

What were the chances it would be this soon, though? I mean, I knew I'd deal with them eventually, those insane narcissists, those sociopath coaches, once I landed a job legitimate enough *to* deal with them. And I wanted that, I ached for it. But who would've thought it'd be right away, the first gig I took after Pullman, here at Dickwater Community College on this depressing spit of coast? And who would've guessed that the coach who fucked me would have such a bizarre genius for it, would be a true Dali of slipping it to yours truly? In all my life, I'd never imagined a coach who would put a revolver to his team's temple and pull the trigger just because fuck it, because why not. Which is exactly what Leonard Kelly, my hoops coach, seems to be about. And yeah, this is *that* Leonard Kelly. University of Iowa Leonard Kelly. Cutting-down-the-nets, bronze-statue-in-front-of-Hawkeye Arena Leonard Kelly. Which, hey—not that

I'm bitching. To be the A.D. who hired Leo Kelly at Fog Harbor Community College? A man with Division I national championships (albeit in the '90s) coaching in the Western Cascade League? Who could complain?

I just wish Kelly wouldn't slash his program's wrists and bleed it into the Harbor. And I wish he wouldn't leave me out in the rain like this, on a bench, waiting to meet with him.

It's just starting—the rain, I mean—though rain never fully starts in Fog Harbor any more than it ever stops. I'm not convinced that Fog Harbor rain even *falls*, to be honest. It's just a hatch, a constant hatch, of wet flecky insects that bother your face and make thinking impossible. Nothing helps but smoking cigs, and with Leonard nowhere in sight, I tap one out. Before lighting it, naturally, I glance up and down First Street and across at the wharf. Nobody's around (it's Sunday, it's December, it's raining), but Fog Harbor is a judgy, backward place and you can't be too careful. Six generations of fishermen-loggers drinking to aneurysm down at Long Pier Saloon, but don't bet against some church hen organizing a coup on the Athletic Director because she saw him spark a Camel once downtown. Shit like that happens, believe me. But what can you do? The king, however sorry his kingdom, is prisoner to the castle.

"Five thousand miles," Kelly says from behind me, and I fumble my Camels into a puddle.

"Fuck, Leo," I say. "Jesus." I retrieve the ruined pack, water drizzling from its corners.

Glancing back, I see Kelly standing in the entryway to Greta's Diner, snug as you please in a black slicker and bucket hat. He gazes past me and past First Street, at the white surf crashing onto City Beach. And this, ladies and gentlemen—weird shit like this, from Leo Kelly—is what brings us here today, to this confab in the rain. Because you can't run an athletic department with coaches who skulk through town like murderers, sneaking up on people lighting cigarettes on benches. You can't run a department with that even in a city, to say nothing of running one in coastal Washington, where everybody's business is everybody's business and peculiar behavior is an affront to God. You can't have it, just as you can't have a coach who not only loses games but who, losing them, strolls onto the court during live action to confer with players and even hand them notes—*handwritten notes!* Just as you can't have a coach who calls timeout only to abandon his players' huddle and roam the sidelines alone, chewing sunflower seeds. Et cetera, et cetera. And with Coach Kelly, there's so much cetera. He hands his players fucking *notes*, for Christ's sake, on the *court*, which I wouldn't have believed had I not seen it myself on game film.

Anyhow, that's why we're meeting. As for why we're meeting here, on First Street, in the rain? You tell me. My assistant requested thirty minutes, to which Leo'd said, Thirty minutes, okay. I'll be at First Street and Bay Avenue, 4:00 p.m. Sunday. Rain or shine, he'd said, as if in Fog Harbor that meant anything but rain. We gave the fucker a nice office, too. Mid-century furniture. And what do I get out of it but a pack of soaked Camels.

"Five thousand what?" I say. "What'd you say?"

Kelly watches the sea. In his husky voice, like a tired farmer's, he says, "Five thousand miles of that. Just that. No islands, nothing. Black water clear to Sendai."

What this has to do with success in the Western Cascade League is beyond me, but then if Leo were interested in success in the WCL, we wouldn't be having this conversation. Scooting down the bench, my pants mopping the wood, I say, "Have a seat, Leo. Come on out from that dark doorway, why don't you? Let's chat."

The man stays standing, his fingers pinching a sunflower husk from his lip and brushing it to the sidewalk. I'm the farthest thing at this moment from starstruck, but it is still surreal, after eight months, to see Leonard Kelly's face in this boonie-ass, rainforest village. Like anyone famous, his face in the flesh appears huge, engorged as it is with the culture's awareness. On top of which Leo's face is actually huge, with a mouth, schnoz, and forehead like three blunt tools accustomed to crude use. You don't expect monuments like Leonard Kelly to push shopping carts up the aisle at Pacific County IGA or chew cod at Ron's Fish Market, and you don't think you'll glance over your shoulder in the rain to see his mug staring out at you from under a bucket hat. Even when you've been waiting in the rain for him to show up.

"Leo?" I gesture at the bench.

"It's right there," he says. "You feel the size of it. And that roar. It roars like that clear to Japan."

Stepping around the bench, Kelly sits with me and crosses his legs. He passes a hand down his jaw. When I open my mouth to speak, nothing comes out, and when I shift my posture to try again, I manage only a helpless grunt. I wonder: Where to begin with this jackass? After all, he is here, isn't he? He's coaching at Fog Harbor. When it comes to a Hall of Famer, isn't that already more than I could expect? Hasn't he already debased himself? At this point, shouldn't I just hand Leo the keys and let him drive his basketball program wherever he pleases, even if it's off a cliff?

The problem is hiring coaches who drive programs off cliffs reflects poorly on my judgment, so I can't let Kelly get up to the shit he gets up to. Not if I ever want a future I can't. What I ought to do, right here on this bench, is fire his ass. And I would fire him, too. But firing the guy you hired eight months ago also doesn't look good, particularly when severance guarantees are involved (as they always are). So it boils down to this: Leo needs to quit acting waterbrained. Fuck winning a conference title. Fuck excellence of any kind. The man needs to blend in so that come next year, there's only one story about the famous coach who took the job at Fog Harbor: against tremendous odds, up-and-coming Athletic Director Scott Darrow hired him. That'd be enough, and I could put this swampy dump in my rearview.

Crossing my own legs, I say, "Leo. So. Tell me about your progress with this basketball team."

"Hang on."

We sit in the rain, Kelly peering at something. Or peering at thin air, lost in thought.

"Scott," he says, "do you feel this mystery?"

"Pardon?"

"I was wondering that about you." He nods over his shoulder. "Watching you just now. Some people, they don't feel mysteries at all. They walk clean through them, clean through the heart of them." He ponders this. "It's part of the mysteries themselves, you might say. Though not an important part."

I stare at Leo.

"You don't have to answer," he says. "We feel mysteries without saying so. Or we don't feel them. It happens."

I say, "I feel the mystery, Leo. You bet I do."

Kelly lifts his face, appraising me from under his hat. His heavy, square face. His face like an aging general's. Nobody on earth, sitting in these drenched pants of mine, could hazard a guess as to what this motherfucker is talking about. But I'll feel his mystery. Why not? Who gives a shit? Leo looks off, bobbing his head appreciatively.

"You've ..." I try again. "I mean, thus far you've been imaginative, Leo. With your approach to this season."

Kelly laughs. And I smile with him, staying light, staying agreeable. "Can we talk about that?" I say. "Your approach to things? Can we get into that?"

"You may be right, Scott," he says. "You may be. Though I'd like to think my imagination's finally wearing off."

I wait for Leo to go on. But the rain falls around us. Nothing happens.

"Tell me about Rupert Ward," I say. Because Rupert Ward, to date, is Kelly's worst coaching causality. A three-star prospect, six-eight and agile, the kid was more celebrated than any Sea Lanterns recruit in history, till a month of Coach Kelly's practices inspired him to drop out and play in Mexico.

"Rupe?" Leo says. "Wonderful young man, lively man. Very early in his journey."

"I'm concerned about the circumstances of his departure, Coach."

"Well. Early in his journey."

A truck turns up First, an old Datsun bleeding its headlights everywhere in the rain. Its tires fan water, and I see at the wheel the same face I see everywhere in Fog Harbor: ball cap, bearded, bitter. It'll be driving the next truck and the next, it'll sit on porches, it'll glare at me at Ron's, chewing its clams. If I lose my patience with Kelly, sitting on this bench, it has to do with yokels like this guy, driving beaters like his. After all, Leo's nonsense punches holes in my boat—wide, jagged holes—and I will not sink in this shitty town with its shitty, desperate people. I will not—end of story. "Leo," I say, the fire coming into me. "I'm going to lay this out there. Okay? I'm going to make this damn clear. It's too weird. Do you understand me? It's too funny. This shit you're doing, with all the weird shit and everything? We're not doing that shit anymore. Do you understand what I'm saying? No more of that. Tell me you understand."

Kelly stares again, at the dusk coming on, at the sea.

"Did you hear me?"

"If you don't know, Scott, I can only try to show you." He wags his finger. "Though you said you felt it. The mystery. You did."

"Okay. And you said you'd coach basketball when I hired you as my basketball coach. Now we've both disappointed each other. Let's get back to normal."

Scraping a seed from his lip, Kelly says, "This is that. Don't you worry, Scott. It's that."

"What?"

"Anything true is normal."

I have no arrows left in my quiver, unless I want to confront Leo with the one thing. But I don't know that the one thing's even a thing. I could float it. I could try. *Coach,* I could say, *is this about Michael? Is he causing all this?* But what's a dead uncle—if that's what Michael is to Kelly, since I'm not even sure—got to do with walking notes out onto the basketball court, mid-game?

"I hope we can find some common ground," is all I manage to say.

And Coach Kelly, *the* Coach Kelly of Iowa Hawkeye fame, squeezes my knee. "It's all ground, Darrow," he says. "Even deep underwater, it's ground."

Oh, Dale. Dale, Dale Clark. I admit it'd feel better, on a day like today, to wear white scrubs and euthanize collies for a living.

There's no light in the sky. Rubbing his jaw, Leo wanders off up First Street, reappearing under streetlight after streetlight.

2.

I SLEEP BADLY, in my condo on Bay Avenue, bad sleep being symptomatic of interacting with Leo Kelly, and symptomatic as well of owning and inhabiting Unit 2F of Sea Breeze Court, South Bay Avenue, Fog Harbor, WA 98525. From the moment I bought 2F, with its octopus door knocker and address plate of infantile blue waves, I knew I'd despise it. It's cheap, near campus and clean (I'd buy it again, if it came to that), but it's also dead, the heart of its deadness being a prehistoric, yolk-colored refrigerator. The appliance runs beautifully, don't get me wrong—it hums along with a soft, linoleum-vibrating purr. But the weight of it, all that yellow steel, anchors my life in a sad, forgotten decade, the seventies or eighties, I'm not sure which. That the fridge runs like it does only aggravates my dread. The seventies must be *now, today,* with *me trapped inside of them,* if this dinosaur hasn't slowed down.

There's the fridge, and there's how night seeps into the condo, night and silence, like tides purling in. The cream walls become dimmer cream walls, walls with dejected faces. Night and silence should encourage sleep, you'd think, but night in 2F isn't entirely night. A blue floodlight on the walkway saturates my blinds, drenching the bedroom in undersea hues. Rain muddles the silence. Always rain. I can't hear it, necessarily, but from my bed

I look out into the living room, where the shadow of rain on windowpanes streaks and stains my walls and the boxes stacked out there. The boxes are loaded and taped shut. They'll stay that way till I leave.

And to boot: I'm a shitty sleeper. Always have been.

If I use an alarm clock in the morning, it's only the thinning of the walkway's light and the evaporation of those shadows on the boxes and walls—it's when the walls lift their faces, the tides ebbing. I shave and shower. Addressing the mirror, I adjust my bearings till the figure before me is pressed and angular, a knife of attainment, a viper (however baggy his eyes).

Hiking up the path to campus (cutting through the woods knocks six minutes off my commute), my Allen Edmonds Oxfords collect the mud I'll buff from them later. Last year, when I started at Fog Harbor, I'd stop on this path, lick a thumb, and remove each splotch as I acquired it. That I've ceased doing this troubles me vaguely. Pacific County, with its endless water, must be eroding my discipline, until, like the state park's bird shitty cliffs, I'll slump into the sea. Speaking of birds, they chitter and call overhead. Rain drips from branches onto my overcoat and neck, and I smack at the droplets as if beset by mosquitos (which, come summer, I will be).

It was on this path, last April, that I first heard the name Michael in connection with Leo Kelly. I heard it straight from Leo's mouth, no less, though he didn't know it. It was a day like today, wet and flat, because all days in Fog Harbor are wet and flat—December, April, whenever. I was walking down the hill toward town, where, believe it or not, I was meeting someone for drinks. Legitimately an actual Pacific County woman, one of eight or so in The Harbor who weren't yet fifty and also weren't enrolled at the college—and of the eight, one of three with teeth.

Though this woman, Jade, just the same was missing one tooth, an upper incisor. A soils biologist, she'd lost the tusk on a mountainside in Canada when a colleague climbing upslope kicked debris into her mouth. Fixing the tooth would've been simple, but Jade liked her disfigurement, liked the prestige of it, the legend. And she was pretty, even with that one black piano key.

Anyway. I was walking to town to meet Jade, stopping to thumb mud from my shoes, when I saw off the path, in the trees, the famous new coach I'd hired for Men's Basketball. This was weeks after Kelly'd arrived in Fog Harbor—months yet before he'd start coaching, and via his coaching, fuck everything up. In a word, it was still pleasant to see the man out and about, even on a chilly day, and even if Fog Harbor otherwise was a drag. Deciding to say hi, I stepped off the path and started toward him, kicking aside vines and ducking under boughs. Kelly would've heard me coming, but forests in Pacific County are so clogged with sound—with birds, insects, water, all that shit—that footsteps approaching won't necessarily catch your ear. Plus, I saw, he was distracted.

Hello caught in my throat. I stopped short of Leo, concealed in some brush. Leonard is a big man, as I've said, and that day his clothes amplified his largeness: he wore a broad, dark jacket, scarf and tweed hat. He seemed very *assembled* for a man standing in a forest, near dusk, as if a briefcase should wait at his heel and at any moment a train pull into station to carry him off. But where the tracks should've run, there ran instead a shallow stream—the same stream that bisected Fog Harbor's campus before tipping off the hill toward town and the sea. Head cocked, Kelly seemed to listen to the stream, to its muttering. Or he was peering up the bank, as if a train might arrive for him yet.

I'm not sure why I didn't greet Leo, except that his manner discouraged it. He wasn't rigid so much as alert, attuned—*vigilant* is probably the word—and I might've unsettled that by speaking. (Plus, nothing keeps me "in the brush" like another person's unguarded, un-self-conscious moments. No thank you.) As I watched, Kelly seemed less to listen to the stream, or to anything, than to listen *for* … what, a voice? A message? Who knows? But what he expected must've been near, by his judgment. It must've floated just beyond detection, because he waited with mouth ajar, scanning the woods for it.

I'd decided to leave, quietly, when Kelly's hand lifted, pinching a seed from his lip. Peering the other way down the stream, rocking onto his toes and off again, the man said, at full volume, "Oh, Michael. We're out here somewhere, aren't we? A lot of somewhere for us to be."

It's hard to explain, but Leo's appearance in the forest, and even his speech to nobody, didn't strike me then as terribly unusual. It still doesn't, taken on its own. Remember, I've encountered over the years my share of maestro coaches, and very few of them—none, actually—have exhibited functional, non-psychotic behavior. Take our football coach in Pullman: eight bowl appearances in ten years, and that man believed that a tribe of ninjas would someday adopt him and teach him their warrior code. I'm not making this up—go read about it. Anticipating his adoption, the guy read widely on ninja culture and customs, and in the offseason traveled to martial arts conventions in Hokkaido and the Philippines. It's not that you don't notice how deranged these people are, it's that they win. Past that, be deranged if you want, fuck it, who cares?

Leo moved upstream, hands at his back, then stepped over the stream and continued into the woods, till he disappeared. I walked to town to meet Jade. That name, Michael, didn't matter much to me, any more than it mattered in June, at the Fog Harbor regents meeting, when Kelly interrupted the proceedings because somebody in the room said it, somebody said the name. *Michael.*

The "culprit," if that's what she was, was Lisa Travers, our provost, and actually she didn't say Michael, she said something else. The chancellor'd posed a question, and not knowing the answer, Dr. Travers had turned to her assistant, covering her microphone, and said, "Might call Olympia on that." I know that's what Lisa said because I sit near her at regents' meetings. Just enough of *might call* leaked through her fingers into the mic, however, that Leo, who'd spent the session staring out the window (he was only at the meeting to begin with because we have a regent from Dubuque who'd insisted we invite him, so he could meet the famous coach in person), swung his gaze toward Lisa, studying her hard. The conversation had moved on when Kelly said, into his own mic, "What'd you say?"

There were seventy people in the room. Nobody knew who Leo was addressing, or why.

Kelly nodded. "Gal in the blue sweater. You."

Dr. Travers, bewildered, glanced down at her sweater.

"That's a powerful name you said," Leo said. "You touched this room with that. This is a changed room."

Everybody held still, not speaking, not breathing. I heard it again in my mind, *might call,* and remembered Kelly's odd remarks by the stream that day. *Oh, Michael. We're out here somewhere, aren't we?*

Eventually, clearing his throat, the chancellor moved down his agenda, bringing the meeting to order. I thought: Okay. So Leo has a Michael thing. That's a thing with him. Only, what would

I do with that information? Kelly's things weren't my business, and I didn't expect them to become my business. I shuffled pages, keeping pace with the meeting.

The name Michael didn't matter to me even a few months ago, when I happened into a classroom in Jubinsky Fieldhouse, the whiteboard of which overflowed with X's and O's, arrows, the sorts of schematics one found on whiteboards in fieldhouses. And under the several plays were written their several names: *Mikey, Mikey₂, Mikey High-Low, Press Break Mikey.*

Given what I know now about Leo's coaching, it's surprising that basketball plays of any sort appeared on that whiteboard, Kelly being totally uninterested in basketball as an enterprise. But that morning, all I understood was: Yeah, it's definitely a thing. Leo has a Michael thing. It didn't *mean* anything till November, when Kelly went off the rails, passing his fucking notes, scaring off Rupert Ward, spitting his seeds onto the court and, of course, losing. At that point, suddenly everything mattered and nothing wasn't my business. As for how a name, Michael, might've dragged Sea Lanterns Basketball into the shitter, I didn't and still don't know. Maybe "Michael" has nothing to do with it. But it was an oddity, and Kelly's oddities were demanding attention.

It nagged at me until last week, when I sat in my office late at night after hanging up with a friend in Spokane, who'd caught that evening's Sea Lanterns game at North Idaho College. I'd caught the score, 42-90, but could only speculate as to the hijinks that'd occasioned it. There weren't highlights from the game, nor articles online—there never are for Fog Harbor sports, which I hate but which has become a blessing.

Before talking business, my friend wanted to catch up. "Tell me about life on the coast, Darrow. Shit, nobody hears from you.

You eating clams yet?" He laughed. "Or do clams still make you blush?"

"You see anything weird tonight?" I said. "At the game?"

"Or, let's cut to the chase."

I sat at my desk, awaiting an answer.

"What do you mean, weird? Weird how?"

Tentatively, this was encouraging. Coach Kelly's species of weird, you didn't need to narrow the question. People saw it, they knew what weird you meant. So had nothing happened in Idaho? Was Leo normal now, besides traveling the Northwest losing by fifty at every stop? It'd gotten to where that problem, the losing, seemed a beautiful problem to have, if it could be my only one.

But then my friend said, "You mean weird like playing Enya on the sidelines, out of a boom box? Because your coach did that. Or do you mean weird like watching the wrong end of the court all game, which he also did?"

I stared out the window, but it was midnight and I could see only myself in the glass, staring back at me. Myself pebbled with rain.

My friend whooped with laughter. "*Yeah*, I saw weird shit at the game, Scotty! Fuck, what's up with this guy? You sure you got the right Leo Kelly? I mean, he looks like Kelly. But Christ, he's out to lunch."

I tossed the phone onto my desk. My friend's voice droned on; I tapped END and stared at the lifeless phone while a janitor entered, piloting a vacuum ahead of him. He nosed it under the desk, bumping my toes, then withdrew into the hall.

Concerning Coach Kelly, the required action, plainly, was to wait at the gym till the team returned from Idaho, then slit his throat as he stepped off the bus. Short of that, I needed another means of domesticating the man. The specifics of what I should do eluded me, but to domesticate anything you needed to sand down what made it feral. You needed—and in this way, what went for hounds went as well for coaches—to purge its hide of ticks. For all I knew, Kelly was infested with ticks. His poor brain function certainly testified to that. But I knew absolutely of just one, and started groping around for it.

For the rest of that night, till dawn paled in the window and elevators lurched in their shafts, bringing my staff up to work, I casted around on my tablet for any Michaels I could find in relation to Leonard Kelly. There was what you'd expect—former players named Michael, former assistant coaches, an associate head coach from Leo's years at New Mexico State, a sportswriter he'd locked horns with in Iowa City. That I could tell, nobody had claim to being *the* Michael, though—nobody, in other words, had any business on Kelly's tongue at dusk in a rainforest, and nobody would "touch a room" or merit plays named in his honor. All night, as I searched, I nibbled unlighted Camels, sucking through them like straws to get the flavor. The smoke detectors in my building, Coleman Hall, probably are decoys to save the college money. Still, I didn't want to gamble.

It wasn't until my assistant, Jeremy, knocked at the door to say good morning, then retreated to his desk to scroll Insta, that I discovered something. In the archives of a defunct student newspaper at Mendota College of Wisconsin was a profile the paper had run decades ago, when Kelly was an assistant at MCW, and going not by Leo, but by "L. Robert Kelly."

I stared at that name a long time. The Camel dropped from my lip, and I caught it and put it back again. My oh my, I thought. L. Robert Kelly. What was he, a railroad magnate? Was he endowing libraries? Going *initial-name-name* in one's twenties required astonishing arrogance, particularly from the low pedestal of Mendota College, but if I was embarrassed for Leo, I also had to admit that, achievement-wise, he had eventually cashed the check that *L. Robert Kelly* was writing.

The profile was trash, unless my interests ran toward L. Robert Kelly's favorite movies and food, or how that year's Mendota Lions would "fight, really fight and contend, at both ends of the floor." I would've disregarded it except that *Mike*, owing to my search, was highlighted throughout the page.

The name first appeared under the super daring question: *What advice can you give to aspiring coaches out there?*

Given the tenor of the interview, I'd have expected Leo to say *Give one hundred percent, one hundred percent of the time*, or even push it further, to a hundred-and-ten percent or a thousand. Instead, the tenor of the interview shifted. Kelly said he had just one piece of advice, and it was advice his uncle had given him—his Uncle Mike, who'd coached football in Chadron, Nebraska, where Leo was from.

The advice was: *Kiddo, only losers want to feel like winners. Winners don't care what winning feels like.*

I don't know if silence descended on the room, the student "journalist" stunned speechless by Kelly's real talk, or what happened. But there must've been empty air, since Leo went on, sharing more about Uncle Mike. It was his uncle, Kelly said, who'd welcomed him into the coaching profession, shaking him awake at 4:00 a.m. every weekday in October to drag sleds and tires out onto the practice field. No sloppy jobs about it, either: sixteen tires, paired rows of four, sleds aligned in fours at the twenty- and forty-yard lines. *And you didn't mess around, no sir,* Leo said. He mentioned the chill of those mornings, his numb hands and nose, and how he'd loved sitting with his uncle in the stands once everything was ready, eating donuts while daybreak warmed their faces.

Not a very cheerful person, Kelly said of Uncle Mike. *Till the day he died, pretty much an a**hole. But boy, he showed me about coaching. He believed in good football.*

After which, the interviewer asked whether Leo'd visit Mars or the ocean floor, given the chance.

It was 8:30, the gray light in my office the same gray light that'd fill the room at noon, at 4:30, at 6:00. A fresh Camel on my lip, I crossed to the window, where students passed below carrying neon umbrellas, or else sprinted building to building, drowning in their hoodies. Mike, I thought. Uncle Mike from Chadron. Are you fucking my coach's brain?

And maybe he is, but I don't know what to do about it. Instead, arriving at the office this morning, shoes fucked and muddy, I grab my tablet and start investigating Kelly's staff, their bios. After all, there's various ways to domesticate a coach. If you can't remove his ticks, you can sneak up with a collar.

3.

HARVEY CROWE, Kelly's associate head coach, wouldn't go for it. He and Leo go way back, to Iowa and farther, and in fact it was Harvey who first approached me about Leo's interest in the Fog Harbor job. Maybe he'd go for it, but not likely, since old-timers like Crowe believe fiercely in loyalty, and anyhow aren't very imaginative.

Kelly's second assistant likewise is out. A bowl-cutted dipshit wearing, in his headshot, an ironed polo shirt buttoned to the throat, the man lists among his "honors" ambassador work for Habitat for Humanity and the Fellowship of Christian Athletes. Rectitude like this can be plowed into darker uses, for sure. It's never difficult to weaponize a believer. But Coach Dipshit quit last month to dig wells in Haiti or something, and they just haven't updated our website.

Kelly's third assistant, Peter Muraro, isn't in Haiti, though, and from what I can tell, he and Leo go only as far back as March, when Kelly hired him. Before that, Peter was an assistant under Leo's predecessor, Duane Olsen. Maybe this Muraro is disgruntled about that, about Duane getting axed so Fuckbrains could take over? That isn't so far-fetched. Plus, given Kelly's zero investment in Sea Lanterns Basketball, you'd have to suspect that the decision to retain Peter Muraro amounted only to indifference, not enthusiasm. In other words, Peter's here because he was here already, and Kelly didn't give a shit. If I suspect that, then it's likely Peter suspects it. And if Peter feels irrelevant, well, then he's my guy. After all, if you seek a puppet, look for the man dangling by a thread. At twenty-four, stubby and bald, with no experience as an athlete besides at the high school J.V. level (an accomplishment featured in Peter's bio, unbelievably), and no prior coaching experience except as a student manager at Sac State, Muraro is certainly dangling. In fact, I would say about Peter what I'd say about practically no one else living: he is lucky to work at Fog Harbor. Now, it's time to lean on Peter's luck. It's time to make him carry water.

We didn't give Muraro an office, that I know of. But it doesn't matter, since crossing campus toward Jubinsky Fieldhouse to find him, I happen upon the kid himself, trudging up the hill from the woods. He wears sneakers, shorts and a t-shirt, all Sea Lanterns maroon. What Peter's doing out in weather like this in clothes like that, I haven't the faintest. He's shivering, his forehead furrowed with discomfort. He's drenched from knees to belly, and yet, weirdly, dry from shoulders down. This makes no sense, but whatever. Smiling, my teeth a white beacon for Peter, I plant myself where his path will meet mine, commanding West Quad in my overcoat and lambskin gloves.

"Pete," I say.

This startles Muraro, who without my hailing him would've charged right by. He inspects me, rain bothering his face, then wags a finger in recognition.

"Scott Darrow," I say.

"Of course. I'm sorry."

"You're a damn bullet train this morning. Where're you headed?"

Nodding up the hill, Muraro says, "Trying to get inside. I'm freezing."

Beyond his sopping clothes, I notice Peter's shins are gritty with silt or sand. He shivers, vibrating in his skin, and I glance past him down the quad to where a line of trees marks the state park boundary. "Hang on," I say. "Pete, were you just at the *beach*?"

Muraro nods, though without the zest of a beachgoer.

"What in the hell for?" I say. Though actually, this beach thing isn't surprising. I'd heard Leo and his guys were fucking around down at the water lately, at what's called The Cove, never mind that it's December and never mind that these aren't clam diggers, but actually a basketball team. Peter and I aren't discussing Leo yet, however, and so I just say: "I don't know that that's such a bright idea, Pete. You know it's almost Christmas."

"I should get inside," he says.

I step aside, waving Muraro on. Then as he's walking away, I call to him: "Listen, why don't you and me get coffee, Pete? That sound good? Get you warmed up, Jesus."

Peter glances around, then squints at me in the rain. "Can I change first?"

"Yeah, get to it. Get in there." When Peter's nearly to the Fieldhouse, I shout after him, "Meet me over at Greta's, Pete! We'll get you some soup!"

I'm crossing campus toward town when the rest of them march out of the trees: Kelly, followed by Harvey Crowe and finally players and managers, the lot of them in maroon gear, soaked to their bellies. Exiting the procession, Leo peers at me across the quad. Then he waves broadly, smiling over the heads and umbrellas of passing students. Some mist obscures him before he's vivid again, smiling, waving. I think: You bet, cocksucker. Have a ball.

Therese at the diner, who once explained to me that she's Greta's great-niece, the greasy spoon having been in their clan since steam engines ran Fog Harbor's logging, shows me to a booth up front. But one booth over sit some pensioners smacking their gums and reading aloud from a paper, and past them sit three cannery grunts in shitty jackets looking mad. When Peter arrives, we'll say things I don't want people hearing, and so it won't do to have such company.

"How about back there?" I say, and Therese hesitates before collecting the menus and silverware she just put down. "Sorry," I say.

"No, no. It's fine."

We make our way back to a cramped, neglected booth by the toilets. I get comfortable and Therese brings coffee.

While waiting for Peter, I think awhile about his position, and about what I'd need to hear in Muraro's position to be ... well, to be *companionable* to an unorthodox professional gambit (unorthodox, in this case, meaning stupid as hell for Peter to go along with, no matter how I sell him on it). Peter Muraro, age twenty-four. Bachelor of Science, Kinesiology, C.S.U. Sacramento. I don't know Peter, but kids his age usually worship breezy confidence. They'll find the man with steady hands and follow him over a cliff. So I'll give Peter that, and give him furthermore the sense that capers like what I'm proposing are standard fare. Third-chair assistants conspire with A.D.s to depose head coaches all the time. Said assistants operate shadow teams for their A.D.s within a team's existing framework. They do, Pete! It's normal business! That'll work on Muraro, I expect, and if it doesn't, I'll find other levers. There's always other levers.

The coffee cools, its steam vanishing (I can't drink the piss at Greta's, which is weak to the point of translucence and probably brewed with rainwater from barrels), and I'm thinking about Muraro, about using him, but also I'm pondering the bric-a-brac lining the shelves at Greta's, the teapots and dolls and spoons and butter churns and trowels and decorative plates and kites and pincushions and harmonicas—generally the mess of shit that blows into diners like this one and stays, like ratty bags accruing in tree branches. The light in Greta's, humming from the dropped ceiling, is a friendlier, sanitized shade of the dullness outside, blanketing First Street and the waterfront. But for the waterfront, this place would remind me of where my parents and I ate pancakes decades ago, after church in Hamilton, Montana. Bedford Street Café, that place was called, and maybe still is, who knows?

Wagon wheels were the thing at Bedford Street Café—wagon wheels, plow attachments and watercolors of fierce peaks. The décor burdened everything, from the walls and windowsills to what should've been the usable square footage (as many farm implements milled around the pie case as customers). Arriving at the café after church, fatigued from kneeling and pretending, we'd claim a table at the window, where leaves blew by in the street. Leaves in Hamilton always blew up the streets, since fall came off the Bitterroots as early as August, and since Montana winds actually ripped leaves from trees in any season, even when they were new and green.

Hamilton. Six years we lived there, from my fifth-grade summer through most of high school, and I loved it—loved its dry, edged light, loved walking to school with no sounds in my ears but my own breathing and the frost crunching underfoot. I loved my friends. I loved Mr. and Mrs. Ahlberg, who let kids play hoops in their driveway late into the night, and who even installed floodlights for us. What else. I loved the mountains west of Hamilton, which loomed over town like a secret nobody acknowledged. I loved the red maples. I even loved Hamilton's wind, which less blew through town than prowled its alleys, waiting to rush up sidewalks and fuck with hair. Not least of all, I loved the pancakes at Bedford Street Café, and the runny eggs, the charred sausage, that one waitress with her trashy perm who always sucked grease from her thumb.

Peter should be here by now. It's been twenty minutes, and Therese wants me to order and the cannery guys want to fight or maybe fuck me, given the bad looks they're shooting my way. Let's get this thing with Muraro going. I don't want to sit here thinking about Hamilton today, and about the nights watching *Seinfeld* with my parents, Mom tossing popcorn into my hair— about walking home from the Ahlbergs under galaxies, just galaxies of stars, or about the mornings I'd walk with Dad to Main Street Bridge to watch logs pinwheel downriver, riding the spring melt. I don't want to think about that, and I don't want to think about leaving Hamilton—about moving to Cleveland with Mom senior year. About enrolling at Kent State, one year later, since KSU was what we could afford. I don't want to think about Mom being mad. I don't want to think about Dad in Hawaii (the halves of my parents' marriage having split like cordwood, landing six time zones and an ocean apart), and the year he sent money for me to visit him in Hilo over Christmas.

That was something. Dad had sent $800, and as I browsed flights in my dorm room in Kent, eyes glazing over, I found myself thinking less about itineraries and more about the few facts I'd learned about Hilo. It was Hawaii's capital—I knew that. Also, the Chamber of Commerce there had stylized Hilo as

"Aloha's orchid capital." But my questions were basically these: what the fuck does Hilo, Hawaii matter to me, and what the fuck is an orchid? All I knew with certainty was that Hamilton, Montana would not greet me at the Hilo Airport with a lei. All I knew about orchids was they weren't red maples.

So, opening an email, I typed to my dad: *Pops, it's been real. I'm happy you were my dad, but I guess it's on to other stuff now. Unless you need it, I'll keep that flight $$. Love you, Pop. Merry Christmas and decorate a palm tree for me.*

After exams, my friends and I took Dad's money to Killington to ski. That felt right and still does. After all, Killington was out ahead of me, far in the distance, whereas Hilo was just where some memories had washed ashore. And, ever since, ahead is where I've kept my attention, alert for what's coming and fine, just fine, with what's over and gone. Enough remains to be decided, believe me, without digging in the ground for what was decided already, by other people. Mom, Dad, we had our years in Hamilton. And that's that.

The door jangles, Muraro entering in a dry hoodie and jeans. I lean out of the booth, hand raised. "Pete. Back here."

—

He eats voraciously, chicken salad to go with his soup and fries. Meanwhile, I watch Peter stuff himself with a keen, almost fatherly absorption, as if nothing pleases me more than to see him nourished. Muraro's embarrassed, as I haven't touched my own soup, but embarrassment doesn't slow his chewing, swallowing, chewing and gulping, punctuated with dainty burps. Incidentally, this is exactly the conduct I'll expect from Peter going forward: I set out his bowl and he eats.

Therese clears our plates, my soup going exactly as it came, except cold. I tell Peter to order pie.

"Pie?" He laughs. "I'm okay. Just more coffee?"

"More coffee," I tell Therese, as if she hasn't heard him.

Alone, without food dividing us, I reach into Peter's space and knuckle the table. "More coffee, I'm not surprised. Shit, you must be hypothermic, Pete. The fuck were you doing down at the beach?"

He shakes his head, gazing out the window. A man out there smokes under the awning, scratching his jaw, and I would enjoy smashing this glass, plucking the cig from homeboy's mouth and swallowing it like candy. But I'm not thinking about cigarettes now.

"Let's just say," Muraro says, "Coach thought it'd be good for us. Wake us up or something."

"Wake you up? Swimming in the ocean, Pete? It's forty fucking degrees out."

"I know. I don't know. It's like a metaphor with him."

Therese fills our coffees, adding just drops to my untouched mug. I say, "A metaphor, huh? You lost me there."

"It's like …" Muraro digs at his ear, thinking. "Waking up *to* something, you know? Opening our minds?"

I let this explanation hover between us like a dumb blimp. Peter laughs. "I know. I don't get it either."

"Seems like you'd wake up to fucking pneumonia."

"Right? Though we didn't *swim* swim. It wasn't like that."

"No? Is that a metaphor, too?"

Muraro laughs.

"You seemed pretty literally soaked," I say. "When I saw you."

"It's more … I guess you'd call it wading? And praying?"

I tilt my head toward Peter.

"I know," he says.

"Did you say praying?"

"You know," Muraro says, "I don't know what it is. Coach has us do lots of stuff. He calls it praying, but then he calls it *encountering* and *witnessing*. I can't keep up."

"I didn't realize we were running a church camp here."

Peter laughs, and this is good, I need him laughing. Each chuckle, each sneer, adds vocabulary to the private language we'll maul Leonard Kelly with. L. Robert Kelly. Soon, it'll be the only language Muraro speaks. I say, "So Leo baptized you this morning in the harbor. Is that what I'm hearing?"

When he laughs, Peter's scalp draws taut in the diner's light, inviting a spear of glare onto his forehead, like a horn. He says, "Yeah, I guess so. I hadn't thought of it like that, but yeah."

I shake my head.

Gazing at his mug, Muraro says, "What can I say? It's odd stuff. All this stuff. But I guess it's Leo Kelly, right? *The* Leo Kelly. I've got to believe it works."

"I still don't get it. What'd he have you doing down there, Pete? Wading and praying? What is that?"

Peter gazes out the window, where the man's pitched his cig and walked off. Pitched it with half an inch remaining, I might add, onto a dryish scrap of sidewalk. Why, an enterprising bum or athletic director could yet salvage that cigarette. Goddamn you, Leo Kelly. Making me drop my pack in that puddle. After lunch, I'll need to go get more.

Muraro says, "It was like everything he has us do. I don't know what it was. Maybe someone else understands it? I mean, some of the guys get pretty into Coach's stuff. They act like they do. Maybe it's an emperor's clothes thing? Who knows. But yeah, it was one of our *feeling* exercises. It's always about *feeling* with

Coach. Feeling, sensing, all of that. Praying. He loves those words. And *mystery*. That's his favorite one."

I nod. "I've heard him say that."

"So he gets us down on the beach." Peter shifts in the booth. "And I mean, it was supposed to be practice. Seven a.m. practice, meet at the Jub. But guys don't even dress out for practice anymore, not really. They know practice isn't practice, even when we do use the gym, which isn't often. So whatever. We're lying around the locker room, the group of us, waiting to see what happens. Nobody knows what's going on. Even Harvey doesn't know. In walks Coach with his, like, thoughtful look. You know the look I mean? His thoughtful face?"

"I do," I say. And I'm happy Muraro's talking like this. After all, he wouldn't have cataloged Leo's faces and pet phrases unless he resented the man, and that'll save me the trouble of convincing Peter he resents him. Instead, I'll just need to water and feed Muraro's resentment, and keep it in the sun.

"It's his *priest* look," Peter says. "Now that I think of it. Which is funny with what you said about baptism and stuff. Anyway, he comes in wearing his priest look and says, 'I believe the tides are speaking to us this morning, gentlemen. Let's go see.'"

I laugh.

"It's not even light out. It's thirty degrees or whatever and we're walking through the woods to the ocean. Carrying flashlights."

"In the rain."

Muraro nods. "In the rain. Yeah."

"Not what I would call basketball practice."

"So he gets us out on the beach," Peter says. "Down at The Cove. And have you been to The Cove? It's nuts down there, Scott. Tides surging everywhere. There's just that one trail out of there, and not everybody swims great, either. Anyway. I guess it's light out by then, but not really. Coach, he doesn't say a word about it. He starts grabbing our arms and getting us in place."

"In place?"

Peter nods. "There's always some way he wants us standing. Or sitting. Or he'll be like, 'Sit cross-legged. Okay, now stand and relax your arms. How's that feel?'"

"I don't get it," I say.

Peter stares at me, face blank.

I laugh. "Sorry, okay. I'll forget about getting it. Got it. So he gets you in place ..."

Muraro sips his coffee. "Yeah. And it was weird this time. I mean, it always is. Weird isn't weird with Coach. But it was weird. He spaced us down the beach, somebody every ten feet or so. Facing the waves."

"And this is everybody?"

"Walk-ons, managers, everybody. Down to that equipment girl, Kayla. Who can't swim at *all*."

"I'm trying to picture this."

"It's weird," Muraro says. "Picture weird."

"And that's it? What, you pray and jump in the water?"

"Basically. Except we stand there awhile first. Like, a long while. Maybe forty minutes. That's always part of Coach's stuff, the standing around. He calls it *surrendering*."

"I don't get it."

Before Muraro can speak, I lay a hand on his wrist. "I'm kidding, Pete. Just kidding. Jesus."

He shakes his head. "It's not funny."

I wait for Peter to go on. And hopefully Muraro feels this waiting, this deference I show him. Hopefully he believes: *Scott Darrow is on my side. All the way.*

He says, "Anyway, so we're standing there. It's cold. I don't know where Coach went, and then I see him up in the cliffs, sort of perched there. He does that sometimes, wanders off. After a while, the sun's coming up. Or it's getting light, anyway. The tide backs up, thank God. Oh and geez," Muraro laughs, "I almost forgot. I'm standing next to Matty Martin. You know Matty, from San Diego?"

I nod.

"He falls asleep. Completely asleep, just locks his knees and nods off. Like a horse. Which, pretty valuable skill if you're playing for Leo Kelly. Anyway, Coach eventually comes down. He kicks off his shoes and starts walking behind us, asking questions."

Therese fills Muraro's coffee. He nods his thanks.

"Questions," I say. "Why do I get the feeling these aren't basketball questions?"

"Well," Muraro says, "you tell me if they're basketball questions. *What waits behind the evening? Is that a basketball question? How about, Where'd you leave your heart when you went looking for a door?*"

"Not hearing basketball," I say.

"*Who collects lost keys? How many yous left you at the station?*"

At the station. Hearing those words, I remember Kelly in the woods, peering up a streambed like his train would come chugging in. Or like it'd departed without him. I remember his cocked ear, the sunflower husk dropping from his hand. As if this memory holds any clue. As if clues are even important, now that I'm past understanding Leo and on to clipping his wings.

"Not that he wants answers to this stuff," Peter says. "He's just filling up the air. He calls it *catalyzing.*"

"My concern," I say, "is that he calls it coaching, Pete. To be honest with you."

Muraro nods. "I know what you mean."

"But keep going."

Peter eases back in the booth. He shrugs. "That's about it. Coach finishes his questions and we're all standing there. Somebody throws a rock at Matty to wake him up. Then Coach gets out in front of us. He says, 'Not a thing on earth didn't come from the ocean.' Some big statement like that. 'Not a thing didn't come from it, and nothing doesn't swim in it still. Including time. Including what's lost.'"

I dig knuckles into my eye sockets.

Peter says, "Then he walked in. Just up to his chest or so. He stood there with the waves hitting him, looking around at the birds. He didn't make us get in, I guess, but then Harvey walked in after him. Harvey always gets it started."

"Is that right?"

Muraro nods. "He won't let Coach look stupid. Not in a million years. So yeah, Harvey walks in. People start walking in behind him. Pretty soon, everybody's standing in the harbor."

I let Peter's account of the morning hang between us, Greta's bad coffee cooling at my wrist. Then I say, "So pretty good practice, all and all?"

When our laughter subsides, I devote a moment to appraising Muraro, my face pensive. Not that I'm lost in thought. Like I said, I hatched my plan for Peter hours ago, reading his bio at my desk. Here, I'm just showing the kid my wheels turning. That way, later, he'll believe we hatched this plan together, right at this table.

"Pete," I say. "Can I make a guess about you? Just a wild guess?"

"Oh," Muraro says. "Okay ..."

I wag a finger at him: "You understand that Leonard Kelly is bullshit. He's psychotic."

Peter laughs, but I don't. When he's finished, I say, "You do. You get it. The shit he pulls? Some people think it's … innovative. Is that the word? Like he's thinking outside the box. But there's no fucking box. There's an old asshole who's lost it. And you know it."

Muraro chews his lip—wincing, or else suppressing a smile.

"Thinking outside the box," I say. "The man's not thinking at all. Thinking isn't a tool in his shed."

Peter isn't smiling, it turns out. He shakes his head, frowning. "I'm not sure," he says, "we should be talking like this. About Coach."

I think, Good for you. Good on you, Peter. You're more alert than I gave you credit for. Not alert enough, though. "Pete," I say, "believe me. I couldn't agree more. Leo's your coach, the man hired you. It can't feel good having this conversation."

He eyes me cautiously.

"Hell, think about it from my perspective." I tap my chest. "He's my guy. You think I want to have this conversation? About prayer time at The Cove? But Pete, college basketball doesn't involve splashing in the waves like a dipshit, it just doesn't. Leo is out of his tree."

"Yeah …" Muraro says.

"If college basketball involved splashing in the waves like a dipshit, then I'd applaud Leo as a leader of men. And we'd win games. But what games are we winning?"

Peter's silent.

"None of the games, Pete. Zero."

Therese approaches, but I wave her off. Leaning forward, I say, "Now I look at Peter Muraro and I think: There's someone like me. There's a sports guy. He believes in contending between the lines. Catalyzing on some beach isn't sports to Peter Muraro."

He shakes his head.

"Is it?"

"No," Peter mutters. "It's not."

"Okay then."

We're silent awhile. Outside, rain blows under the awning, pecking and marbling the window. Finally I say, "Then let's turn this back into sports, Pete. Do you understand me? Damn it, let's do it right."

Muraro lifts his eyes. I stare straight into them.

"What do you mean?" he says.

"What it sounds like I mean. Do you know where the gym is, Pete?"

"What?"

"The gym. The basketball gym. Jubinsky Fieldhouse. You know where that is?"

"I'm not sure what you mean."

"Take the guys," I say. "The basketball players. Or as many of the basketball players as you can round up." I point through the wall. "Take them to Jubinsky Fieldhouse and *play*."

Muraro squints at me. "Okay..."

For the first time since sitting down, I sip my coffee. "Do it every day. Keep doing it. Get them as good as you can, then during games, make. Them. *Play*."

Muraro laughs at this, but he's laughing alone. "It might not be that easy," he says.

"Yes, it is."

"What about Coach? What about Harvey and...?"

"Fuck those guys. Take the kids to Jubinsky and play."

"And Leo? He'll just give me his team? He'll say, 'Here, take my basketball team?'"

I shake my head. "I don't know what Kelly'll do. He's insane."

Muraro laughs. "Well, that's a comfort!"

The cannery guys peer over at us. Therese's chubby face peeks out from the kitchen.

"But you're a basketball coach," I fairly whisper. "Is that right? Do you coach basketball, Pete?"

Muraro's fingers drum the table.

"Coach," I say, "basketball. That's your thing. I'll handle Leo."

Minutes later, leaving Greta's, I say, "By the way. What's Kelly's deal with this Michael?"

"Who?"

"Mike. It's his uncle or something."

Muraro shakes his head. "I don't know about any uncle."

4.

I BUY MY CAMELS in Aberdeen, thirty miles from Fog Harbor—distant enough nobody'll see me at the register, but near enough to be back with smokes before anyone at Coleman Hall notices I'm AWOL. Those ignorant Coleman Hall cowards. All careerists but headed nowhere, they're capable of just two obsessions: how they might incur blame and where they might assign it. I left the office maybe ten minutes ago, and if any Coleman Hall lemmings are starting to wonder where I am, I hope that Jeremy at the desk sets them straight. I hope he reminds everyone that I spend nights in Coleman Hall regularly—not sleeping, either, but working as fuck. Meaning: when they show up yawning with fuzzy teeth and bedhead at 8:30 a.m., I've already slammed out a federal workday, plus thirty minutes' O.T.

The drive to Aberdeen takes way longer than thirty miles should, however, the highway getting there being two-laned, potholed, poorly painted, jungly and slick. Twenty minutes in, driving breakneck, I've covered just twelve of the thirty miles. You can't top fifty on Highway 111—breakneck or not, you just can't. On a straightaway you could push fifty-five, but if there's a straightaway between Fog Harbor and Aberdeen, I haven't seen it.

Driving a Buick LaCrosse doesn't help matters, but administering an athletic department means personifying, in every dimension of your being, that bland, reptilian-heartrate constancy that makes regents swoon. Accordingly, it was Buick LaCrosse or Chevy Malibu for me, and Malibus lately look too European, too sporty and slick. My Buick drives like a waterbed, and cresting the rise into Grays Harbor County, I need to smoosh the ungainly bulk of it down through hairpins and twists into the valley below. It's a beige sedan, with beige upholstery and trim, and had they shown me a model with more beige on or in it, I'd be driving that. More bland, please. More ho-hum, more limp. More sleepy, if you have it.

Fourteen miles to go. I see it in my mind, the glowing canopy of the Mobil station off 111, where Camel cartons fill up the shelves like ingots. Now thirteen miles. Banging over a bridge, the Buick sponges underneath me—I'm not hydroplaning, but it feels like it. Climbing the next grade, the accelerator dumbly ignores the stomps I give it, like it speaks one language and my Oxford another.

"Let's go, let's *go*," I say, the needle grudging upward. The klutzy windshield wipers whip and fold, whip and fold.

With twelve miles remaining, I think: Possibly I should own two cars. That might be the solution to this. One, the Buick, I'll park at Sea Breeze Court with FOG HARBOR CC tags on the windshield. That'll be "my car" so far as everyone in town is concerned. Then, when I need Camels, I'll fire up the GTO I keep hidden under a tarp in the woods.

The rain this far inland usually thins, but it's hammering down today, pooling in the ruts. With true hydroplaning a possibility, I drop to forty-five, then forty, the wipers kicking senselessly. Nine miles left and I think: Sure, that's what you need, Scott. A car devoted to buying cigs, and an acre of land in the forest where cig car waits at the ready. Because people in town, and at the college, care so desperately about what you drive. Don't they, Scott? Don't they? Imagine them now, all four thousand residents of Fog Harbor and two thousand students, staff, faculty, and administration, worrying not about their lives but about the modesty of your wheels. How it would horrify those souls if you turned up driving a Honda, or something red.

Not above laughing at myself, I chuckle at the woods flying by. "Yeah," I say. "Fuck you, Darrow." Because of course it's stupid. Who cares, who even *notices* whether I drive a Buick, Honda, Bentley, duck boat or donkey? I walk to work anyhow, and only drive to hit up Aberdeen (in which sense, I already own a cig car, just a shitty one). Who notices my transportation, and who notices or cares if I'm late getting back to the office today, or don't get back at all? Or don't go in tomorrow? Who notices or gives a shit if my appearance one day isn't pressed and angular—*a knife of attainment!*—and who cares if I smoke?

It's purely stupid. But it's stupid moreover because the answer to those questions, every last one of them, is: Everybody. Everybody gives a shit, and giving a shit, they notice. I'm not saying photographic observations lodge in peoples' minds: *There's Darrow, driving his sensible midsize. There he is in his office, and there he goes up the sidewalk, not puffing cigs.* I'm saying that human beings, beneath their thinking, in realms of awareness they're unaware of, interrogate the worth of others. Endlessly, they do. And one's ceiling in life is where those inquests into his worth cease to yield favorable impressions and start yielding contempt. People won't know why they dislike you, but they will dislike you, and that'll be fate stepping into the road to shake your hand. So yeah: I'll obsess over LaCrosse or Malibu. I'll barber my hair weekly, buy exfoliating soap and wear suits just once before dropping them at the cleaners. I'll drive up the coast for smokes, goddamn it, and hurry back before lizardy eyes start blinking at my vacant desk.

Or else people don't care. That's possible. But fuck that most of all. Give me every worry there is, every vanity and neurosis—that's preferable to a world I float through unseen, immaterial as a ghost.

The number on my phone, rattling coins in the console, isn't an area code I recognize. Probably it's a solicitor, but in my business one answers exotic calls, since good news arrives no other way (just as bad news, predictably, is local).

"This is Scott," I say. A voice garbles in my ear, the reception along 111 being atrocious. But it is a voice, a woman's voice, and not a bot. I lean toward the window. "Hello?"

Somewhere in the crackling, I hear "... Darrow ..." and while a telemarketer might know my name, the next phrase I hear is "... make overtures ..." and salespeople, in my experience, rarely drop fancyisms like that.

"Hang on a minute," I say.

"If this isn't ..." The voice cuts out. "... happy to ... is there ..."

"Let me call you back. I'll call you back."

Dropping the phone, I see up the highway only shaggy forest, rain pattering asphalt and a gloom that's not fog, but has the sag of fog. Nothing anywhere advertises cell reception. Retrieving my phone, tapping the mysterious number, I get only a *call failed* message. When it fails again, I resort to the voodoo that's my best understanding of technology. Swerving off 111, I barrel down a sideroad in search of higher ground. Within a mile, the pavement becomes dirt and what passed for daylight in December in Grays Harbor County becomes full dusk, the vegetation closing over me so that not even rain sifts down. My wipers croak the dry windshield. Streams splash under the tires. "Fuck, fuck, fuck," I say, since it isn't possible I'm driving *toward* better reception. All around me in the forest, orange ribbons dangle from trees somebody aims to cut down, or spare. My thumb paddles through failed calls, one and the next. "Wake up, motherfucker," I tell the phone. "Wake up."

Lacking options, I veer up a narrow track marked only by numerals on a post. It's a Forest Service road, I assume, but minutes later, cresting the rise with the Buick's fan whining, its temp gauge needling red, I see that actually I've steered up someone's driveway. Ahead, the road becomes twin ruts of gumbo curving through weeds to a trailer, one wall of which is painted blue, the rest a dull orange.

I lever into park. Probably I should leave, but private land or not, this ground is elevated and cleared of jungle. Rain again drums the windshield, and little sparks of reception populate my screen.

After two rings, the voice says, "There you are. I'd abandoned hope."

"A little network challenge. I'm sorry."

Into the silence that follows, a younger me would've poured words, words, words, smothering the silence with everything I could think of to say. But if this call is what I suspect it is—and it is—nobody who couldn't withstand silence would receive it.

"Well," the woman says, her voice meticulous, glassy. "I don't know how much you caught, Scott. A moment ago."

"We should start over."

"That's no trouble," she says. And it isn't. And she does. Though there isn't much to cover. The woman represents a firm out of Raleigh facilitating the Athletic Director search for Leighton University in Albany, New York. "In the Pine Hills District," she says. "Are you familiar with Albany? Or with Leighton?"

It rises to my lips autonomously, no thinking required. "The Runnin' Wolfhounds," I say.

She laughs. "Correct! The Runnin' Hounds! I'm impressed, Scott."

I know Leighton and its Wolfhounds because I know them all. Not all the jucos or Division IIIs, nor the NAIAs and not *quite* every Division II, but if it's an NCAA Division I institution in the United States, I know its name, location, mascot, colors, conference and more besides. This call might've concerned Sacred Heart University, for instance, and its Pioneers playing out of Fairfield, Connecticut in the Northeastern Conference. It might've concerned Alcorn State, whose Braves and Lady Braves, purple and gold, call Lorman, Mississippi home. Morgan State Bears, orange and blue, Baltimore, Mid-Eastern Atlantic Conference. Cal Baptist Lancers, navy and gold, Riverside, California. It's not that I memorized this info with flashcards or something. It's that, wanting a thing, the quantity of its availability, and where it's available, flows into your consciousness just naturally. It can't be helped any more than an owl can help knowing where voles burrow in snow. In fact, I'm not convinced want and consciousness are separate notions at all, one always mapping where the other sails.

The woman says, "We're establishing the framework for our search now, and contacting select applicants. And I'll be upfront: Scott, you come impeccably recommended. I spoke with Dr. Clark at Washington State. He said he didn't know of a more committed young administrator anywhere in the country."

"I'll have to thank Dale for that."

"*Dogged* is how he described you. And we see what he means, in terms of your development savvy, your knack for attracting talent."

I stare at the rain streaking my windshield and at the weeds nodding in the clearing. If we can leave it at that, I think—at *attracting* talent—then I'll do fine. Let's leave it at that, okay, wonderful, and not muddy the waters with talk of talent coming unglued and setting teams on fire.

The woman says, "You understand what I'm driving at, of course. Scott, on behalf of the Leighton team, we'd love to see an application from you. No answer necessary today. I'll send along some details for you to consider. In the meantime, if you have questions ..."

I note the woman's name and her firm's name and thank her for reaching out. The call finished, I sit at the wheel under a sky suddenly vaulting into the stratosphere, never mind the lid of clouds thirty feet overhead. I sit before a broad plain extending to the planet's edge, even if actually the clearing ends at a sloppy trailer. Leighton U. of the America East Conference. Running Wolfhounds, navy and silver.

I know fuck-all about Albany. Still, buildings there must exceed three stories. Restaurants must number past two. Sidewalks must fill occasionally with human activity, rather than just puddles, and a man in Albany at night must sense beyond his walls ... something. Something.

The Buick's fan whines, drawing down its temp needle. Birds rake into the clearing, little swifts or whatever that bristle in the grass before scattering again. I've sat here I don't know how long, but rather than reverse the car, I dance through photos on my phone of Albany (*Cradle of the Union*, one page calls it) and of Leighton's campus. Tall buildings—not skyscrapers, but close—preside over a river, and also invert in the river, the blue water recording their form. Row houses ascend a hill, alternating peach, green, burgundy and brick-colored brick. From what I can tell, Leighton's grounds extend radially from an abbey-looking chapel, its sidewalks passing old halls, fountains and beds of landscaping—tulips, poppies, dahlias. One edge of campus fronts a thoroughfare leading through town toward the river (which I see now, on a map, is actually the Hudson River, the big one). Elsewhere in Albany, avenues nudge into pockets of retail: kitschy storefronts, pear trees, doggy bowls, Teslas. By next year, I'll stroll among those Teslas, wearing a golf shirt and chinos, lighthearted.

It's a weekday, but to the teams and budgets of Leighton U. I've imparted momentum enough to cover me for an hour. What choice did I have? Breezes combed the oaks shading my office window, and I floated from the office into fragrant neighborhoods, parks. I drink coffee now. I admire ants marching past my shoe. Clouds sail by—just occasional clouds—and bells jangle as I enter a barbershop. Do something with it, I tell the guy. Do what you like. But give me those towels on my neck, the hot towels. Astringent scents fill the air, and the tidy, termite-ish *snicket* of scissors. Wearing aftershave into the day, and less hair, breezes cool me nicely. I browse shop windows with no urgency in my step, no purpose. It could've been coffee I drank—the yummy, pretentious kind wrought into thimbles from machines the size of suitcases—but more likely I sipped vodka at a patio table, and now am cruising Albany for lunch: bread, salad, sandwich, another vodka.

This is idiotic, childish dreaming, but while I'm at it: halfway through lunch, a woman with eyeglasses and tumbling hair walks into the bar, hitching her purse up her shoulder. She plucks a menu from the stand, browsing it idly. We're not here to meet each other, this woman and I. Our vodka lunches are independently undertaken. But one life intersects with another because cities past a certain size always nourish a certain magic. No hostess seats the woman. She simply carries her purse to my table. Rummaging her hair, settling into the booth, she frowns at the stranger seated across from her, chewing his cocktail olive. She laughs. After all, adults of conscience do not, we do *not* spend weekday afternoons sipping Ketel One. Except sometimes to certify our freedom, we do. And sometimes, ducking into a bar, you meet someone.

—

Wading in dreams is like wading in oceans; your toe flicks the water and immediately sharks, or the knowledge of sharks, swims your way to crash the party.

Across the clearing, on this mountainside in the clouds, a shirtless wretch bangs open his trailer and charges into the meadow to scowl at me. It's raining, but the man is indifferent to rain, even contemptuous of it. His face is gums, a meaty forehead and no blinking. For a time, we watch each other in the gloom. And the question this beast poses to me is not: What're you doing on my land? The question is: How will it ever change, Scott? Can it change? Say you land Leighton, say you take it and move east. After Leighton, you land the next, better Leighton and cash stains your hands green. Would your heart feel different, any more than your kidneys, spleen or lungs would? Would you sleep? Look at me, Scott—look at me standing in this downpour. What could you bring to this meadow that would ever change *me*?

Inside or outside makes no difference to this man, but to let him go back inside, I reverse into the trees and turn around. Little streams braid over the driveway; setting my tires to their course, I bump and splash down the hill. And listen: I'm no dipshit. However Leighton would feel—whatever walking through Albany, sunny afternoons or else late at night, passing lighted windows, would do to my spirits—it wouldn't be what I think. I get that. Shit, give me some credit. I know something waits for me there, if I make it there, that'll stop me in my tracks like a club to my chest. It could be bad winters. It could be the stench of an alley, or the glare a stranger gives me. Some freighter, dragging up the Hudson one morning, could crush my breath with ugliness. If nothing else, Leighton itself would disappoint me. Division I or not, it's a petty school: worthless facilities, low-major, no football.

What do you expect me to do about it? Yeah, seeing through dreams, knowing them for lies, is a higher plane of enlightenment. So what? The highest plane is knowing dreams are bullshit and pulling the wool over your own eyes anyway, since the world might have nothing for you, but you'll still make it empty its pockets. I'll live in a brownstone when I get to Albany. I'll eat breakfast at an east-facing bakery, where sunrises scorch my corneas, and fall in love a thousand times, whenever somebody glances my way in a crowd.

Aberdeen's just five miles farther, but I've been away too long. And I should spray this mud off the Buick before driving it in town. Turning south, I follow 111 back to the coast.

PART II

5.

EVEN IF KELLY WEREN'T UNHINGED—even if *the* Leo Kelly reappeared to walk and coach among us, in lieu of his crackpot doppelganger—still, we'd have all we could handle in Big Bend College from Moses Lake. They're a vicious squad, and I'm tempted write off tonight's game at Big Bend and pin my hopes to next Monday instead, against Yakima Valley. But the Sea Lanterns are 0-5, and if I'm shipping off to Albany next year I can't have them going 0-very many more. We need to dirty up that wins column, just scribble some numbers in it. That's how it's done. Scribble shit in both columns and suddenly a season camouflages itself, masking its scent, allowing eyeballs in Albany to drift down one's résumé to shinier laurels. *Oh, Darrow's Sea Lanterns win some, they lose some. Look at this coach he hired, though, that's Leo Kelly!* It's when nothing appears in a column—and this goes for losses as well as wins—that eyeballs linger. After all, if you haven't lost a game—or won one, in our case—then your supremacy or else decrepitude is as yet unmeasured and could prove immeasurable, without ceiling or, in our case, floor. *Huh,* Leighton would say, seeing 0-7 or 0-9, *who died in Fog Harbor and when will Darrow notice?*

I should drive over the mountains, five hours, to watch the game in Moses Lake. Nobody walking earth needs Sea Lanterns victories like I do, and that yearning, in person, might register somehow. It could influence a ball's flight toward the basket and soften or stiffen rims, as needed. I could use the trip, too, since past the Cascades this time of year, there's no rain. It's only blinding, crisp sunlight and stubbly fields for miles. It's like Montana in the winter, and I could lower the windows to singe my ears with cold. I could smoke Camels en route, though there'll be other spectators at the game (at least one or two of them), and I wouldn't want somebody sniffing my collar and spreading rumors about me. That wouldn't happen, I realize, but things unlikely to happen fuck people all the time by happening anyway, so paranoia's a virtue.

Ten hours out and back, twice over Snoqualmie Pass, and I'd go except that Peter Muraro has been sweating his role in this all week, texting and calling and dropping by my office for pep talks (as if I were the fucking coach), and I shouldn't harm Fog Harbor's chances more than they're harmed already by sitting behind Peter in the stands, freaking him out. We'll let Muraro handle tonight and see how it goes.

It won't go well. But this week Peter has done things, at least. That's what he tells me. After Greta's on Monday, he toured campus, going dorm-to-dorm and classroom-to-classroom, finding players where they lived and learned to enlist them to our effort. He succeeded with seven guys, he said, telling them: *Look, Coach is trying things, some new-age stuff. That's cool but Dr. Darrow and I—the A.D., Dr. Darrow—thought fellas should just play hoops, too. Keep that part of things up. So listen, I'm opening the Jub tonight around eight. Stop by. And yeah, keep this under your hat for now. We want to keep things simple.*

I'd have preferred, for simplicity's sake, Peter keep my name out of his goddamn mouth when organizing his insurrection. But anyway, he'd mustered a gang. They played Monday, Tuesday, and yesterday nights, till late, leaving them exhausted for Leo's 7:00 a.m. practices. But when practice, as it did this week, entails lying on wrestling mats in a dark room while Kelly projects sitcoms onto the ceiling (*Growing Pains*, *Who's the Boss?*, and *Alf* being this week's selections), then exhaustion doesn't hinder one much. Muraro said his guys slept straight through the shows every morning, which Leo noticed but which, oddly, pleased him.

Standing over the sleeping players, Peter told me, Kelly'd smiled at their faces like a dad. When one twitched, he'd laughed. "One dream of many," he'd said. "One of many."

It was last night, ahead of today's trip to Big Bend, that Peter floated to his group the idea of playing basketball during games, too. That nutty idea. Muraro said he was nervous to bring it up and that his guys were skeptical. "But Coach has stuff he wants us doing," one kid said, "during games. Now you want us to do this other stuff?"

Peter's response sounded good to me. "Well, keep doing what Coach says," he'd said. "Definitely do that. But do the basketball version of what he says, you know? When Coach says something, interpret it as basketball. And play ball." Which could only mean "play ball," since there isn't a basketball version of chewing seeds, blaring Enya, tugging your cock into the ocean or watching *Alf*.

Muraro relayed this stuff in my office earlier, before catching the bus to Moses Lake. He stood at my desk in his shitty slacks, worry stamped on his face like a cattle brand. "So that's where we stand," he said.

The best approach might've been for Peter to shove in his chips and tell his guys: *Look, Leo's out of it! This is your chance to play actual basketball again!* But I just nodded at Muraro. "Terrific. Great work, Pete."

He eyed me suspiciously, as if my confidence in him were dubious. It was and is. It forever will be. But with the game in ten hours, it wasn't too soon for Muraro to start believing in himself. Staring at the kid, not fidgeting or blinking, I said, "You're going to kill it, Pete. Damn it, I know you will."

When Muraro left, I pulled on my coat to shoot up to Aberdeen—for real this time. The headaches this week have been rough, and I didn't think I could watch a Sea Lanterns gamecast without puffing something, while Big Bend cranked up the score like a winch. I made it nearly to the elevators, but then Jeremy called my name. Returning to his desk, my temples thudding, I said, "What? What do you want?"

Jeremy Harrington. A good kid but too peppy lately, he wore a cowl sweater, his hair pinned back like a tennis star's. "Did you see that thing?" he said.

I thumbed the sweat from my forehead. "What thing? What're you talking about?"

Guiding his mouse around, clicking, Harrington turned his laptop for me to see. He tapped the screen. "Tuesday. Chancellor Toren wants twenty minutes."

"Twenty minutes with who? Me?"

"That's why we're having this conversation."

"Don't snark me, Jeremy." Studying the screen, I saw only a calendar event for Tuesday: RODNEY TOREN, 8:30-8:50. "What's he want?"

"They said he wanted twenty minutes. That's all they said. It's about Men's Hoops."

I stared at my assistant.

"That's all I got!" Harrington said. "That's all they said!"

"What do you mean, Men's Hoops? What about it?"

Jeremy shook his head. "I don't know."

"Did you ask?"

"I said, 'What shall I tell Dr. Darrow the meeting concerns?' And they said, 'Men's Basketball.'"

Unraveling my scarf, I walked back into my office and sat. I placed a hand on the desk. This wasn't unexpected, of course. A team showing goose egg wins attracts its chancellor's attention sooner or later, and if said chancellor shelled out beaucoup severance guarantees to said team's coach recently, then you can bet it'll be sooner. I pinched my eyelids till white spots swam behind them. At least this wasn't a complex situation. Because it wasn't, really. Between today and Tuesday were two games, and if we won even one, there'd be no issue. I'd sell Toren on progress. We also could win both games, in which event Rodney at our meeting would tap a sword on my shoulders, anointing me to the Realm of the Chosen. But we needed to win. The situation wasn't complex, we just strictly needed to win.

I stayed at my desk all day—fuck cigarettes—and still am here, with Coleman Hall empty and night fallen. Pretty soon, they'll tip off in Moses Lake. But what I'm thinking about is showing up 0-7 Tuesday, and everything that'd mean for me. Because that'd leave me ... I don't know where that'd leave me. Guys in jeopardy at their current jobs don't vault to better ones—I know that much. Also, guys in jeopardy at their jobs often stay that way. What starts as a crisis becomes a proclivity, then a lifestyle. Except, Scott, you're not in jeopardy. Don't think *jeopardy*. Two games in five days—two forty-minute games—and you only need one of them.

At 7:00, the game's first points register on my phone: two free throws for Big Bend. Dozens of Big Bend points follow, and instead of smoking I brew mean coffee, pouring the joe through the machine a second time, over fresh grounds. Munching chips and Tylenol from the cupboard, wrappers accrue in my lap. Big Bend wins egregiously, 91-59. The box score shows not even a pulse on our part, nothing I can seize on to believe we're alive.

The HVAC hums in my office, then clicks off. I say to the room, "Christ, you people break my heart."

6.

JUB FIELDHOUSE on Friday night is a silhouette against black sky, security lights studding its perimeter. Nothing's happening there, nor anywhere on campus—crossing West Quad, I see just one person, a girl with bare knees under her poncho, rollerblading. Being a juco, Fog Harbor evacuates most weekends, its students fleeing inland to what holes they came from, or else sheltering in place with drugs. Plus finals are next week, and kids are trying to remember what courses they enrolled in.

Muraro's guys wanted tonight off, after a rough week, and Peter would've allowed it, but I said Fuck That. At 0-6, we're not chillaxing in fuzzy clogs and Snuggies. "Get those motherfuckers down to the Jub, Pete," were my words. "I'll see you at seven."

Entering the Fieldhouse—at 6:35, not 6:59—I roll a ball rack onto the main court and fire up the lights, their mustardy glare seeping into the hardwood. Surrounding the court, two tiers of seating wait in the shadows. The Jub isn't terrible for a juco venue, I'll grant it that. At 5,200 chairs, it nearly rivals Gonzaga's barn in Spokane, which seats 6,000. The largest crowd I've seen at a Sea Lanterns game is twelve, though, so Lord knows why they ever built this place. Tapping a ball off the rack, I dribble and loosen up.

For what it's worth, I played basketball—throughout high school and one season at Kent State. The rubbery melon in my hands still feels stupid, though, as if in fifteen years they switched from a round to ovoid ball. Sailing a clean, spinning jumper from the elbow, I'm confident in its chances till the rim fires the ball sideways. Strolling after it, my loafers *clop clop* underneath me. My next shot twists strangely from my hands, striking the glass and bouncing back my direction. Dribbling to the opposite end of the court, the ball jumps clumsily to my palm, jamming a thumb.

This should piss me off, having once been skilled at this sport and now being oafish, but athletic prowess belonged to an earlier, now discarded Scott Darrow, and if I'm pissed tonight, it's only because six losses hang from my heart like grief. Six losses, and all the jackasses causing those losses. With that to worry about, who cares how I handle a basketball? Plus—if I'm telling the truth—I never cared how I handled a basketball, or how I anything with basketball. Even all those years ago, as a kid, when I was excellent at the game and played all the time and smiled and laughed as I played and dreamed about hoops when I slept and shot a ball at the ceiling every afternoon in my room— even back then, I didn't care about it. I thought I did. I thought I cared about basketball exhaustively, to the exclusion of all else. Those nights after playing at our neighbors' house, the Ahlbergs, I would walk home under Hamilton's cold stars with the ball in my backpack snug against my spine. And I would think: This is it. Basketball is The Thing. I will carry this ball on my shoulders just as far as I can carry it. As far as it can carry me.

I've known for years that all that was bullshit, naturally. Basketball wasn't *it*. It wasn't The Thing. All I needed then and have ever needed was some kind of Thing, and it could have been basketball or anything else. The Ahlbergs could just as well have had a drum set in their driveway, or a fly rod or pottery wheel. My thing now is athletic departments, but it could just as well be astronomy or medicine or tech startups or robbing banks. The important thing isn't what thing. It's having the thing. And having a thing that goes on and on.

People forget the on and on part. They get bogged down in things themselves. Take the guy from Kent State I ran into at SeaTac last year, who'd kicked ass on our college squad but who couldn't get through that to the other side. Barry, his name was. And basketball remained his Thing.

We ate tapas together in the terminal, and practically the first words out of Barry's mouth were: "So how's the cross-over, Scotty? I remember you had that quick step." He feinted his shoulders some.

"How *is* it?" I said.

"You had that floater, too. The teardrop." Barry made a swan's neck of his arm. I didn't say anything.

"Son of a bitch, though," Barry said, sipping his sangria. "I mean goddamn, Scotty. This one league I play in? My Monday league? It's all younger guys. And they rub it in so hard. They don't know they're doing it, but that's all they do. Dunking and shit like that. Fucking pricks."

I thought I'd misheard. "This what league? What did you say?"

"They don't even play. They just run for two hours, like cheetahs. Little young cheetahs. What? Oh, this one league. My Monday league."

Barry popped a croqueta into his mouth.

"Your Monday league," I said. "Barry, how many leagues do you play in?"

He shrugged. "Just the three. Mondays and Thursdays, then Saturday mornings."

They called a flight over the speakers, and even though it wasn't mine, I shook Barry's hand and walked off. Some hours later, waiting at baggage claim in Pullman, I still was nauseous over what the guy'd said to me. Three fucking leagues. Mondays, Thursdays, Saturdays. Who needed three occasions weekly to fan the flames of what he wasn't anymore, and couldn't be again? Who needed to cling to a thing when the thing was dead in his hands? Right there in the concourse, I said "Dipshit" aloud, and know I said it, since a woman hauling suitcases off the carousel glared at me. Jesus, though. Joining three leagues, what else did Barry manage to do? Did he squeeze in a life around the life he made believe? Did he at all realize he blundered through the universe backward, gazing at what was lost while trampling under his heels everything he still could have?

I sail a three-pointer past the backboard, which knocks over a chair behind the hoop. It's important to me, somehow, that I don't stand the chair upright again. Leaving it there, I trot after the ball, my shoes clopping the floor.

———

It's 7:12 before doors bang in the hallway, and those lost minutes say everything I need to know about the kids now entering the gym, tossing gear into the stands and unzipping their jackets, as if I weren't already familiar with these nitwits' deficiencies. Dropping my ball on the rack, I watch Peter's crew change into their sneakers. With tortured slowness, they pick at laces. Tossing one shoe aside, they pick at the other, yawning and stretching like a family of overfed koalas, their hair misshapen from what one assumes were daylong naps. Wondering when these assholes will succeed with their shoes—wondering *whether*—I understand vaguely Kelly's abdication with his team. If a group of kids shows such limp devotion, being twelve minutes late, then eight minutes lacing shoes, slumping by the moment deeper and deeper into the bleachers, till fully half the team is horizontal before me, then why not fuck it and beam *Alf* onto the ceiling? But Leo's not abdicating—whatever he's up to, it isn't that—and anyway, no, I don't understand the urge to give in. People without fire in their chests don't make me throw up my hands; they make me ball my hands into fists.

Muraro's guys feel me watching them—one or two glance my way before scratching their noses and glancing elsewhere. Nobody says hi, though. Nobody waves. They're thinking: Take forever with our sneakers and Dr. Darrow will vanish. But fuck that, boys. Cock up your own lives, if you want, but lose Monday and that's my life. You will not cock up my life.

Peter appears, crossing the court with his hand raised in greeting. "My bad," he says. "Little confused about the time."

"Why?" I say.

"Excuse me?"

"What about 'seven o'clock' confused you about the time?"

Muraro offers no reply since no reply will do. He didn't care enough to be punctual, period.

In the silence that follows, I wait for Peter to animate his guys. He doesn't, and meanwhile his shooting guard, Matty Martin, reaches a ceasefire with his Jordans; leaving the laces sprung, he reclines luxuriously under Jubinsky's lights, forearm shielding his eyes. Matthieu Martin, Cathedral High, Mira Mesa, CA. Like other Golden State mimbos, this one's hair curls lusciously to his shoulders, falling in ringlets like Sleeping Beauty's—Matty being as pretty as Sleeping Beauty and as spry. Crossing the court, I crouch at Martin's side, tie dangling between my knees. He peeks out from under his arm.

"Scott Darrow," I say, thrusting out my hand.

Matty eyes my hand. Then he shakes it.

I say, "Question for you. Why is this taking so long?"

"What?" Matty says.

"I'll put it this way. Why are you not doing fucking anything right now?"

The other guys watch us. Muraro inches forward to intervene, wringing his hands, but does nothing. Eventually, Martin swings his feet to the floor. "Sorry, homie."

"Zero wins in six games," I say. "You expect me to tie your shoes for you?"

"I'll do it." Reaching down, Matty cinches his laces. "There we go. We're good."

"Yo big wig," someone else says—someone farther down the bleachers. "Man with them Argyle socks. You can save all that shit. Fuck that." It's Odie talking, one of Peter's forwards. He sits with arms extended down the bleachers, his eyes half-mast. I stand, smoothing my tie.

"Coming at us," Odie says, "talking about losing games. *Us* losing games." He shakes his head. "Not having that."

"You want to share how you feel, Odie?"

"Who gave us a clown coach, huh? Who did that? We speaking on that?"

Besides Odie, nobody in the gym looks at me. In the silence, Muraro shifts his weight foot-to-foot, hands crammed in his pockets. Doing this without trashing Kelly would be preferable—I know Peter'd like it that way—but how could we? And anyway, Leo deserves trashing. "I hired Leonard," I say. "That's true. And yeah, he's shitty. He's a shittier coach than anybody could've imagined."

Odie watches me.

"It's my fault," I say. "You bet it is. Now what're we going to do about it?"

"Pshh…" Making a phone of his fingers, waggling it, Odie says, "Call me when you know, baby. That's on you."

"Yeah, okay."

"Call me when you know. I'm a patient motherfucker."

"You're going to lose a lot of games, Odie. In the meantime."

He turns up his hands, shrugging. I stare at Odie. Pivoting to the group, I say: "Not that it wouldn't be my fault. I get it. Every game you boys lose is my fault."

The team's eyes start finding me.

"I need to put you in a position to win, and I haven't done that. I'd have thought you still wanted to play, though. I'd have thought you wanted to come here and work."

Nobody speaks.

Counting on fingers, I say: "I'd have thought you wanted to work tonight. I'd have thought you wanted to work Monday, against Yakima." Pointing down the court (who knows why?), I say, "Next weekend, Shoreline comes here. I'd have thought you wanted to work those fucks. Unless this other shit's more important to you." Another of our forwards, a cornfed hog from Vale, Oregon, sits off to the side. "Is that what it is, Sam?" I say. "Is this other shit more important to you?"

The kid stares at me, his mouth slack. "I don't know what you mean."

I stamp my heel. "Figuring out who's to blame, Sam! Whose fault everything is!"

The team's silent, unblinking. Scanning their faces, Muraro's too, I say: "Goddamn it. God fucking damn it. Let me tell you people something. Not everybody knows this, but everybody who's done something knows it: you'll waste your life worrying who did what and waiting for the people who fucked shit up to fix it. They won't. They will not. They're who fucked it up to begin with, and all you're waiting for is the next time they fuck it up. And fuck it up worse."

I pace the sideline. "Not that it even matters," I say. "Because as soon as you're waiting at all," I finger-stab the air, "the *moment* you start waiting, then you're not living anymore. Do you understand? You're nothing. You're luggage. The real people— the people who *are* living—will drag your asses around wherever they want to go. And that should turn your stomachs, each one of you. Listen to me: Fuck whose fault this is. Fuck me. Fuck Leonard Kelly. Be the kings of your lives." Planting my feet, I glare at their faces. "Be the kings of your lives and tie your fucking shoes."

Returning to the rack, tapping balls onto the court, I hear Dajuan behind me—Dajuan Simms, Fog Harbor's stout point guard. "He's saying it, man," Dajuan says. "He's right."

"Dajuan so serious," someone says, but nobody laughs. Guys are cinching their laces.

Muraro works his group through warmups, lay-ins and fast breaks, then organizes some three-on-three, shirts and skins. That's more like it, I think, gripping my knees and watching. Let's break some arms. Let's chew meat. What Peter's crew trots onto the court hardly qualifies as nasty hoops, however, with its sloppy focus, friendly manners and charitable view of defeat. Starting a play, Matty flips the rock underhand to Austin, who cradles it at his hip, yawning. Somebody cuts. Somebody hops in place. Asthmatic, bony Austin heaves a three-pointer, its rebound striking hardwood before anyone reacts. The next play, timid James Hicks doesn't budge two steps from where he started, creeping forward then retreating again, creeping sideways but creeping back. James raises his fist for a screen then simply drops it, his initiative dying on the vine. I drop my head between my shoulders.

Dajuan hustles. When Sam backs him down, Dajuan presents his chest, knocking that Oregon tubby to his knees. Odie loses the handle and Dajuan dives for it, his body smacking wood with a thud. There we go, I think. That's basketball. But everyone else disgusts me.

Matty lingers at the wing, blowing in one fist then the other, his dribble hopping beside him like a yipping terrier, untended. He wipes his soles, contemplating a move, and strolling onto the court, I punt the ball away from him into the stands. It ricochets among the bleachers, echoing up there. Everybody stops what they're doing, which was nothing.

"Matt," I say, "are you chilly? Can I bring you a sweater?"

On the far sideline, Peter's mouth forms an O, like I've jerked a Tootsie Pop from his lips.

"Uh," Martin says, "I'm good?"

"If you're chilly, I'll bring you a sweater. Otherwise, quit blowing in your hands."

"Blowing in my ...?"

"Your hands. In your fucking hands." Lifting my fists, I blow in one, then the other, then the first again, then the other. "That shit. Cut it out."

"Ah." Martin wags a finger. "I got you."

"Get me or don't. Just quit doing it."

The kid opens his mouth, but doesn't speak.

"What?" I say. "Say it."

Matty shakes his head. "It's nothing."

"Fucking say it."

"It's just ... I was going to drive." Martin gestures at the lane. "In a second there. I was about to."

Rubbing my forehead, I say, "Damn it, Matt, I know you were about to. I didn't think you'd wipe your shoes all fucking night."

Matty's silent.

"*Do* it, is what I'm saying. *Do* it. This other shit isn't *doing* it. *Do* it."

"Matty blows in his hands so much," Odie says from the sideline. He laughs, and backpedaling off the court, I shout across at him: "Odie, you like jokes? Jokes make you happy?"

He pretends not to hear me.

"Tell your jokes to the wall, if you're telling jokes." I point at the back wall. "Walk over there and tell jokes. Or else shut the fuck up."

Odie doesn't go to the wall, but also he quits laughing.

To everyone else, I say: "Is anybody going to act like he *wants* something tonight? Christ, you people are cool with everything, huh? Everything's peachy. Well, stay the fuck home if your life is peachy. Don't come here unless you're mad."

James Hicks, with his dangling, weird arms, eyes me strangely, puzzling out my meaning. The scrimmage resumes around him.

"I don't know what you're staring at, Hicks," I say.

Dajuan drags James into position, then scrambles to defend his man.

Moving up the sideline, brushing past Odie, I position myself near where Hicks is defending the wing. "You need me to explain myself to you, Jamie?" I shout at the kid's forehead. "I said don't come here unless you're mad. Do you know what 'mad' means? Are you fucking thick?"

Play reverses, James dropping into the key. Stepping onto the court, I shout over the action: "Plenty of people must get mad at you with that dumb guppy face, James! You ever get mad back, or do you just swallow it? I bet you swallow it." Hicks double-teams the post then cheats off. I shout, "You're a milky soft mother-fucker, I knew it the minute I saw you, James. Get off the court. Get the fuck off the court!"

On a skip pass, rushing toward me to check the wing, it's as if Hicks has yanked on a mask: his eyebrows crash together, teeth bared like fangs.

"*There* it is, James!" I shout. "There it is, goddamn it!"

What small distance separates Hicks from the ball he erases immediately, jailing his opponent, Matty, against the sideline, blinding him with flurried hands, yelling: "Yeah, baby! Yeah, baby! Get it!"

Martin's sneaker crosses the sideline, and swatting the ball from his hands, stepping around him into James' face, I scream, "You bet! You bet, motherfucker!" Spit flies onto Hicks' lip, my spit, and who cares? I shove the kid. "You did that! You!"

Dajuan trots by, smacking James' ass and retrieving the ball for their team. "Go do it," I say, and Hicks dashes this way and that, unsure where he's going but going full bore.

Finished with James, I ignore the scrimmage awhile and stare up the sideline at Odie, who stands with his fists balled into his jersey, his eyes indifferent. Odie Bowles. At six-eight, with square shoulders, lean muscle and lacrosse scoops for hands, the kid is everything you'd want in a forward, but for sucking dick attitude-wise. We'll see about that, though. Shitty attitudes translate into shitty players only if you mismanage them, after all—if you detonate them in your own hands rather than lobbing them at other teams.

I've stared for several minutes when Odie, not returning my stare, says, "Man, you got a problem out here?"

I shake my head. "No problem, Odie." Then, stepping closer, I say: "But you just don't have it, do you? You don't. What you saw James do? Lighting someone up like that? You don't have that." I stare at Bowles' face. "Because you don't have shit, Odie."

Puffing his cheeks, Bowles exhales noisily. He shakes his head. "I fucking hate even looking at you," I say.

Peter appears, touching my arm. "Scott, let's ease up a bit. Come on."

"Is that what you need, Odie?" I wonder. "You need me to ease up?"

Bowles laughs. "I don't need shit from you, big wig. Except you stepping off."

I laugh with him. "Okay. Yeah, okay. But you're not getting that. That one thing you need, you won't get it." I stare at Odie's mouth, waiting for it to say anything. But the kid walks away, circling around to the opposite sideline, where he stands as before, fists in jersey and eyes watching nothing. Between us, his teammates hustle and sweat.

Speaking at my ear, Muraro says, "Odie's pretty sensitive, Scott. I wouldn't push him too hard."

"No time for that, Pete."

"What?"

"There's no time not to push Odie. Quit thinking like a therapist."

Circling around midcourt, I call to Bowles as I approach: "You feeling emotional, Odie? What's up?"

The kid shakes his head. "I told you to step off."

"I said I was going to fuck with you. Now here I am. Let's do it."

Bowles laughs. "Keep it up, baby. Just keep it up."

Standing at Odie's side, nose level with his shoulder, I hitch my pants and stare at him. As he watches the court, his expression doesn't flicker at all. He could be waiting in line at the post office. I say, "Get out of here, Odie. Leave."

"I'm cool," he says.

"You're making me sick, being here. And you're not going to try. Look at you. You'll never try."

Bowles hikes an eyebrow at me, then watches the scrimmage.

"What you want," I say, "is to curl up like a puppy. And I'm saying you can, Odie. Go home."

The kid shakes his head. "I'm a crack that ass, my man. Keep going."

I wonder briefly if Bowles is sincere, then barrel ahead, outrunning the knowledge that he certainly is sincere—no question he is. "Odie, I've never felt safer in my life than when I'm busting your shit," I say. "You won't touch me. You'd never touch me. Think how much work that'd be. Lazy motherfucker like you, I could—"

At the Ravalli Fair in Hamilton one year, I smashed the High Striker so flush that its puck dented the bell. Instead of ringing it *buzzed*, knifing everyone's ears, and by that same signal, I know now that I've found the mark with Bowles. His knuckles surge at me like that puck, ramming my eye, and laid out flat on the court, my world spinning, I hear it like I heard it twenty years ago: a harsh buzz deep in my ears.

Odie towers over me, his shape dividing and merging, and legs race past to drag him away. Stumbling to my feet, I attack whoever's intervening, which happens to be Peter. "The fuck are you doing?" I shout, my own voice sounding far-off.

"You all right, Scott?" Muraro says.

"Back out of it, Pete. Christ."

The buzz thins to a whine, my vision sharpening some, and I notice the scrimmage has stopped, its six players rooted where they stand like pillars of fear. Off to the side, Bowles watches me with chest heaving, his hands ready and loose. I totter slightly, but I'm good. "Did you see that?" I ask everyone. "Did you fucking see it?"

When nobody speaks, I say, "If it came to it, I hope each of you motherfuckers would do that to me. Or to anyone."

The guys glance at each other. Touching my eye, ensuring it's not cut, I say, "So let's do this. Odie, you're in for Sam. Check the ball."

7.

WE PRACTICE SATURDAY, then Sunday morning and a final time Sunday night. Nobody hits me again, but I keep my jaw out for it and by Sunday it's not unthinkable that several other of Muraro's guys, not just Odie, would oblige me. It's not because they hate the asshole who showed up this weekend to belittle them (though certainly they do). It's because, simply, they start playing like kids who'd hit people, kids with grievances. Shots bang off the rim and the ball doesn't find hardwood anymore, vanishing instead into the knot of bodies scrumming for a rebound. Or it finds hardwood, but only because someone horse-collars someone else out of position, and the two guys end up ignoring the ball and butting foreheads instead, talking shit and flaring their nostrils like rams. Possessions stop wasting time, as even Matty starts turning his drives downhill, conceiving of the court as a steep funnel leading on all sides to the rim. Guys just quit dicking off, is what it is. They shout at each other. They tie their shoes. At Sunday night's practice, the closest thing I see to a smile is when Austin spanks Sam's jump hook clear into the stands, after which he struts up the key, licking his teeth.

They're not fully there, of course. How could they be? Skills-wise, these are materially the same players Big Bend College waxed the floor with three days ago. If they're fighting and hustling now, it's only because they choose to, and being a choice they could discontinue it anytime. These kids aren't killers, is what I mean, the virtue of killers being that choice doesn't factor into it—their knives bury in opponents' throats before decision-making even kicks in. Peter's crew doesn't have that and won't have it come tipoff Monday. Still, I hope they liked tasting blood this weekend. I hope they decide to taste some of Yakima's.

—

Monday morning, I shower, dress and stand at the mirror in 2F, nicking stray hairs from my chin. Rinsing the razor, straightening my four-in-hand and shooting my cuffs, I look pristine besides the fat lump folding my left eye shut, the bruise curing this morning into eggplant and wine hues. Surprisingly, I don't hate the look of this shiner. Situated on a groomed face, with neat hair above and pressed threads below, the wound testifies to what I traded for everything else. Or would happily trade. It's like a price tag stamped into my flesh. Studying the mangled eye, what I actually see are questions, however, and suspicion and gossip. Show up Monday with a wrecked mug and people assume you stayed out all weekend brawling. That happens to be exactly what I did, but the brawling in this case was work-related, so people can spare me their judgy shit.

Gesturing at the eye, I audition some alibis for the mirror. "Ran my car into a ditch," I say, and "Walked into a tree," though these suggest idiocy and intoxication, which aren't any better than someone just popping me one. Plus, it could get out that Odie's responsible, so whatever lie I concoct needs to be, at a minimum, truth-esque. In other words, if the real story gets out, it needs to seem like Scott Darrow, all along, was already telling it.

I'll figure it out. Meanwhile, I wait in 2F till it's bright enough outside to justify wearing shades, then call a breakfast order into Greta's and walk to pick it up. It's not actually bright enough for shades, nor ever is in Pacific County—walking along under drizzly skies, I resemble in my wayfarers a blind man or G-man— but what're my options? The food's not ready, so leaving the diner, I cross the street and walk out onto the wharf, where I'm unlikely in December to encounter any citizens. I even remove my shades, in case briny air does something for the swelling. At the end of the wharf, waves toss over the decking and suck back into the troughs below, slapping pilings. It's unclear in the distance where sea meets sky, but from that soupy zone, riding onshore gusts, seabirds zoom along as if on cables. I spot a ship out there, rounding the point, till I see it's actually Fog Harbor's lighthouse, swatting its beam through the gloom. Then I hear myself say, strangely, "Five thousand miles, clear to Sendai."

No islands, Leo'd said. *Black water.* Why he was volunteering nautical data at night on a street corner in the rain is anyone's guess, just as his motivations for making players pray at dawn at The Cove are mysterious. Standing on the wharf, oxfords gripping the planks, I do feel in my chest the scale he described, though. Five thousand miles, and how black it'd be at night, how blank at day. There's *magnitude* out there, and were I God this morning, the lighthouse on the point would indeed be a ship. It'd collect me from this wharf to carry me on the high seas till I hit something, anything—till Fog Harbor vanished behind me over the lip of the world.

Maybe Kelly feels something like this, this lust for escape, when he gushes about the ocean to anyone who'll listen, but a wave drenches the wharf, skating over my shoes, and my next thought is: Then what's stopping him? Why's he staying? Leo's nothing if not a millionaire, he hasn't got family to think of. If he wants out of Fog Harbor, why doesn't he go?

The wave drains through the slats, leaving behind clots of foam, and I realize the question isn't what keeps Leo here, because nothing does, but rather what would've brought him here to begin with? A legend, wealthy, crowding eighty years old—what business does a man like that have coaching two-year ball at a crap school in rural Washington? "Huh," I say aloud, watching terns ride the swells, because it's the obvious question to have asked about Kelly, yet I never asked it. Such a famous talent, I only cared that he was *willing* to coach at Fog Harbor. Past that, who gave a fuck?

Well, I should've looked into it. I should've demanded sensible answers—answers that didn't entail Enya and sunflower seeds. A little due diligence, and I'd have saved myself tremendous grief and a black eye. Though who knows, who knows. You could've told me how Leo'd be, after all: I still would've hired the guy. A name like Kelly's only floats within reach every so often, and when it does, you grab it, schizophrenia be damned. But whatever. It's finished and not worth pondering. We need to beat Yakima, end of story.

Slipping the shades onto my face, I retrieve my omelet and waffles from Greta's and start up Bay Avenue. I'm nearly to Sea Breeze Court when somebody shouts at me from across the street. "Well, there he goes! Old Hoot Owl Darrow!"

A car passes, hissing mist behind its tires, and on the far curb stands Jade O'Neil, hands in jacket and scarf heaped to her ears, her grin like a white plate with one Tootsie Roll on it. It had to be Jade, both because there's no mistaking her untimid voice and because nobody else on earth calls me Hoot Owl anymore. My friends in Hamilton christened me that and my parents threw the name around, but those people wouldn't remember twenty years later. I hardly remembered myself till Jade pressed one night for the identity of my spirit animal (she's bizarre like that), and *Hoot Owl* coughed out of me. "If nicknames count as spirit animals," I said, to which Jade said, "What else would they be?"

Another car turns toward us as Jade crosses the street to say hi. Jamming his breaks, the motorist thrusts a finger over the dash, using his other hand to pound the horn. Jade gives no fucks at all. She claimed the street first and this numbnuts could wait his turn.

"That guy's pissed," I say.

Jade watches the car speed off. "Too bad. Nobody ever died from courtesy."

"You sure about that?"

We smile at each other.

"I didn't know you were in town," I say.

"Well, Hoots. You didn't ask."

"I didn't know you were here for me to ask you."

"You should be swinging by my place and checking on these things."

I tilt forward slightly, almost imperceptibly, since there's a draw to Jade and I can't help it. She eyes my face.

"I know," I say.

"Is there an eclipse today?" Jade inspects the sky. "Do I need mine?"

I should beta-test my lie right now, the brilliant lie I just contrived, which is *I practiced with the team this weekend and things got physical*—brilliant since it's pure truth and since it depicts me as an A.D. in the trenches, hooping with his team, rather than as an abusive prick. But Jade reaches up, plucking the shades from my nose, and I'm silent.

"Whoa, whoa, whoa," she says.

"All right."

"Is that a goiter? Jesus Christ."

I retrieve my Ray-Bans.

"Is your head growing a head?" Jade says. "Who did that to you?"

"You're one to talk," I say, "with that tooth."

Jade claps a hand over her mouth, some hair falling across her eyes. Slipping the wayfarers onto my face, I say, "You know I don't mean that. I'm sorry."

She drops her hand.

"It was one of the basketball kids," I hear myself say. I shouldn't be saying this. "One of the players."

"A *player* hit you? In the *face?*" Jade's clearly impressed.

"So," I say. "How long are you in town?"

She studies my wound through the glasses. Then she shrugs. "I don't know. For a bit, I think. For the winter."

"No trips?"

Jade scrunches her nose, wincing but smiling too. "They offered me something in the Ozarks, but meh. Banjos and all that. I want to hold still."

"Good place for holding still."

"The Harbor?" Jade glances around at Fog Harbor's dreary streets. "I think so. Except for the tea. Which, actually, is basically my schedule today. Walk in circles till someone opens a tea place here."

"You'll be walking a long time."

"I know. It's on my schedule for tomorrow, too, though."

A door opens up the block and a man I don't recognize strolls our way. Shifting my stance, I avert my shiner till he passes, as if the Ray-Bans weren't precaution enough.

Jade nods at my bag. "You got food?"

"Yeah. And I'm running late, actually."

"Of course you are, Hoots." She smiles. "Nice seeing you."

"I like your tooth, Jade. I wouldn't change anything about it."

"You know, I was going to think about that later? I was going to sit by the fire and brood?"

"Don't do that."

"I was going to."

"Don't put brooding on your schedule."

We stand together, unspeaking. Jade studies me curiously.

"What?" I say.

"Nothing. I was just wondering if you're still ... you know. That way."

"Excuse me?"

She looks off, smiling.

"And what way would that be?"

"Oh," Jade says. "Like you'd strangle a baby panda to get ahead. That sort of way."

"What!"

"Hoots, I've got to know these things! If I'm going to flirt with somebody on a sidewalk, I need to know what he's capable of."

"Is that what we're doing? This is flirting?"

Jade shrugs, pursing her lips.

"Why would I strangle a baby panda," I say, "when I could sell it?"

Jade laughs. She wags a finger at me. "You think I'm kidding. But I'm on to you, Scott."

"Let's talk about this flirting thing."

Jade bobs on her toes. She stuffs her hands in her pockets.

"We should get together," I say.

Eventually, she nods. "I like that idea. So long as you know that I don't care about any of it. None of it, Scott."

"No?"

Jade shakes her head.

"None of what?" I say. "What do you mean?"

"All that getting ahead stuff. Butchering pandas."

"See, that's what I like about you," I say. And it is.

"Well." Jade thinks about it. "Then I'll make us dinner some night. How's that sound?"

"It's a date." And actually I'd like right now to drop Greta's shitty waffles in the gutter and follow Jade home for a meal. Or follow her in circles for tea. I'd like to drop It All, but it's 8:40 a.m. on a Monday, and I won't do that.

"I bought that house, by the way," Jade says. "The one you saw. I don't know why I'm telling you that. But I bought it."

"I like that house," I say.

"Well," Jade says, "let me know about dinner. Any night."

8.

NOBODY ATTENDS SEA LANTERNS GAMES, particularly during exams. I could sit front-row, I could drag a sofa into the Jub and relax on it courtside—nobody'd wonder about my purple eye because nobody'd see it. Given my activities with Kelly's players, I maintain some distance, though, and watch the game not from the stands but from the press box in Jubinsky's rafters—a press box no journalist has ever used, to my knowledge. Janitors at some point hijacked it for storing supplies, and arriving before the game, I need to drag aside stepladders, WET FLOOR signs and crates of disinfectant to make room at the window overlooking the court. It's an hour before tipoff, and though the scoreboard counts that hour down, I see no one on the floor preparing, not even a ref. Smacking on the press box lights, dust whirls underneath them and stinks on the heating bulbs. I smack the lights off again and sit in the dark, so nobody sees me up here.

I've gotten comfortable when knuckles pound the steel door behind me. What the fuck, I think, as Harvey Crowe lets himself into the box, pulling the door shut behind him. He carries a chair over to mine—Roman-nosed Harvey of sixty years, maybe sixty-five, with fluffy hair that may've once been curly. He wears the coat and tie I assume he'll wear tonight on the sidelines. Harvey's coached with Leo since the eighties, maybe longer.

When he doesn't speak, I nod at him. "Harvey."

"Did anybody look at that eye?" He has an offhand, southerny voice. "You don't want pressure building up in there."

"It's fine."

"Why don't you get it checked out? What's the harm?"

I'm about to ask Crowe what exactly I can help him with, here in this press box tonight, when he jumps right in: "But setting aside your injury, if I might. You're interfering with our basketball team, Scott. You and Peter Muraro."

I stare Harvey down, though with my eye swollen shut, it could seem like I'm merely pondering something, reflecting. I'd hoped this wouldn't happen right away, but naturally it was coming. "That's one way to look at it," I say.

"It's what's happening."

"The smart way to look at it is we're playing hoops. Since Leo won't."

Crowe's mouth twitches faintly. He rubs it away. "I understand what you mean, son. I do. But it's Leo's team. He decides."

"He doesn't decide if they play *basketball*. Are you from fucking Mars, Harvey? He decides what plays to run, that sort of thing. He checks people into the game."

"It's his team."

"Not when he smashes it with a wrecking ball, it's not. Come on, you know that. I don't need to explain this to you."

Crowe considers me awhile. Then he nods. "Fair enough."

"Excuse me?"

"It's your rodeo, Scott. So when should we expect you to fire us? Should I clean out my office?"

We fall silent, Harvey waiting for me to answer. When I don't, he shifts on his chair, leaning forward to speak earnestly. "Listen, I'm no moron, son. Leo isn't either. Despite how it seems."

"I never said he was."

"I know the position you're in. I know you had to act. Hell, I'm not even asking you to stop. That's not why I'm here."

"Then why are you here, Harvey?"

Crowe searches my eyes, the bad one and good one, then relaxes in his chair, straightening his coat. "I want to be sure we understand each other. That's all."

"I don't think we do."

"You can run your things," Harvey says. "You and Pete. Your workouts. Coach the boys, Peter can coach them during games. Leo won't mind and I won't stand in his way. But that's as far as this goes."

I'm confused. Since obviously that's as far as this goes. Where else would I take it?

"What I'm saying," Crowe says, "is you leave Leo out of it. He works with his team how he wants to work with them. He doesn't owe you explanations."

I search my mind for any reason that won't work, and find none. Harvey's asking only for what I'm already doing anyway, and that's a concession I'm always happy to make.

"Shall we shake hands?" Crowe says. And we do.

He's nearly to the door when he turns, running a thumb along his belt. "If it's worth anything to you," he says, "I hate putting you in this position. It's too bad."

"You didn't put me in any position."

Harvey smiles. "Isn't that the truth? We do it all to ourselves then try to hang on."

"Just win this fucking game," I say.

9.

FROM MY LIPS TO GOD'S EARS. The Sea Lanterns show up pissed and stay pissed all night, accruing thirty-one fouls to go with their rebounds, blocks, steals and copious points—most of which points arise in the paint, from guys thumping skulls. It's feverish. It's electric. And everybody eats some flesh, the seven guys from this weekend each totaling eight points or more to complement his hefty creel of fouls.

Of the team's thirty-one, two of the fouls are technicals, including when Odie mashes on a Yakima guard in the second half, then backpedals onto defense with biceps hoisted in a muscleman pose—not an inexcusable taunt except that Odie maintains his arms in the pose throughout the ensuing possession, executing defensive slides with his knuckles on his shoulders, till whistles blow. The five players who skipped our workouts also catch the bug, or most do, diving for loose balls, attacking the rim, yelling, fouling, glory being as communicable as any disease. In light of our treaty with Crowe, I'll send Peter around to these kids' dorms next week to recruit them again. No more whispering about it. Sound the bugles, get a switchblade in every fist. By all indications, Muraro himself is ready to stack bodies. He spends the game out of his chair, directing traffic with fierce gestures, stamping his heels, acting by God like a coach.

Harvey ignores Peter, but Leo clearly relishes his young assistant's antics, watching from the bench with hands composed, beaming, as if Muraro were some Branagh-in-training, breathing life into a classic role.

We win, and not by any hair's breadth. At 72-51 it's a mauling, and the vibes of it must radiate far into the universe, because Tuesday, walking to my meeting with Chancellor Toren, I get a call from out east. I'm following the trail between town and campus when my phone rings, and its chimes sing more melodiously than any wren in the trees. "This is Scott," I say.

The voice I hear lingers in its sentences—a trait of educated speakers who shape their talk rather than honk it. I love hearing from people like this, both because their voices soothe and because, inevitably, they're calling from somewhere *above*. "Dr. Darrow, I wasn't convinced I'd reach you," the man says. "I understand it's early where you are."

"Early's fine," I say. "I prefer early."

The man is Ed Goodwin, Vice President for Personnel Management at Leighton University. He's calling this morning to acknowledge the materials I forwarded, and to thank me for my receptiveness to his school's overtures. "Headhunting can be an unsavory process," he says. "We appreciate your generous spirit."

What I appreciate is Goodwin's interest in an Athletic Director at a shit college who undermines his coaches and tells student-athletes they have "dumb guppy faces." So everybody's grateful today. "Well," I say, "it's lucky timing. I've decided to take lunches this year, Ed."

"I'm thrilled to hear that. Thrilled."

"I haven't committed to leaving. My current position, I mean." Did my lips just form those words? "But I'll admit I'm curious."

"The curiosity is wholly ours, Dr. Darrow. Reviewing your materials this morning, I could envision nothing but success for you here. Or elsewhere, if that's where your road leads."

I'd bat my lashes at Goodwin's praise, if my lashes weren't enfolded into a bloated hematoma. "Well, that's kind of you, Ed," I say.

"Not that I should get out over my skis. This is a housekeeping call, primarily, just confirming receipt of your file. Though confirming with great enthusiasm."

"I understand."

"As of this morning, Scott, we've solicited materials from a shortlist of applicants. From that pool, we'll invite finalists to visit our campus and community. That should happen in the coming weeks. For now, I'd hope to answer any questions you have."

The question I should ask Goodwin is: Why, when I'm seducing you people—every time when I seduce you people—does it feel like I'm mainly seducing myself? And why, Christ help me, don't I ever play hard-to-get? But I just whistle Dixie. "I'm sure questions'll come up, Ed, but I don't have any now. I appreciate your call."

"It's been a pleasure matching a voice to the name, Dr. Darrow. You'll hear from us soon."

—

Entering Toren's office, the win from last night and call from this morning rest in my coat pockets like derringers, and I'm almost embarrassed to have arrived today carrying such firepower. Rodney shuffles out from behind his desk, a brittle geezer in pilling wool, and what chance does he stand against me? What threat could Toren make today that I wouldn't chew up and spit out on his floor? "Rod," I say. We grip hands vigorously. Arranging ourselves at the desk, I note that even Toren's office broadcasts his defeat. From the upholstery and carpet to the wall art, paint, and curtains, every hue and theme in the room obeys the law of surrender set forth by its occupant's shitty posture. The seat cushion underneath me is patterned with sailboats, for Christ's sake, the lampshade on Toren's desk grainy and brown. On the windowsill behind Rod, a red Dala horse gapes at the room like an idiot. I think: Bring it on, dotard, with your fuzzy fucking ears.

Like Crowe before him, Toren indicates my eye. "Got a nasty bonk there, didn't you? Look at that."

I smile. "Occupational hazard."

"Yes," Rodney says. "I heard that. Someone told me that. You were playing with the team?"

"Just a few practices."

Toren wags a pencil at me. "Now you were a basketball player yourself, upon a time."

"I was. In school."

Rod's grinning teeth are disarranged and yellow. "Contemptuous of health and safety, he roars out of retirement," he says. "You may color me impressed, Scott. I'd take a hundred more with that nerve."

"Thank you."

"Though my goodness, protect your face."

As our laughter subsides, Rodney shakes his head, dissolving into thought. "It didn't used to be so rare, you know? Moxie like yours. The way I learned it, why everybody manned an oar. If you were in the room, you were a teammate, by God. You'll remember Pete Rose for the Reds of Cincinnati? He was the skipper, but he ran onto that field every inning, same as Larkin or any of them."

"It's so true." While the sailboat chair isn't uncomfortable, I wish Toren'd wrap this shit up so I could drive to Aberdeen.

Raising his pencil, eyebrows arched, Rod says, "Not that Mr. Rose represents *every* value we espouse."

"Of course not." Though actually Pete Rose's ugly side is what I admire about him. Who better than Rose, after all, understood that rules aren't any different than, say, the ninety feet separating first base from second? The game presents opportunities and when no one's looking, you steal. You cork a bat, lay bets, fuck it. They throw you out, fine, but if you're not exploiting opportunities then you're not playing ball.

Toren aligns his pencil on the desk. "But rolling up one's sleeves," he says. "Digging in the soil, with your two hands. That's what produces results, Scott."

"Oh yes," I say.

"You tussle with this basketball team, you get in the trenches, in the mire? By God, last night they cut down the nets. Excellent progress with those young men, Dr. Darrow. Terrific initiative from you."

Teams rarely cut the nets after improving to 1-6, but I accept Rod's compliment for the white flag it is. Any confrontation he'd planned for today is kaput, and what lies ahead for me now is a quiet December of agitating Kelly's players into three more, or even just two more wins, at which point Leo Kelly as a subject will erase itself from my brain. Goodwin, if he wants, can investigate my tenure at Fog Harbor. My record will bear scrutiny, and to hear Toren today, the old vulture might even go to bat for me, like a vintage Charlie Hustle. So that should about do it. That should cook this goose. Scooting forward in my chair, patting a knee, I say, "Well, Chancellor, I appreciate this chat. As always." I'll be to the Mobil station on 111 in fifty minutes, driving with windows down and rain blowing in. Afterward, I'll call Jade about dinner.

My hand floats over Toren's desk, but Rod's own claw stays in his lap. "Off so soon?" he says. "I'd hoped to visit another minute or two. One minute longer, if you would." Toren glances at my hand, and withdrawing it, brushing my trousers, I settle back onto the sailboats.

"Our schedules these days." Rod shakes his head. "I understand why you'd rush off. Probably eight appointments waiting for you back at your office. Oh, I understand. A thousand demands, a thousand ..." Plucking his cellphone from the desk, Toren deals it away with disgust. "... instruments. What I wouldn't give for my father's life. He practiced estate law in St. Paul, estate and taxation. If there was a letter to draft, or petition or filing, he'd sit at his desk in silence and compose it longhand. Hours of concentration for one document. Why it's unimaginable anymore. But forty years at that desk and not one complaint against Dad at the Minnesota Bar. Was he a conscientious attorney? You bet your socks he was. But that unblemished reputation owed something to the fact that his fountain pen never chirped at him or played web videos."

I should muster some interest, but only stare at Rod's head.

He's embarrassed. "You're wondering if I kept you here to share stories about Dad."

"I don't mind."

"No, I'll come to the point. 'More matter with less art,' as the Bard said. I'll come to the point."

Something in my spine, where it meets my skull, seizes up. Because Toren already came to his point earlier, when he said: *Excellent progress with those young men, Dr. Darrow. Terrific initiative.* That's all Rod had for me today. So why is he clearing his throat now? Why's his gaze troubled?

Toren's fingertips descend to the desk—gently, as if addressing piano keys. "Mr. Kelly," he says. Abruptly, he retrieves his hand. "Coach Kelly. What can you share about his conduct, Scott?"

"His what?" I say.

Rod and I lock eyes. Then he twirls his hand. "We receive reports. With *regularity*, we receive reports concerning Mr. Kelly. And they're unwholesome, to put it bluntly."

"I don't know what you mean."

There's a long silence before Toren smiles, nodding thoughtfully. "Okay. Let's try it this way, then. I understand that Leo Kelly is erratic."

"He is," I say.

Rod waits for me to continue. When I don't, he squirms in his chair.

I say, "Chancellor, I won't dress this up. Leo's a basket case, you bet he is. You remember this summer with the regents. That's Kelly. Those are his feathers. The man opens his mouth and ... well, you saw it. But his team's about to win a lot of games, Rod. This is going the right direction."

Toren steeples his fingers at his lips. "So we leave it at that, do we? His team wins games, so that's it?"

I sit forward in my chair. "I don't follow."

It's the same meek Rod it's always been—ratty wool and fucked teeth—but for the first time maybe ever, the man's jaw ripples. His gaze settles on me like collapsed earth, and however feebly, Toren is pissed. "I didn't know," he says, "that accruing basketball wins excuses a man from decorum in your book. Excuses him from respectability."

This does happen to be true in my book. Why else win, unless it sets you free? But I say, "Rod, Leo's not lighting fires around here. He's kooky. He's eccentric."

Toren spits the word back at me. "Eccentric..."

"If he were wrecking the program, I'd feel differently. Or if he went too far. But Kelly's—"

"Why don't you quiet down now, Scott," Rod says.

I think: Why, you snaggle-toothed prick. Shushing me.

"You'll listen to this, I think," Toren says. "And you will listen with both ears. Eccentric. You said Kelly's eccentric. Well, I had my fill of eccentrics in the 1960s when what passed for enlightened thinking was wagging your body parts on every street corner and eating from another man's plate because you thought you deserved it. I've seen enough of eccentric. The world's seen enough of it. At this institution, a man will comport himself with a mind to propriety and coherence." Rod points at me. "Particularly when he represents this college in a public way. Do you know Commissioner Pucek, Scott? Arnold Pucek?"

"I don't know Arnold Pucek," I say.

"The commissioner and I serve together on the Rotary board—twenty years we've served on the board—and if anybody grasps the essence of this community, believe me it's Arnie."

"I don't doubt it."

Toren lifts his chin, observing me. "Twenty years. So you'll appreciate my displeasure when Commissioner Pucek informed me that a coach at this institution has been sighted around town—*repeatedly* sighted around town—flouting decency. And neighborliness."

Passing a fingernail through my hair, razoring my scalp, I think: Rod, for Christ's sake, don't do this. Don't need Leo to be *right*. Need him fettered, ok. We both need that and I've fettered him. But not right. The man will never be right. Don't send me into his brain with superglue.

"You're aware of Cook Park, Scott?" Toren says. "Behind our middle school? The nature park?"

I'm aware that Fog Harbor probably has schools and parks, but past that I'm taking Rod's word for it. "Okay," I say.

"Well. Several homeowners near Cook Park, good homeowners, looked out their windows the other night and saw Mr. Kelly walking in the trees with a kerosene lamp. Not with a flashlight, mind you—a lamp. They said he stayed out there till morning, freezing cold and all. That's *your* coach, Dr. Darrow. That's a leader at this college, stalking through the woods in the dead of night like a ghoul. Now I suppose those families should remember Kelly's basketball wins? Rather his basketball *win*? That should content them? What if you visited those homes to explain your thinking, Scott? You could lay it out so everybody understood." Toren flicks his hand. "'Mr. Kelly gets to scare you, I'm afraid. That's his right. His team has momentum.'"

Listening to Rod, it's as if the lighthouse yesterday indeed were a ship, and indeed spotted a man waving from the wharf, only to weigh anchor and sail without him. "I'll talk to Leo," I say, my breath hardly catching the words.

"In point of fact," Toren says, "you will do more than talk to him, Scott. This *stops*, and it stops today."

"Yes."

"The Cook Park incident came to mind, but that's not the extent of this by any means. George Haslett at the IGA tells me that Leo Kelly follows customers up the aisles, harassing them with riddles and so on. Now that's uncivil behavior, I'm sure you'll agree. And it isn't restricted to local complaints, either. My office yesterday fielded a call from Portland. Portland, Scott. A gentleman there answered his door and Mr. Kelly barged into his home talking gibberish about the man's family, refusing to leave. Why the fellow had never so much as laid eyes on Leonard Kelly. We're lucky he didn't call the police. I won't stand for it, Scott. I will not."

I shake my head. "No."

"Control," Rod says, "this man. You're a gifted administrator and we hope to keep you, Dr. Darrow. But if this comes to dismissing Mr. Kelly and paying his absurd guarantees—guarantees *you* supported—then his won't be the only spinning chair. Do we understand each other?"

We do.

Toren nods. "Splendid. Now if you'll excuse me, I have other appointments."

10.

JADE'S HOUSE WAITS back in the trees, its living room a small glow under the towering firs, hemlock, whatever they are. Woodsmoke drifts from her chimney, flattening itself through the forest and out over the beach, where the tide's low and where Jade trudges in her Wellingtons, humming songs I don't recognize and whapping the sand with her shovel to spook clams.

She gave me a shovel, and mesh basket, but also gave me spiced wine and I'm working that instead, whapping it against my face to spook calmer feelings to the surface. The shovel I poke here and there like a gentleman idling his cane.

Jade should say, "Bend that back, you sorry shit, I'm not your digging slave," but instead says, "A couple days ago ..." *whap* "... I tried ..." *whap* "... doing this by sonar. I stood out here listening for an hour. Listening to the sand."

"That's how herons do it. When they fish," I say.

"Well, no it's not. But I see why you'd think that." *Whap.*

"It's how bats do it."

Jade pauses, peering out over the flats, before again hoisting her shovel. "That could happen. A little bat could wriggle its snout into a mollusk. Tell you what, it'd only take one time and they'd never look back. It'd be chiropterans as far as the eye could see out here, every night."

99

A coin of sand near Jade's boot sifts away into a dimple, and kneeling beside it she levers her shovel into the muck, hauling out glops of it. Jerking up her sleeve, Jade probes her arm into the beach like a veterinarian palpitating Mother Earth's own calf. "You want to reach behind it," she says. "Or it'll gash your hand."

"Razor clam," I say.

"Worthy of its name."

I sip some wine, myself feeling like an invertebrate buried in goo in Pacific County. Like one who'd slice you if provoked, or perhaps like one who'd lie in hot butter to be fried. Chancellor Toren certainly fried my ass, no doubt about it, and I'll need to address that soon, but for tonight I'm happy standing on this beach—this deserted beach—nothing but nothing stretching into the distance. *Happy* overstates it, but I like Jade and like the loose fit of her thoughts. I like wine, and how this woman ambushes clams like some ravenous coastal monkey. Grunting, she drags the thing up into God's daylight, or God's dusk, thumbing gunk off its shell. I offer my hip, where the basket hangs, and Jade drops it in.

Farther up the beach, again whapping sand, she says, "What's it, three weeks till Christmas? Two? I'm lousy with calendars."

"Two weeks."

Whap. "A fortnight. And why do I get the feeling you haven't put up a tree, Hoots? And watered it? And busted out tinsel?" *Whap.* "And bought gifts for your loved ones? And wrapped them creatively?"

"I don't see you doing all that," I say.

"Not yet." *Whap.* "I'm pretty sure I might, though. I might tomorrow."

"I don't want a tree in my house. There's trees everywhere already, now I need one in my house?"

"Well, get a cactus. There's actually native cactus on the coast, if you know where to find it. Prickly pear."

"I don't know where to find it."

Whap. "Obviously not, but I'll show you. I'm generous with my time. And I'm a biologist."

"I don't have a cactus stand. Or ornaments. Or wrapping paper."

"Or loved ones!" Jade sings, and my face melts into a droopy, juicy frown. It's not strictly true—my dad still lives near Hilo, and Mom's retired with her second husband in Clearwater, Florida. But we don't exchange Christmas gifts, that's true. Littering the sand at our feet, in manic jumbles, are thousands of sandpiper tracks. As nimbly as one of those birds, Jade dances up to kiss me. Her lips are restful, almost merciful—they're how pillows feel on those stray nights I sleep like the dead—and my mouth, as Jade ends the kiss, chases her somewhat. Rubbing my arm, she returns to clamming.

"It's getting dark," I say. Back down the beach, Jade's living room gleams in the trees.

"So it gets dark." She kneels to dig a clam, tossing it into the basket.

"What about … seeing?"

"We'll see with our feet, Hoots. Relax."

Personally, I see with two eyes and the brain behind them, not with my feet. But I wouldn't mind getting lost out here tonight, and even swept out to sea. Swept far enough, to Polynesia, I could look up Dad and trade gifts with him. We could eat papayas. Jade walks up the shore, vanishing into the dark; I only spot her again, her movements, by gazing off to the side. When I catch up, she drops two more clams into the basket with a clatter like money.

The basket holds six clams when Jade sprays them off under the spigot in her yard. She leads us across the grass toward what is more accurately her cabin, not house, with its snug living room, kitchen, one bedroom and bath. Inside, my cheeks prickle from the heat. "Play us some music," Jade says, dumping our clams into the sink.

After scrubbing my face and hands, the bathroom's water sulfuric, I return to Jade's living room and flop on the sofa. I've forgotten the music but fuck it. Who wants to stand again? Gazing around at the bookshelves, stacks of blankets, lamps and twin glider chairs (both ratty), I call into the kitchen, "I like what you've done in here, Jade!"

She glances over her shoulder, then pries a shell. "Done? You think I did something?"

I look again, this time at the woodstove and night-black windows. I don't know if she did anything. The room seems better than when I was here in July—more inviting, though in July no woodsmoke scented the air, cozying things. Also, I'm more tired now than I was then. As a rule, homes speak more powerfully to the exhausted. "You folded those blankets," I say. "Is that what it is? I don't know."

Jade carries wine into the room, wrapped in a towel so her hands don't slime the mug. Sitting against me on the sofa, she sips some then passes it off. Perhaps three clams lie shucked in the kitchen, no more, and once the full haul is shucked, Jade must clean, bread, and fry the fuckers, plus cook everything else besides. Yet she's in no rush, nor ever is. I am. I can't help it. Even sprawled in a seaside cabin, medium drunk, the core of me races on toward something. But while this lasts, I'll float with Jade in her peace. May it last and last. Nudging my ribs, she says, "Thanks for hanging out, Hoots. This has been nice."

"That's it? You're booting me?"

"What?" Jade smiles. "No. No boots for Hoots."

"Thank God." I wriggle deeper into the sofa. "I can't walk right now."

Some time passes before Jade rests her hand, the unslimy rear of it, on my chest. "It's that same old thing with you, huh? Running your battery down. Burning yourself up."

"I'm not burned up," I say.

"Maybe not burned. But you fucked your face up pretty bad."

"Me? I didn't do this."

"Of course you didn't."

"I didn't. Plus that's the point of batteries. You use them up."

Twirling a finger over my shiner, an inch off the skin, Jade says, "Is this the point of your face?"

I sip our wine. Claiming the mug with her towel, Jade also sips, the glogg and hot room igniting radishes on her cheeks. "You don't believe that anyway," she says.

"Believe …?"

"That that's what your battery's for. Running it down."

I gaze at the ceiling, the wine's nutmegy tang calling to mind what my parents drank, cold nights in Montana—wine they offered me Dixie cups of. "I don't know what I believe," I say. "I'm too pooped for believing."

Knuckling my sternum as if rapping at a door, Jade says, "Well, it's your life for the living, Hoots. But you're missing a lot if you think your battery's for running down, and not soaking up."

"I know."

"You don't act like you know."

"I know. But I know."

After a while, I say, "Jade, you really sell the shit out of this."

"Excuse me?"

"Your life. All this stuff. Unemployment in a fishing village isn't everybody's dream, but you really sell it."

She laughs, flashing the pit of her absent tooth. "I'm employed," she says. "Sort of. But thank you."

"You can't want to stay here, though. Really? Come on, you'll move to California." Jade grew up in Kentucky, but I've always imagined her bound for Santa Cruz or Big Sur. She only landed in Fog Harbor incidentally, for a work stint last year.

"No, Hoots, this place feels good. And I bought the house."

"Yeah, but you'll sell the house. Why don't you level with me, Jade: you're depressed and bored as shit out here. You can admit that, right? For me?"

She laughs. "Scott, I'm happy."

I shake my head. "I'm sorry to hear that."

Dragging a knuckle down my ribs, watching it go, Jade says, "There is one thing about living here."

I drink our wine.

"Sometimes ..." She studies her hand. "... if I don't see anybody for a day or two, or a week, it starts to feel fake. You know what I mean? Like everything's made up."

"Okay," I say.

Jade dims an eye. "Like I'm not looking at a world anymore. Like everything's just painted on the inside of my head and I'm trapped in there."

"I don't like that."

"It doesn't happen all the time," she says. "But it happens."

"So I'm doing you a favor, coming here and drinking your wine?"

"I already said thank you, Hoots."

Gripping Jade's sweater, I draw her toward me for a kiss, throughout which she curls her briny hands underneath her like a hatchling's talons. "What happened to playing music?" she says.

"I was getting to it."

Squirming off the sofa, Jade returns to her preparations in the kitchen. The woodstove hisses and pops, and now and again wind sheers the cabin, whistling its corners. Wrapping a blanket onto my shoulders, I cross to Jade's computer and flick on songs, then join her in the kitchen. Her hair dangling down, she lifts clams out of panko crumbs like sandy organs and arranges them on a sheet.

The music says:

You crept down the hall with our warmth in your bed
And made your way out to the street
But I never quite lived even once you were dead
And I still hear your whispering feet.

I say, "It doesn't fuck you up, Jade? Not working?"

She flops a clam around then shakes off the excess crumbs. "Oh, it does sometimes. That's definitely where I'm at my coolest, anyway. As a person."

"Yeah?"

Jade shrugs. "You wouldn't believe what I know about dirt, Hoots." Her fingers bulbous with egg and panko, Jade scrapes them into the trash and washes her hands.

"Yet here you are in Fog Harbor," I say. "Where cool is illegal."

She loads the clams into her freezer, then works a hand in the overlay and every which way of her black hair. Then: flinging out her arms, addressing the ceiling, Jade says, "But holy shit, do I feel my heartbeat, Scott! I do!"

I should kiss this woman more earnestly now, and elsewhere but on her lips. Instead, Jade refills our wine and says, "Let's drink this. Then let's smoke."

"Now you're making sense," I say.

It's not the Camels I've craved, but smoke of any kind racing hot over my tonsils, as we sit together on Jade's stoop, rain nibbling our socks, is enough to sand my edges. "This is hardly anything," Jade says, admiring the papery stick in her fingers. "It's just barely, barely. I love it."

I take the thing from her hand.

"I noticed you quit the other stuff," she says.

"Cigs?" I smoke. "Not if you've got one for me, I didn't."

"You could've fooled me."

The rain tapers off, then rides a sudden gust into our laps. "That's one of those … best practices," I say. "Fooling people about cigs."

Jade claims her weed. "Best practices. You mean for work?"

"For work. Yeah."

"I wonder," she says. "How is it that people at your job can kick your ass, but you can't smoke tobacco?"

"It seems like the whole universe is questions like that. Lately anyway."

Jade stubs out the joint on her stoop. "Then you need to see more of it, Hoots."

"More …?"

She pats my foot. "Of the universe. The terra."

Taking my hand, Jade leads me off the stoop and across her driveway. I don't ask where we're going, the gravel underfoot chewing my heels and mud wicking up my socks. Reaching the trees, we skid down a ditch to a path through the brush, where roots and pinecones start in on my feet. I hear wind, but when the path finds a stream, I realize it's water sounds filling the air, not zephyrs—water tumbling a last few yards to the sea. Behind us, Jade's house throws light onto the front half of everything— every leaf, every trunk, every stalk, every twig.

"What am I looking at here?" I say.

Jade kneels in the undergrowth, pawing around.

"Are we eating snails?" I say.

But she hands up grips of plant life instead, wet plant life, the leaves as round and shimmering as coins. "Miner's lettuce," Jade says. "With some sesame oil and nuts? You'll see."

She fills my arms with the stuff, and it's a surreal few moments, this woman hunkered in the forest in the rain, offering up doubloons.

It's a simple meal—greens, clams and oiled bread—that we don't eat till after midnight, needing first to hang our wet clothes by the stove and warm ourselves in the shower, and also needing more wine and to warm ourselves further in the musty quilts on Jade's bed. After dinner, dishes strewn on the table, we drop into a black sleep that I don't emerge from till late morning, when my breath floats ceilingward in the cold house, the room's only moving thing. Through Jade's window, I notice the tide has come in, its rollers combing downshore, toward town.

PART III

PART III

II.

Strolling First Street with the hot tea Jade made me, I notice everywhere the rough material people use to fashion livings—poinsettias for our florist, crooked teeth for the dentist, a zonked junkie some policeman can arrest, crates of eggs riding a dolly into Greta's for Therese to crack. No one profession, given this bounty, hems anyone in. God as my witness, I could trim flowers. I could drag lowlifes to the slammer. By Pacific County standards it's a brilliant winter's day, the cloud ceiling high and scalloped, scraps of blue managing almost barely to appear. Oh, I could be anything in this life, starting now. Why not? It's just that what I am underflows such drugged thinking, and survives it. It survives one excellent night's sleep and the ensuing good cheer. It survives a king's helping of love by the sea. So my best wishes to you people with your *jobs*; I'm headed now to hogtie a legendary hoops coach, because I'm Scott Angstrom Darrow, born 1983 in Longmont, Colorado, and while any life out there might've been mine, this one is.

It's exactly the center of the workweek, midday Wednesday, the time of all times at which employees should occupy their desks. But I've never witnessed Leo at his desk at any time on any business, and so instead of calling there, I call Muraro.

"Scotty," Peter says. "Scotty, hey. Tried swinging by your office earlier."

"I was busy." I sip my tea.

"That's what your guy said. Jerry or whoever. He wouldn't even let me knock on your door."

I think: Good man, Jeremy. Goddamn it, good man. I don't show up in the morning, then that's exactly what you do: shut the door, shoo people away.

"I was stopping by," Muraro says, "because you must've said something to Harvey. Shoot, he gave us the green light. He said to run our practices. Run *day* practices if we want, with all the guys. I'm running one in ten minutes."

"That's exactly what you should be doing," I say. "That's your team, Pete. Show them how."

"Can you make it?"

"What?"

"We had great energy finishing up last weekend," Muraro says. "I thought we'd keep that going."

"I'm not coming to your practice, Pete." Some people approach on the sidewalk, and I nudge the Ray-Bans up my nose. "You're the basketball coach. You're doing this."

"You should come," Muraro says. "But anyway, check this out. I have some ideas to run past you. So Dajuan's a genius, right? He's smart as hell. And Matty's coming along. I say we get into some dribble exchanges, swing the floor left and right."

"Like you said, it's a green light. Just stay on their asses, Pete."

"We add that side-to-side confusion and maybe free up the lob to Odie? Sam seals the backside—"

"Stay on their asses. Listen, where's Leo right now?"

"Coach?"

"How many Leos do you and I talk about? Yes, Coach. Where is he?"

Peter clicks his tongue in my ear, thinking. "He had the guys this morning for one of his things. Then I don't know. Maybe check The Cove?"

"Okay. Go coach your team, Pete."

"I'll let you know how it goes."

"I'll know how it goes. Just do it."

Dropping the phone in my pocket, I stare down the shore toward Harbor Point, over the hump of which and somewhat farther is The Cove. Kelly might be down there, but it'd take hell to reach him and anyway who cares if he's there? Leo can splash in tide pools if he wants. He can catalyze and say poems to the birds. With luck, a rogue wave will happen along and solve my problems. It's only in town, finally, that Kelly fucks me up, acting waterbrained where everybody can see him and fracturing Arnie Pucek's cosmos. Leaving the waterfront, I start up Terrace Street toward what I understand is Leo's home address. He might not be there, but even if I just find his car, I can slash the man's tires and limit his range. Or I could sabotage his brakes.

Climbing Terrace, the ocean yawns open behind me—far to the north, south, and a compass swath in between. It's vertiginous, glancing over my shoulder at that vacant horizon, and reminds me of scaling lookout towers with friends in Montana, wind singing through the trusses, quivering the steel, the rungs in my hands so immediate, yet the valley below me so vast. It reminds me of that and also of Dale Clark, who joked that professional advancement amounted only to a cliff wall for suicidal people, who weren't particular about their route up the cliff so long as they put a sufficient drop beneath them. Well, Dale, here goes nothing. Here goes your protégé, reaching for higher ledges.

A school bus descends Terrace, easing to a stop, and it's in the crosswalk where the bus stops that I happen to spot Kelly: maroon sweats, barrel chest, his hair askance and face lifted to the sky. Waving to the bus driver, Leo looks like Emperor of the Dumdums. Trotting after him, I practically knock the man over as he turns, recognizes me and offers his hand. "Scott," he says, his grip pressureless despite his enormous paw. "Out in the open air, are we? Good to see you, good to see you."

"Good to see you, Leo." I glance around, but we're the only people anywhere on Terrace. "Listen, I'm glad I ran into you."

Leaning sideways, Kelly peers around my shades.

"I know." I gesture at my face. "It's nothing."

"Looks like you caught one in the eye."

"A little bump. It's nothing."

Leo frowns. "I wouldn't say that it's nothing. It happened in your life, didn't it? It's part of your sphere."

"Okay, it's part of my sphere. That is true." I think: Ten seconds into this and I'm ready to die. "So, Leo." I shift my stance. "Listen, I'm glad I caught you—"

Squinting at the sky, Kelly says, "The sun wants to come out. I don't know that it will, but it wants to."

I stare at Leo, right up the hairy barrels of his nostrils.

"It might come out," he says, "or it might not. But we can feel it up there, its wanting."

A mail carrier trudges up the block, sorting envelopes, and ushering Leo aside, I smile at the woman as she passes. Ready in my throat is some idle chitchat, in case Kelly ambushes this stranger with his gobbledygook and I have to drown him out. But she doesn't notice us standing on the curb and Leo doesn't notice her. For nobody but anxious Scott Darrow has anything almost happened. Still pondering the sky, Kelly says, "Or it doesn't want to break through. It moves behind the clouds on its own time, in its own story. That's good, too."

What I've decided to try on Leo today I have misgivings about, both because I'm not convinced it'll work and because if somebody already speaks aloud to his dead uncle in a forest, you should be cautious about fucking with his brain. But the longer Kelly goes on about this peekabooing sun, the fewer reservations I harbor. "Coach," I say, "listen. Really. I need to ask you something."

Kelly's gaze flutters down from the heavens, meeting mine, and this is it. *This* is what counts. If I can hold Leo's gaze, I have him leashed. "What do you know about that patch of woods over by campus?" I say.

Kelly studies me. "There's a lot of woods by campus. What woods do you mean?"

"Those ones off the hill. By Azalea Street."

Nothing registers on Leo's face. It's possible the woods mean zilch to him, but they're where I saw him that day by the creek. *Oh, Michael. We're out here somewhere, aren't we?* The woods are a long shot, but they're what I have to go on. "I was walking back there this morning," I say. "Headed to work." I laugh, both to feign disbelief at what I'm about to say and because I truly can't believe I'm about to say this—can't believe my life and career have so thoroughly demeaned me. "I think," I say, "I heard something back in there. In the trees."

Kelly lifts his chin, inspecting me over the bulge of his nose. "Heard something?" he says.

"A voice," I say. "I couldn't quite make it out. But it wasn't talking to me. I don't think it even knew I was there."

Leo's silent.

"This sounds crazy, I know. But you, Coach. I had this feeling the voice was asking for you."

After a while, speaking at a whisper, Kelly says, "Can you show me where this was?"

I nod. "Yeah. If you're not busy, we can go there now."

Leo shakes his head. "I'm not busy. Not anymore."

12.

IT BUYS ME an afternoon, anyway. An afternoon and cockleburs on my socks.

Being nearly the shortest day of the year, it's not much of an afternoon, though. We're in the woods only an hour or so before dusk thickens in the trees, last night's frost still clinging to the earth even as another night comes on. All around us, nearby and far off, that thawing frost drips onto stumps, leaf mulch and brush, filling the forest with tapping sounds like the settling of a creaky mansion. I stand behind Kelly, off to the side, while he inspects the dirt where I said the voice spoke. His gaze traces invisible wires out into the trees, then follows those wires back to the soil at his feet.

"It might've been somewhere else," I say. "It could've been anywhere in here."

Leo shakes his head. "No. Something's here."

Okay, I think, then it was here. We'll stand here. There's no houses around and nobody hiking the trail. We'll stand here for weeks, if that's what it takes—till Kelly falls over dead or Goodwin calls.

Nodding vaguely, Leo picks his way into the brush, angling upslope. Since it's not viciously cold out and since prolonging this into the evening makes sense, I cup a hand at my mouth and shout after him, "It said something about the stars, Leo. The voice did. Or about the moon or nighttime or something." Not that stars or the moon ever shine in Pacific County. Knowing that Kelly appreciates a lyrical touch, I add, "It said it moves in darkness. Or it speaks to darkness, something like that."

Up the hill, hands in his pockets, Leo surveys the trees like a birder. In profile like this, he reminds me dimly of the Kelly I remember from years ago on TV—the Kelly we all remember, presiding over sidelines as if the games unfolding before him issued not from the sweat of players but from his own blunt will. As if they weren't basketball games at all but foosball matches, his eyes turning the rods. Who would've thought, all those years ago, that someday I'd lead this titan on a snipe hunt through a jungle? Yet every step from there to here has made sense to me. Oh well. Every step from there to here probably made sense to Leo, too, and look how he turned out.

I trek my way up to him, accumulating those burs on my socks, and on my pant legs and sleeves too. We stand together in the twilight under a rocky overhang. Patting the stone, Kelly says: "To or from?"

"Pardon?"

"It speaks *to* darkness," he says, "or *from* it?"

The distinction wouldn't matter unless Leo hoped for what I hadn't said. "From," I say. "It said from, now that you mention it."

Kelly nods. "Mysteries live in the dark. Or in our dark. They have no choice but to speak from there. Or else behind—did it say behind?"

"I think it did," I say.

Leo rubs his jaw, peering into the trees.

"It said it speaks from behind the darkness," I say. "I remember it now. From and behind."

Kelly touches my wrist to silence me. Ear cocked, he scans the woods around us, though nothing moves out there and besides the pit-patting frost and creek's trickle, nothing makes a sound. Through the trees, I see red lights pulsing on Fog Harbor's radio tower. Leo laughs then, one bursting laugh that's nearly a sob, and though it's dark, I see the man wipe his eye quickly, or his nose. I wonder if anyone from campus, namely Harvey, is out looking for Kelly yet. Or for me.

"He's here," Leo says.

Unless "he" is a skunk or porcupine, he is definitely not here. But I whisper back, "I hear it, too. That's it, Leo. The voice."

Leaning forward into the dark, Kelly says, "Oh, would you listen to that? His sweet laugh."

It's not the aspect of Uncle Mike I'd have expected Leo to hallucinate, given that he once described his uncle to a student reporter as an "asshole till the day he died." On the balance, this isn't any weirder than the rest of Kelly's shit, though. I say, knowing the answer, "Who is it? Do you recognize him?"

And Leonard says, "That is Michael Phillip Kelly."

It won't happen often that I stand in a forest at night in December—filthy with burs, pretending to hear voices—and think: *This is going better than I could've imagined.* But where we stand, under this overhang, nobody on the trail could spot Kelly or hear his voice. Even in daylight nobody could spot him, and that's if anyone used the trail this time of year, which they don't. Now, I just need to nail Leo's feet to this ground.

Touching my ear, I say, "Did you hear that, Coach?"

He listens. "What is it? What'd he say?"

"I'm trying to make it out."

"Tell me," Kelly says.

Leo's eyes search mine in the dark, and seeing his credulousness, his open-faced, child-like belief ... well, the man should break my heart with his pathetic sincerity. But I'll save my heart to break against something better than Leo Kelly, thanks very much, and anyway if Leo wants to stand in these woods wringing his hands over some dead Chadron coach, then that's his problem and his own fault. "I don't know," I say. "I think he said he comes here. Or lives? Lives here? I don't hear him now. But I think he said he lives here, Leo. Like this is his home."

Kelly studies the trees, breathing heavily. "His home," he whispers. "His home."

"He said you can find him here when you want to talk to him."

I lean against the rocks, hands in my pockets, expecting with these good lies to be here all night. Instead, stepping past me, Leo starts down the hill toward town.

"Coach?" I call after him, his rustling moving farther and farther off. "Coach?" I descend through the dark, vines whacking my face. "Leo!" I shout. "Where're you going? Michael said he was up here by these rocks!"

I catch up to Kelly down the trail, near where it meets Azalea Street. Headlights sail by in the night, and only when Leo shrugs off my hand do I realize I've grabbed his arm.

"We're not just leaving him up there, are we?" I say. "Coach, this is *Michael*."

"You don't need to remind me." Leo continues down the path, and following at his shoulder, I say, "We didn't even hear him out. We don't know what's on his mind."

We spill onto Azalea Street, our soles clopping the asphalt like hooves. We're as noisy as cavalry out here, and people are going to come to their windows. They'll see us. "Leo," I say. "I want to go back up that hill."

Kelly stops in the street and faces me. "You? You want to go back?"

"Michael spoke to both of us, Coach. There's a reason for that, and I want to know what it is."

Leo continues up the street.

"Coach!" I shout. I'm aware of the living rooms on both sides of us, casting gold squares onto their lawns.

"The reason," Kelly barks over his shoulder, "is the easy part, Darrow!"

"Keep your voice down!" I hiss. And I think: Especially when you say *Darrow*.

Leo marches back up the street, his finger trained on me like a lance. "Michael has been out there," he says, "for years. Now it's time I be with him. That's why he's speaking. There's your reason."

"Good," I say. "Great. Let's be with him."

But Leo turns, dragging his old knees on up the block. "Once I'm ready. It won't happen till I'm ready, Darrow."

Kelly recedes down Azalea. Trotting after him, then tailing him up Fourth Street, we come eventually to Terrace. There's cars and pedestrians everywhere on Terrace, and I keep close enough to Leo to headlock him in case he tries any wacky shit. But he just hobbles along, head down and hands in pockets, clear up the hill past Fifth Street and Sixth, past Seventh, to his house.

Kelly's house is lousy—a cracked stucco façade behind a flimsy iron gate and shaggy lawn—and leaving him there would be nice. I could shoot home for a consecutive night's sleep, or effort at that, and come find him again in the morning. But what's to keep Leo from venturing out again in ten minutes, or twenty, or an hour or five hours? What's to keep him from turning up in Commissioner Pucek's garage?

Stepping over the gate, I trot after Kelly up his walk. "Coach," I say, reaching the porch just as he's shutting his front door. He hesitates, his face hovering in the dark.

I say, "Can I come in?"

"What?"

I glance behind me at the streetlights spaced down Terrace and the cars prowling underneath them. "I wasn't sure I was going to tell you this ..." I say, still unsure what it is I'll tell him.

"What do you mean, tell me?" Leo says. "Tell me what?"

I scratch my nose. And fortunately the muscles I use for thinking sometimes double as the muscles I use to speak, eliminating the lag. "It's not just Michael," I hear myself say. "He's not the only one."

Kelly's silent in his doorway.

"I heard someone for me too, Coach. Someone I know. And I'm freaked out. I don't know what to do about it."

Eventually, Leo says, "Did it say your name? Did the voice say your name?"

"Well," I say. "I think that's what it said. It sounded like my name."

Kelly ponders this.

"It said my name," I say.

And he ushers me inside.

13.

SOMETIME NEAR MORNING, Kelly folds closed the ATLAS VAN LINES box he's kneeling over, and has knelt over (together with his sixty other Atlas boxes) obsessively since 8:00 last night. Settling onto his ass on the floor, groaning, he scans his disordered living room for what I suppose is his missing sixty-second box. That one certainly will contain the objects eluding him: Braun electric shaver ("The Eighty-Six model," Leo has clarified for me) and Koss HV headphones. "That shaver is here," he says, not for the first time. He taps his ear. "And I hear those headphones."

Your question might be: What are we doing at 5:00 a.m. on Kelly's floor, rifling through moving boxes? And my answer is: Make up an answer for yourself and it'll make more sense than anything I could tell you. But eating time is what we're doing. Or, if you ask Leo, we're exhuming knickknacks from his life in Las Cruces, New Mexico, where in the eighties he coached New Mexico State University's Aggies. This has something to do with Michael, somehow. Having heard his uncle's voice today, Kelly believes he needs to round up old trinkets. Do I understand this? I understand that if Leo's in his house, he's not abroad in Fog Harbor fucking up my future. So I understand it as well as I need to. Earlier, Kelly suggested we compile mementos at my place, too, seeing as I heard a voice of my own out in the trees—my Aunt

Audrey's voice, I've told him, though if I have an Aunt Audrey, it's news to me. "It's a plan," I said. And it is. Once we're done here, we'll spend as long as Leo wants indoors at 2F.

"What're they playing?" I say, seated across the floor from Kelly, my shoulders against the wall.

"Pardon?"

"You said you heard your headphones. What's playing?"

Leo wags a finger. "Now you're thinking, Darrow. Listen for the song, it'll lead us to the source."

Actually, what I'm thinking is: Fill up the air with bullshit. Command this moment with bullshit. It's 7:00 a.m. out in Albany. Goodwin will finish breakfast soon and reach for his phone ...

Eyes closed, his eyelids fluttering, Kelly listens to the silence. His furnace whooshes alive, breathing up through the grate in the floor. He nods. "There. There it is."

"What is it?"

Leo touches his lips. Then—with steady pitch, I'll admit—he sings:

*"A childhood of dreaming of being on horseback
A bedroll, some whiskey and beans.
Riding up high in the mesas and hoodoos
I traded my homestead for dreams ..."*

He cups an ear as he sings, as if relishing his Koss HV sound. "What's that?" I say.

Parting his eyes, Leo notices me sitting across from him, as if he'd forgotten he had company. "You can't tell me you don't know what that is, Scott. That's old Barlow Jeffers."

"I think I knew that. The name's familiar."

"Man about invented country music."

"What else did he sing?"

But Kelly ignores this. "My office in Las Cruces," he says, "looked out at the mountains. The Organ Mountains. All that rugged country spread out in my window. I'd lock the door and play western songs."

Leo's elbow rests on his knee, his hand dangling between us. We watch his hand, the two of us, its knuckled mass hanging midair like dressed beef. Then Kelly pats his knee and struggles upright. Limping into the kitchen, he bangs drawers and cabinets, rattling porcelain, before returning to the living room carrying an old, chipped mug. On its side, a faded bandito aims one pistol while reaching for another, his chaps ballooning. Leo tosses the cup into my lap. "And that." He nods at the thing. "I'd drink my coffee out of that."

"It's Pistol Pete," I say. "Go Aggies."

Kelly stares at the mug. "Darrow," he says, "do you realize how much of it there was?"

I set the mug aside. "How much ...?"

"Love," Leo says. "For that life in that office. And I'm not talking about loving the coaching. I mean the feeling of it, Scott. The sensations. The *doing*."

"Well, you were one hell of a winner." Then I say, "Are. Are one hell of a winner."

Kelly laughs. "I'm a hell of a lot of things, aren't I? I'm just plain hell. But the winning, I don't know."

At a loss, I again inspect Leo's mug, turning it in my hands. "I like this," I say.

But Kelly snatches the mug away from me. Crossing the room, he tosses it with some other bric-a-brac he's accumulated in the corner—the fan from his desk in Las Cruces, the nameplate from his office door, a tie pin, a plaque, refrigerator magnets from La

Cocina this, El Toro that, wherever he ordered delivery from. "My phone would ring," Leo says. "And I'd slap on those headphones." He surveys his pile of crap. "I didn't answer calls. And I never left. I shaved right in the office, over a trashcan." At the bottom of the pile, like a checkered tablecloth under the rest of it, are the red-and-white plaid trousers Leo in the eighties was famous for. They're the pants he wore to Denver for the Final Four, and they belong not in a heap in Pacific County but behind glass at the Hall of Fame in Springfield.

Kelly doesn't see it this way. Collecting his shit, pants included, he totters past me to the door. "Open that," he says, then shuffles off the porch and around to the side of the house. From the doorway, I hear his fan bang into the trash, along with the rest of it.

"We can still find your headphones," I say. But Leo marches past me into the house, shaking his head. "Fuck the headphones. And fuck that shaver."

I pull the door shut behind us. "You said we had to find that stuff."

Standing under the bulb in his living room, exhausted, Kelly's face and neck are slabs of shadow. Gooseflesh covers his arms. "Have you not heard a word I've said, Scott?"

"Coach?"

"It was love. I *loved* that life. And I still love it. It's what I need to get shut of."

"I'm not sure what you're telling me," I say. And it could as well be everything I ever say to Leo.

He passes a palm over his face. Going to the wall, he lowers onto the floor where a sofa would've caught him in a house with furniture instead of sixty-one moving boxes. Though I'm one to talk where unpacked boxes are concerned.

"Forget it," Kelly says.

I sit beside him on the floor. "No," I say. "What is it?"

"Let's go to your house."

"Tell me what's on your mind, Leo. We have time."

Eventually, Kelly draws a long, shuddering breath. "It won't happen, Scott," he says. "It never will. Not if I keep hanging on."

"It?"

Leo glances at me.

"Michael," I say.

"He's out there. You heard him, Darrow. And he wants to take me but I need to be right. I need to let go."

Behind us, through the wall, a motorcycle rips up Terrace Street, fading away into the hills. Fog Harbor is lousy with bikes, which puzzles me given the rain, and given that everything else about life here is slow. "In that case," I say, "let's get you right."

Kelly's silent.

"Let's do it. And this is important, isn't it? It's more important than coaching or the rest of it. That's the point you're making, if I understand you."

"I need to be with him, Scott."

I push away from the wall, arranging myself on the floor at Leo's feet. "Coach." I set a hand on his ankle. "Then let's do this. Let's say fuck everything else. Fuck basketball. Peter can handle that."

Kelly smiles, and I wonder momentarily if I've blown it, if he's seeing through me.

"All your practices?" I charge on, waving a hand. "That's off. Let's do this now."

"It's funny you'd mention practices. You've never liked how I work with those boys."

"No," I say. "I don't like it. But this is about Michael now, and Audrey. We can't waste our time with other shit."

"Let go of my foot," Leo says.

I do.

"What you're not understanding, Scott—what you've never understood—is that other shit counts. You hear me? That's part of it. That's how we *release*."

"Then fine," I say. "We'll practice. I'll practice with you."

"I expect you would, if you're serious about your aunt."

"But we're not practicing tomorrow." I glance at my watch. "Today. We're not practicing today."

Grunting, Kelly hauls himself to his feet. "Yes we are."

"It's five a.m., Leo. We're not practicing in two hours."

"You just have no idea what it takes, Darrow. No idea."

Massaging his quad, Kelly crosses the room and disappears up the hall. I hear him back in his bedroom, rummaging.

"*I* have no idea?" I charge after Leo and stand in the doorway. Ignoring me, he rifles through his dresser, tossing items onto the bed. I say, "Coach, how long were you down there, anyway? In Las Cruces."

Kelly flops a maroon hoodie over his shoulder and keeps ransacking his drawers. I know how long he was down there, but wait for him to say it.

"Eight years," Leo says.

"Eight years. And you think you handled all that just now? Throwing out some old pants?"

Kelly straightens up, facing the wall two feet from his nose.

"What about those headphones?" I say. "What about your Braun? And that has to be just scratching the surface."

"I never said I handled it."

"Yes you did. You said you were done. You're ready to fire up a practice in two hours."

"I told you, Scott. It's part of the same thing."

"Yeah," I say. "Part of the same fucking it up."

Leo looks at me.

"Are you with him right now, Coach? Are you with Michael? Then maybe you should listen to me. Let's do a real job on this Las Cruces stuff. We'll practice some other day."

Dangling from Kelly's fingers is a white sock with gold and maroon stripes. He notices it, then drops the sock to the floor.

I say: "Goddamn it, I believe in this so much. In what we're doing, Leo. But we've got to give a hundred percent."

"A real job of it," he mutters.

"What was it you said? You needed to get shut of this thing? Well, we'll start at the beginning. Whatever the beginning is, you'll tell me and we'll start there. We'll cram it *all* in the trash."

Kelly examines the ceiling. Wincing, he eases himself onto the edge of the bed.

"We need to rest first," I say. "That's the first thing. After that, we'll go do it."

"I don't know," Leo says. "I just ... I don't know."

"I'll stay here tonight. Out in the living room. Then in the morning, we'll do it."

"Your aunt ..." Kelly says.

"No, no, no. No, no. One thing at a time."

14.

IF ANY OF THAT MADE SENSE to you, then you're doing better than I am. But I leave Kelly in his bedroom and walk up the hall to sit with his boxes, and pretty soon bedsprings creak through the wall. And that's all the coherence I need from this moment. Time passes, maybe thirty minutes, and when I don't hear his springs again, I slip on my jacket and walk out into the morning.

It's raining, the streetlights down Terrace Street racing with it and the asphalt beneath them jittering with a zillion splashes. Lacking hat or umbrella, I'm soaked in three seconds, but the storm relents as I turn down Seventh toward Sea Breeze Court, till it's a prickly mist choking the air. Black as it is, it could be midnight but for the headlights streaming off the hills into town, Fog Harbor's beggarly workforce starting Thursday's labors before the sun even does. Though my own labors today started the instant yesterday's finished, at 12:00 a.m. sharp, as I dug through Leo's boxes. So in the final analysis, who's the beggarly one?

Rooting in my jacket pocket, underneath the tea mug I'm still carrying from Jade's, I get out my phone and check for calls or messages. But there's nothing—no pings from New York or anywhere. I should chill out with this Goodwin shit, it being only 9:00 a.m. in Albany on the second day since we spoke. Patience, I remind myself. Patience, dickhead.

I call Muraro.

"There he is," Peter says, his voice at this hour less snoozy than I'm expecting, and more chipper and dumb. "The Phantom," he says. "Phantom of Fog Harbor."

"What?"

Peter crunches something in my ear, making a noise like tines dragging through gravel. "Were you actually in your office yesterday?" he says. "I walked by later. Your window looked pretty dark."

"Pete, when I need you snooping under my window, I'll let you know. Christ."

"Hey, hey, hey. Relax. I was walking by."

"How much air is in your brain, wasting time on shit like that?"

Muraro's silent.

"What's the story with Shoreline?" I say. "You got the guys ready?"

"Time will tell," Peter says. "But it was some workout yesterday, I know that. Dajuan, geez, he is a *wolf*. Getting in people's ears, grabbing jerseys. And Kayla did the stats—nineteen for twenty-two in the scrimmage. He missed three shots in two hours, Scott."

"I don't want to lose to Shoreline. Win that game, okay?"

"We'll do our best." Muraro's spoon rings in the bowl.

"Listen to me," I say. "You're running the session this morning."

"You mean later on? We're going at three."

"If I meant later on, I would've said that. This morning's session, in an hour. That's you, Pete."

"Coach runs those morning ones," he says.

I stop in my tracks under a streetlight, as if aliens from Planet Waterbrain were abducting me. "No!" I shout. A face appears in a lighted window, and I move up the block. "Leo won't be there. You're running it."

"Okay, okay. I get it." Then Muraro says, "Wait, do I do a normal one, or how Coach does it?"

"Which one do you think I'd like more? If you had to guess."

"Look, Scott, relax. I'm trying to find out what you want."

"A normal practice. Run a basketball practice, Pete. In an hour."

"Okay," he says. "Ten-four. I'm there."

I continue down the street. "And there's one other thing. Harvey doesn't know about this."

"Doesn't know?"

"He thinks Leo's coming. Leo is *not* coming, and you're going to explain to Harvey that Coach had stuff to do today. He said he was busy and you—you, Peter—should take the team and run practice."

"That's what Coach said?"

"It's what he said when you tell Harvey about it. Don't complicate this, Pete."

"Okay," he says. "Okay."

We're silent. Then Muraro says, "Scott, is there anything else I should know about? All of this seems pretty weird."

"Nothing you don't know about already. I'm handling Leo. You're winning basketball games."

"I can do that."

"Yes, you can. And don't tell Crowe you talked to me, either. Leave me out of this."

"Read you loud and clear. Tell Harvey I did *not* discuss this with Dr. Darrow at six this morning."

I say, "We're not on joking terms, Pete. Do you not understand that? You and I, we don't joke together."

"Sorry," Muraro says.

"Run practice. Tell Harvey what I told you to tell him. Beat Shoreline."

I drop the phone in my pocket and jog up the steps to 2F. Inside, stripping off my jacket, pants, shirt and tie, I hang it all from the ceiling tiles in my kitchen, using clothespins. It's an ugly sight, my good attire dangling under fluorescent bulbs near a gross yellow refrigerator, but in Fog Harbor, anything you leave damp for two hours never smells right again, and molds. I smack on the stovetop fan, in case that does something, then shave, shower and dress in a clean suit. With luck, Kelly's still sawing logs. Trotting down the steps to my car, I again take out my phone.

"Hmm?" Jeremy mumbles, groggy.

"It's Scott. Listen, when you get to work today, turn on the light in my office. And leave it on."

"The light?"

"Around the clock. Leave it on."

"I got you," Harrington says.

15.

THE SOUND I HOPE FOR, returning to Kelly's with bags of groceries, is the sound that greets me: no sounds at all but rain tapping the windows and, faintly, behind Leo's bedroom door, breath whistling. It's 8:30, and with luck we won't need breakfast—Kelly will sleep past lunch—but if I'm smart enough to capitalize on luck, I'm also not stupid enough to expect it. Setting the groceries down gently, so nothing thumps, I set about readying a spread should Leo stumble up the hall.

Nothing in this house is unpacked, but thankfully Kelly's scattered some items throughout his kitchen—a bowl here, some mugs there, one drawer of utensils, a pan. The coffeemaker under his window requires filters but I brought those, and grounds. It'll be enough for eggs, pancakes, bacon and joe. It'll be enough for an hour, and maybe longer if the carbs knock Leo flat again.

It's an uncomfortable experience, prepping food in this sparse kitchen with rain falling in the yard. I need to be quiet, for one thing, and beating eggs quietly is a special kind of tedious, akin to the torture some Greek hero or military cadet with his toothbrush might endure. Also I'm bushed, my good sleep from the other night starting to wear thin. Mainly I dislike Kelly's gear, though, his kitchen gear. The whisk I'm using is a nylon embarrassment from the seventies, for example, its orange handle still wearing a dot matrix price tag (SAV-N-LOW $2.99). It's the whisk my parents might've owned in one of their grubby kitchens, and that I might've gummed on their linoleum floor in my diaper. Leo's coffeemaker sucks, too, its tank made of that opaque, dim plastic that everything once was made of. Just the sight of it screams videocassettes and station wagons, and my dad in a shimmery windbreaker pouring himself a cup.

My being uncomfortable doesn't count for shit, though. I have a meal to distract Kelly with once he emerges from his room. It's been 48 hours since my meeting with Toren and nothing's happened to get me fired. Rolling my suit jacket into a loose pillow, I stretch out on the floor in Leo's living room, rain drumming the roof and minutes ticking by.

—

I awake to an open front door, misty wind blowing in, and that's alarming until I spot Kelly on his porch, in jeans and a sweater, gazing at his yard—Leo's own porch being a better place to find him than Cook Park or the IGA or Portland. It's 10:15, my watch says, meaning I slept for an hour. Climbing to my feet, I unfurl my jacket-pillow, shake it out and slip it onto my shoulders again. I pour two mugs from the pot in the kitchen and carry them outside.

Leo's freshly showered, his soap's harsh scent wafting off him and the remnants of his hair slicked back in white needles. He doesn't look very alive, though, his eyes droopy and lips hanging open. Standing at the edge of the porch, Kelly's shins and feet catch the rain slanting under the eaves, and he doesn't notice or doesn't care.

"Pretty gross day out," I say, putting a mug in Leo's hand.

He glances at me, then at the coffee he's suddenly holding. He sips.

"Maybe we should hang low today," I say.

From this high up Terrace Street, the harbor on a clear morning would be visible, along with the wharf and sooty brick of the cannery. But nobody in this town knows what that is—a clear morning—and all we see around us is soup. "It's a beautiful day," Kelly corrects me.

I choke back some coffee, the kick of it much needed even if Leo's machine gave the brew an oily film.

Kelly nods. "A lot of it has to do with rain, actually. This work we're doing."

"Is that right? You'll have to tell me more about that."

Leo gestures with his mug. "Look at it out there. Right in front of us, Darrow. Everything we can't see."

"Come on." I walk Kelly inside, shutting the door behind us—shutting it and throwing on the deadbolt. "I've got some food for us. We'll want our strength today."

"It's not something you've thought about?" Leo says. "Rain?"

I clear boxes off Kelly's table, stacking them against the wall. "It's not that I haven't thought about it. But I'm not thinking about it the right way, it seems like. You'll need to teach me how."

Leo's chairs also are saddled with boxes. I clear one off and pat the back of it for Kelly. Sitting down, he says, "It's plainly physical. The rain hides what's there, what is behind it. But it's right there. We can touch it with our hands."

"That's amazing," I say.

"We have to walk in the right direction. We have to know what's there and walk toward it. And what's behind us? We have to walk till that disappears, Scott. Does this make sense to you?"

"It's starting to. I'm getting there."

"Your aunt. She's out there in that rain. It's hard to imagine, but that woman is lacing up your little baby shoes."

"You want to start with bacon," I say, "or flapjacks?"

It's once we're eating—Leo shoveling grub by the mouthful, I'm happy to see, helping himself to seconds and thirds of everything—that Kelly says, "So I thought about it, Darrow. What you said last night about starting at the beginning. It's been on my mind."

"Yeah?" I say. "Terrific. Well, that's what we'll do, Coach. We'll start at the beginning."

He dabs his mouth with the toilet paper that's all I could find for napkins. "And I know what it is," he says.

"It?"

"The beginning. Where everything started. I know where that is now."

Crossing to the coffee, I pour us both fresh mugs. "Well," I say, "let's hear it. And don't leave anything out, Leo. We're doing a real job of this today."

The joe steams under Kelly's face, his body rocking in concentration. He blinks, his saggy eyelids not needing to drop much for a blink. "Pioneer Park," Leo says. "In west Las Cruces. It was Sunday, and a cold Sunday. There wasn't anybody around."

I think, Now we're talking. Now we're like razor clams, digging into the muck. "You were at the park ..." I say.

Kelly nods.

"And it was just you. It was cold."

He shakes his head. "No, Susan was there. We were there together. She wanted to tell me about Michael."

I should ask who Susan is and what about Leo's uncle she hoped to impart to Kelly, but from the looks of him, this man is about to sit in his kitchen and spin yarns forever, and as long as he's on that train, I'll cheerlead rather than interrogate. "So Susan was there," I say. "Okay. She wanted to tell you about Michael ..."

Leo fidgets, adjusting the rim of his mug like a dial.

"Coach?"

"I listened to enough of what she said to know what she was saying, Scott. And that was plenty for me. This was in January. Have you been to New Mexico?"

I've visited the Land of Enchantment two or three times. But I shake my head. "I haven't, no. Tell me about it."

Kelly says, "It's so wide open there. You can see a hundred miles, particularly when the cottonwoods drop their leaves. The willows. And this was in January, as I said. I could see right through those trees in Pioneer Park, clear across the valley to the mountains. The same mountains I saw from my office."

"The Organ Mountains," I say.

"Those very ones." Leo ponders this. "She had so much she wanted to tell me, Darrow. Susan did. She had a plan for how everything could go. And God as my witness, I heard her out. I listened to her plan, every word of it. But you probably know how this goes. You're about that age. I knew what she was saying, so by the time she finished saying it, I'd cleared right out. I was up in those mountains, or at least up in my office where I could see the mountains, even if I was drinking coffee on a park bench."

Kelly gazes at the window, where raindrops nose along the pane like fleeing worms.

"I'm trying to picture these mountains," I say. Though naturally I'm not. I'm not picturing any mountains, unless they're the sleepy Catskills that crop up occasionally in search results for Albany. "Tell me about them," I say. "Give me some idea."

Frowning, Leo shakes his head. "You don't need an idea. If you've seen a mountain, you've seen these."

"I can't picture them. Are they ... what do they look like?"

Kelly glances at me, then again eyes the window. "They're mountains, Scott. Everything's flat, then they shoot up into the sky."

"Coach, I'm just saying: this could be part of it. You keep mentioning the mountains, I'm trying to understand how they fit in. Let's not race ahead of ourselves, remember? If you're getting shut of this, you need to—"

Leo knuckles the windowpane. "Have a look at that," he says. "It's pissing out there."

"—do a real job."

Rain lashes the glass, curtains of it dragging over the lawn and street like some stagehand somewhere doesn't know which ropes to yank. As if playing up for Kelly, the sky at that moment flashes blinding ivory. Thunder rolls off the hills—electrical storms in fucking December—tumbling into town like clumsy boulders. I pat the table. "Okay. So Susan wanted to share her plan …?" But, leaving the kitchen, Leo carries his coffee into the living room and stands at the farthest window.

"Coach?"

Eventually, Kelly says, "People don't realize it rains in New Mexico, too. Quite a bit, it rains. And when it does, watch out."

"You were lucky to be inside then," I say, just grasping. "I mean … always being in your office."

Leo sips, watching the storm. "One year," he says, "in March, it poured for eight days. Didn't let up for an hour that whole time. The streets turned into rivers, brown rivers. Floods happened every year down there, little floods, but this one carried off cars and trees, undermined houses. As you suggest, Darrow, I was in my office." Kelly shakes his head. "But no Organ Mountains were in the window. Not that week. I could see maybe twenty feet, twenty-five. The whole world was horchata."

Carrying the pot into the living room, I again fill Leo's mug. He salutes his thanks, and we stand there. "It's true," he says. "Quite true. I was in my office wearing dry loafers while he was out in town in those floods." The rain on the window blots shadows onto Kelly's face. "Isn't that something to think about? Isn't that—" and the word Leo uses is exactly the word I'd use to describe his behavior in any circumstance, in any weather, "— insane? He was out there. Michael was, with Susan. I could've gone to him. It wouldn't have taken anything. I could've changed shoes, or not even changed shoes. I could've walked to where he was."

How it happened that Michael Kelly was present in Las Cruces in the eighties, having died in Nebraska in the seventies or sooner, is beyond me. But what isn't beyond me, where Leo Kelly is concerned? Stepping closer, standing the coffeepot on Leo's mantle, I say, "There's no reason we can't do that, Coach. We can walk to Michael. Take us back to your office. Take us to Las Cruces. It's horchata outside. Okay, so you change your shoes. Now how do we get to him? Take us on that walk. Tell me what you see."

Kelly rocks onto his toes then settles back on his heels, ignoring me. "That was '91," he says. "March of '91. Then they were out of there by '92. I don't know where she took him. She did write me a letter once." Leo squints vaguely. "Not that I could be troubled to read any letters. Envelope sat on my desk for a month before somebody threw it out. Then I was out of there myself in '93. But you know what, Scott? You want to know something?"

In fact I do want to know something, and it's: When will Ed Goodwin call? "What's that, Leo?" I say.

"I made it up to Iowa, to Iowa City. And it rained there plenty. That's one hell of a wet place."

"Interesting," I say.

"And I didn't realize it at the time," Kelly says. "But he was out in that rain, too. That cornfield rain. Just like he's out in any rain." Leo nods at the window. "Just like he's out in this, as we speak."

"Come on," I say. "Let's sit down."

"Michael's in the rain because I put him there, Darrow. Do you understand what I'm saying? I staked out a warm, dry place, and staked it out just for myself. That left the cold weather for Michael. So that's where he is. That's why you heard him in the trees. That's why he said he lives there."

"Coach," I say. "We're speeding up again. Let's backtrack some."

Transfixed at the window, Kelly eventually says, "Probably what I should do is cut everything away. How's that for a plan? And not nickel and dime this. Cut everything off and get out there with him, in the rain."

I was afraid that outdoors was where Leo wished to be. Setting his mug on the mantle, the man steps past me and crosses his house to the back door.

"Is that why you came here, Leo?" I say.

He fumbles with the deadbolt.

"To Fog Harbor, I mean. Did you come for the rain?" It's the question I should've asked Kelly months ago. Why was he here?

"Fuck the rain," Leo says. "I came for Michael."

"Let's catch our breath, okay? I'll make some more eggs ..."

But Kelly wrenches open the door and storms out into his backyard, never mind the downpour and never mind that he's in stocking feet.

"Leo?" I say. "Leo!"

I trot after him into the yard, my shoes immediately fouled in the marshy grass and puddles—my shoes and the lower third of my trousers. But it's a private lawn, thankfully. Kelly's neighbors to either side lack second floor windows, and their main floors are obstructed by shrubs. Across the alley, only shitty garages stare back at us.

"Coach?" I say.

Leo stands near his own garage, where two spindly fruit trees are staked with twine. He gazes at them and at the rainy sky, his arms at his sides and muck wicking up his jeans.

"Let's go inside," I say. "We'll make a plan."

"You're looking at our plan, Scott."

"I thought we were taking this one step at a time."

Leaning against his garage, Kelly tugs off one of his ruined socks. Returning his bare foot to the grass, he says, "There's a step." He removes his other sock, tossing both into a puddle. "There's another one."

My phone chooses this moment to burst into song, whirring and jangling in my pocket. Leo glances over his shoulder, then stares out at the towering evergreens several streets away, their limbs collecting scraps of fog. "I should get this," I say, despite the screen flashing Georgia instead of New York.

"That's a mistake, Darrow. You should stuff that thing in the trash."

"I'll be right inside."

"That's not the direction we should be moving."

And I'd heed Kelly's advice except that just one person in the world would call me from Georgia digits. Retreating to Leo's kitchen, where I can spy on him through the window, I put the phone to my ear. "This is Scott."

"Darrow," Crowe says. "Just what in the hell are you doing?"

"Harvey, nice to hear from you. What can I do for you?"

143

"I want to know what the hell's going on. Are you in your office?"

"Not at the moment. You sound upset, Harvey."

"Fuck you," he says.

"Excuse me?"

"Sending Peter Muraro to lie to me? That boy is a cupcake and you know it. You should know better."

Harvey's on the money with that one. Entrusting Peter with a basketball team is one thing, but I couldn't have expected him to pull the wool over anyone's eyes, least of all a pair of shrewd eyes like Crowe's. Luckily, Muraro needed only to complicate Harvey's life some and jam up his footwork, delay him. Which he did, because it's 11:45 a.m. He needn't actually have *duped* Crowe any more than I need at some point to procure a dead uncle for Kelly. Or a sane coach for Rod Toren. None of this needs to *work*, ultimately. It just needs to keep going awhile. So I say, "Harvey, back up. Hold the phone. I need you to start over from the beginning."

"What's your play, Darrow? Where are you taking this?"

"My play? Harvey, I'm making fundraising calls this morning. I'm calling assholes and begging for money. What do you mean, play? What play?"

"You know goddamn well I'm talking about Leo. Son, we had a deal."

Through the window, I see Kelly pacing his yard, his hair dangling in wet spines from his otherwise baldness. "Leo's not my business," I say. "That's your responsibility."

"I want to know what happened this morning. And you're about to tell me."

"This morning? Okay, let's talk about this morning. Three boosters pulled their checks because our hoops coach acts stupid all day. Now I'm tugging dicks to get that revenue back. That's one thing going on this morning. Is that what you mean?"

"Scott, you don't know what you're doing with this. This isn't a game."

It's hard not to laugh. Because of course I don't know what I'm doing with this, except to know I'm doing it, which puts me one step ahead of anybody trying to stop me. And of course it's not a fucking game. "Look," I say. "Leo came by my office last night. Is that what you're talking about? He said he wanted a day to himself to catalyze things. A day or two. That's the word he used—catalyze. And he said Pete could take the team. Why, what'd Muraro tell you?"

Crowe's silent.

"You there?" I say.

"Son," Harvey says. "You need to level with me right now. Did Leo say that? What else did he say?"

"I can't figure out why you think I have time for this shit. You and Leo both. *Talk* to each other. Leave me out of it."

After a while, Crowe says, "I hope you're as smart as you think you are, Scott. And not just for Leo's sake."

"If you find him, would you tell him to call Peter? Kid's sitting on his thumbs waiting to hear if he's running practice tomorrow."

"What do you mean if I find him? I didn't say I couldn't find him."

"Goodbye, Harvey."

"Scott, goddamn it—"

Dropping the phone in my pocket, I walk back out into Kelly's yard. Across from me, the man stands at his shrubs inspecting leaves with his fingers. He looks beautiful this way, hunkered in a sheltered lot where nobody can see him. But Harvey's not a dipshit. He'll be here soon.

I step closer to Leo. "Coach," I say. "I think you're right. I think we need to get out there."

Kelly shuffles around to face me.

Twirling the Buick keys on my finger, I say, "Let's really do it. Let's go."

16.

By eleven that night, the LaCrosse's floor mats, upholstery, armrests and console are as soaked with rainwater as the suit I hung from my ceiling tiles seventeen hours ago, and the suit that replaced my drenched suit is demolished—sodden, like everything else, but also mud-spattered and torn in the elbows and shins from the nettles we wrestled through while fucking around in the national forest north of town. (Nettles and also one lone patch of cactus, if you can believe it, which I've made a mental note to report to Jade. No need for any guided botany tours, thanks very much, I've shown myself to the prickly pear.)

Our destination initially was the forest near campus, where Michael "lives," but once in the car I encouraged Leo in the belief that relying on woods near his house constituted fainthearted-ness on our part, and that our loved ones, Michael and Audrey, needed to know, needed to *see*, that we were all-in and would die to be with them. "They can't think we're chickenshit," I said, accelerating up the hill leading out of town.

"But that's where he lives," Kelly said. "In those woods off Azalea Street."

I shook my head. "Michael lives in the rain. You said it yourself. He lives in rain, wherever it's falling."

And Fog Harbor disappeared behind us.

How to explain this next part? Or have you, like me, abandoned the quest for explanations where Kelly's concerned? It doesn't matter. This is what happened: I parked the Buick at the end of a deteriorating two-track, where the canopy closed over us and streams washed out the road. Exiting the car, groaning with stiffness, Leo stood in the forest and—bear in mind, I'm just telling you what happened—stripped to the waist, tossing his sweater and shirt into the brush. Already wet from his time in the yard, Kelly's full torso was gooseflesh. His thick hide, with its white fur and liver spots, shivered like a horse's. "Are we going swimming, Coach?" I called through the window. "What're you doing?"

Lifting his face to the rain, or what rain sifted down through the trees, Leo said, "You could say that we are, Darrow. We're leaving behind the shore."

Exiting the Buick, I stood with Kelly with folded hands, waiting for him to lead us somewhere. With Fog Harbor far behind us, all my requirements for the day were met. We could swim, if Leo wanted—metaphorically, literally or both. We could roast marshmallows, forage for leeks, count woodpeckers, fuck it. Kelly could be God of this trip to the woods, provided he didn't cut it short.

Stirring a finger at me, he said, "You too."

"What?"

"We didn't come into the rain to wear raincoats, Scott. Off with it."

Possibly Leo expected me to shed my suit jacket and shirt, too—and possibly I should've, to save them—but I tossed just my overcoat back into the car. Then, with no further commentary, Kelly scrambled down the ditch and up the other side into the trees. I ought to have hopped in the Buick right then and burned rubber back to town. Leo could've lived his final hours as a geriatric sasquatch—another breed of legend altogether. But we'd passed some cabins down the road, and if Kelly failed to die in the woods, I couldn't have him showing up on a stranger's doorstep, nipples bared. Cinching my laces, I ran after him up the hill.

And I'd have followed Leo into far, far worse, for the afternoon and evening it bought me—afternoon, evening, and chunk of the night. It wasn't pleasant. My suit was a goner with the Buick still in view down the hill, and by an hour later we'd lost all visibility, dusk in December in Washington arriving at 4:00 p.m. Twisted ankles, wildlife attacks, hypothermia—all were in play, but I didn't object and spectacularly 76-year-old Leonard Kelly didn't either. He didn't mind or even notice the darkness any more than he minded or noticed the nettles and that one cactus taking from his hide the same pound of flesh they claimed from my excellent wool (except literally). Overtaking him once, in a clearing, I saw on Leo's chest the hundred nicks and abrasions he'd suffered, the deepest of which seeped tiny threads of blood, transforming his torso into a sort of lurid river map. Beyond the cuts were the rashes he hazarded, and the interest that insect life might've taken in his skin and blood. There was the cold. The dicey footing. None of it affected Kelly. A total and unredeemed barbarian, he sucked air and charged ahead into the brush, not calling out to Michael but keeping his face lifted, on a swivel, receiving in the center of his sensory palate all available traces of his uncle—the sum of which, I don't have to tell you, was none.

Our whole time in the woods, Leo spoke to me just twice. Once, gesturing brashly at the night, he hollered over his shoulder, "We won't make it anywhere if you don't pick up those feet, Darrow! Move it!" The experience of which—a man better than twice my age screaming at me to hustle—was thrilling in its way.

The second time Kelly spoke to me, hours later and three drainages from where we'd left the Buick, the rain was intensifying. Though I'd have gladly kept up our frolicking till morning or longer, we obviously were done. Gripping his knees, spitting between his feet, Leo swayed like a drunk.

I grabbed his elbow. "Coach?"

"That can't have been nothing," Kelly panted. "All of that just now. That has to be something."

It was nothing, though—just some fucking around in the hills. "I don't know how you could say that," I said. "Something? You know it was something. You don't feel it out here, this energy?"

"Then where is he?" Leo gestured at the dark before again gripping his knees. A rope of spit hung from his mouth.

"Let's wait here a minute. We've come this far, let's hold still. Let's listen."

I was mulling how to work *mystery* and *prayer* into our conversation when Kelly straightened up, wincing. "Let's go," he said.

"We can't leave it out here," I said. "This thing we're feeling, this ... we've got to give it some time."

But Leo picked his way back toward the car. We wouldn't make it there directly—no chance of that. One vestigial skill from my years in Montana is I can drop a pin in my mind and trek back to it over peaks and ravines, night or day. And if there was one direction we weren't moving in, it was the correct one. That was terrific. I'd let Kelly roam the wastes for hours longer, like Grendel or whoever. Except thirty minutes passed, and up ahead of us over the berm of a road, someone's Buick LaCrosse came into view. We'd circled back to it from the far ridge, somehow. I'm not sure how.

"We'll go find him where he is," Leo said, waiting for me to beep open the doors. "Where we know he is."

"I feel him here, Coach," I said. "I feel Audrey here, too. I don't think they're far."

But Kelly had nothing to say to that. He waited while I found my keys.

Driving back to town, rounding the headlights into electric-eyed deer and raccoons, I hoped Leo would sleep. He was old, and I directed the heating vents onto his skin (his sweater and shirt being back where he left them, in the forest). If Kelly did nod off, I planned to drive clear to Oregon or farther, and when he awoke, plead idiocy. *Shit, I don't know where we are, Coach. I must've missed the turn. Let's pull off and get some rest.* And then in the morning keep barreling south, till Friday went the way of Thursday and we were a thousand miles from Fog Harbor. Instead, defying sleep, Leo nixed the heater and punched down his window, insisting I lower mine as well. The frigid weather thundered into the car as if from a cannon, but Kelly offered his face to the wind and rain like he smelled blossoms out there, like he smelled honey.

——

Leaving the Buick on Azalea Street, parked some distance from the trailhead (using the woods after dark violates posted ordinances, and we don't need one of Pucek's finest jacklighting us tonight, with our hair bonkers and clothes destroyed or missing), we start up the path into the trees, pursuing—if I understand this correctly—exactly what we left in the trees an hour ago and fifty miles north, which is to say: nothing that eyes can see or hands touch. Mercifully, the rain has abated into that smoldering, rude mist that Fog Harbor residents consider to be not rain at all, not that Kelly and I benefit much from fairer weather, being already drenched. We can see our footing now, at least, with the sky returning to earth some of downtown's orangey haze.

Leo should've slept in the car, however. Or stayed home all day to sleep. Struggling up the trail, his vigor dissipates like a pneumonia patient's, and soon he's slopping his sneakers through the mud from one tree he can lean against to the next—a pneumonia patient, which given the man's age and escapades lately he might soon be, God willing. Or else Kelly's fine physically and just sad (and who wouldn't be sad, hauling his ass over the countryside after fictitious bullshit like this?). Meanwhile, I'm doing stellar. Thursday's almost in the books and the woods in every direction are devoid of inquisitive eyes. My clothes and Buick are fucked, and I require Camel unfiltered cigarettes with an almost medical urgency, but the game now is to trade every resource I have for every next day. And it's working. It is working.

Ahead of me, pausing to rest, Leo scans the dark hillside above us, the dim sky swirling creamily into the trees. Nodding, he says, "We peeled it back, Darrow. We laid it bare."

"I was just thinking that," I say.

"It's unvarnished. It's more vivid than it was." Kelly glances over his shoulder. "You should do it now, shouldn't you? Shouldn't you go to her?"

"Her?" And then I remember Aunt Audrey. "Oh," I say. "Yeah, I should do that now. You're right."

"Find her voice, Scott. Listen for it, then when she speaks, you go to her. Wherever she is, you *go*."

"That's the best way to do it. What are you going to do?"

In reply, Leo steps off the trail into the brush, floundering through what looks to be more nettles. It's fine. He's moving so slowly after a day on his feet, and so noisily, that he couldn't exactly slip away from me. Minutes pass and Kelly's still just spitting distance from the trail. It takes a half hour or longer for him to become a smudge up there in the dark, and even still I hear his rustling, and could run him down in no time. Brushing off a log, as if I might yet salvage my pants, I sit. Rooting the phone from my pocket, I confirm that there haven't been any calls, and then to confirm that my phone still works (despite recent adventures in my pocket), I place a call to the first number I think of. It happens to be the 406 number of our landline in Hamilton from years ago, and no sooner does it ring, verifying my phone's integrity, than I end the call and slip the phone back into my pocket. I'll skip the conversation with whoever owns that number now, since who gives a shit?

Leo's silent, up in the trees, and I wonder briefly if I've lost him before again hearing disturbances, tacking now to the west, back toward the trail. My log is luxuriously comfortable—I could germinate on it, like a shiitake—but I can't have Kelly making the trail, turning up it and stumbling out onto the campus lawns at 1:00 a.m., with their security cameras, the man being shirtless, bloodied and mental. Starting up the path, my quads stiff, I make it only a short distance before hearing, down the trail behind me, a separate commotion of rustling and snapping. Then I hear laughter.

This life was never going to be easy.

"Who the fuck?" I mutter, peering hard into the dark. Flashlights swat through the trees a hundred yards downslope, and while there's too much giggling for it to be anyone official, everyone in a fuck-all town like Fog Harbor, its rumor mills being what they are, might as well be official. Charging up the hill, straining a glute in the process, I make it to where Leo will reach the trail in a moment. But he's still struggling with the brush, kicking his way so deafeningly through the groundcover and vines that I'd need to yell to get his attention. And what would I yell, in any case? Act normal, people are coming? If plain English worked on Kelly, I'd have resolved this situation two weeks ago on a city bench in the rain and saved myself an Italian suit and major blood pressure points. Besides, how normal could Leo act when he's not wearing a shirt?

The flashlights snap off, one then the other, and whoever's lurking down there simply cannot come up here and find Kelly barebacked and raving, they just can't. Inspecting myself by the glow of the sky—my sleeves, lapels and pants—I decide that under cover of darkness I don't look as pulverized as I am. I'm like one of those bums you're not positive is a bum until you look closely, and maybe after midnight in a forest people won't look closely? Maybe before they look closely, I can scare them off? Not that I have any choice in the matter. There's nothing else to try. Raking a hand through my hair, straightening my collar and cuffs, I start down the trail, limping some with the glute.

I'm not sure how far down the path I saw the flashlights, and in the dark I'd have shuffled past their owners, but for the ruckus they start making in the trees. Ducking behind a boulder, I peek around it at the excitement going on, and if there are two unwholesome motivations for lurking in the woods in the wee hours, kidnapping a basketball coach is one and I bet you can guess the other. They're like bears in those trees, bucking around, pawing and moaning. I rest my cheek against the rock.

Believe it or not, there once was a Scott Darrow who would've relished this spectacle just to relish it, who'd have cowered in a forest and watched fucking for no grander a purpose than to watch fucking, full stop. That Darrow had no prize he was chasing, though, and if the fucking is thrilling tonight, to the man I've become, it's only because it preoccupies the jackasses doing it. Leaving them there, I sneak up the trail to hustle Leo off to the rocky overhang where Michael lives, or even deeper into the woods. I only reconsider my strategy because I remember what town I'm in, and remember the degree to which gossip in this town draws water. And if I need to make certain that these fornicators, should they spot Kelly or me, won't say shit about it, then they need to know what I know about them.

There's no elegant way to do this. Striding back down the hill and into the brush, I shine my phone light into the perverts' faces. I don't know what I'm expecting will happen, but one of the lovers turns out to be Jeremy Harrington, of all people—my assistant, Jeremy Harrington—behind whom, buckling his jeans while trying to shield his eyes from the light, stands a mean-looking cannery grunt I've seen around town here and there, at the barbershop, at the IGA.

"Get that out of my face," Jeremy says, squinting. He fumbles with his boxers.

Dropping my arm, the light pools in the grass. "Shit," I say. "I didn't know it was you."

"Me?" Harrington says. "What?" Then he says, "Wait, *Scott?*"

"You know this fucker?" the grunt says, pacing nervously, his belt rattling in his hands.

I say, "Listen, if I'd have known it was you … I didn't know it was you."

Jeremy tugs up his jeans. "Well, it's me," he says. "Surprise."

"We weren't doing anything!" the other guy shouts. "Stop acting like we were!"

"I know you weren't," I say.

"Stop acting like it! I know what you're thinking!"

"I've got to go," I say. "You weren't doing anything, I get it."

"Scott …" Jeremy says.

"Forget it, Harrington. You're fine. It's none of my business."

Clutching his jeans with one hand, Jeremy gestures with the other. "It's just … I mean, if people … you know."

"Look," I say. "Did you turn on the light in my office today?"

"What?" Harrington says.

"I called you this morning. I said to turn on the light in my office. Did you?"

"What the fuck is he talking about?" the grunt says.

Jeremy nods. "It's on," he says. "I left it on. Yeah."

"Well, there you go." I walk away, then come back a few steps. "That's what I care about, okay? Just that."

Harrington stares at me in the dark. Finally he nods. "Okay."

"I'm sorry." And I apologize to the other guy, too. "I'm sorry. You didn't need this from me."

—

Back up the trail, with the flashlights behind me organizing themselves and descending through the trees in silence, I find Leo resting in the path, a palm in the mud as if he hopes to stand but can't remember the maneuver. He nods down the hill. "Was that her, Darrow? Audrey? I couldn't make out your voices."

"Something like that," I say. "It was some people who said they saw her. They saw a woman in the trees."

Kelly nods vaguely.

"They saw a man, too. They think they did. They heard a man's voice."

Leo shakes his head. "He's not here, Scott." He gazes at the earth between us, his forearm resting on his knee.

"Now why would you say that?" I say. "Of course he's here. We know he's here. We heard him yesterday."

"I would say it," Kelly's gaze rises, his voice rising with it, "because he's not *here*, Darrow! Do you see him here? Point him out to me!"

"That doesn't make sense," I say. "We know he's here. It's like you said, his presence is vivid."

Glancing at his hands and legs, Leo finally remembers how to operate them. He labors to his feet. "His presence," he mutters. "You can keep his presence. I want to see his face, Scott. And where is that?"

"You'll see it, Leo. You'll see Michael's face. Keep believing."

Kelly totters a few steps before regaining his balance. He continues down the trail. "I'll see his face," he calls back to me, "once I deserve to see it. That's all this is."

—

By way of deserving to see his uncle's face, Leo, when I deliver him to his house at 2:00 a.m., drops a legal pad on his kitchen table, brews coffee and spends the dead hours concocting schemes for Friday's practice—by which I mean the practice scheduled to begin in five hours, at 7:00 a.m., Kelly having refused to cancel it. And by which I mean "practice," not practice, since the drills Leo mutters about, and that I peek at, craning my neck over the table to read his berserk notes, incorporate nonsense like *muscular erasure, cognitive masking, memory breathing* and even *fasting,* with no mention of jump shots, team defense, picks-and-rolls or rebounding. *Neural purge,* Kelly scrawls so brutally that his pen tears the paper, and while I can't visualize what specifically neural purging entails, I'm confident that Leo should neural purge in private, alone, if neural purge he must. The activity likely doesn't qualify as "decorous, respectable and coherent" in Rod Toren's view.

At least Kelly's put on a dry hoodie. It's his one comprehensible act of the last twenty-four hours, even if he pulled the hoodie over his bare torso without yanking it fully down, so that, hunched at his notes, a fuzzy mutton of tummy spills out of the sweatshirt into his lap.

Patting the table, shaking my head, I say, "I don't know. Something about this doesn't feel right to me, Leo. Don't you feel that? It's like we're turning down a dead end."

Kelly rips back a page, his fifth or sixth, and starts scribbling on the page underneath it.

"I can't understand why Michael would want you to practice, is the thing. Or really to do anything with other people. This is between the two of you, right? Why would he want everything," I flick a hand at Leo, "splashed onto the front page?"

"Fill this up." Without lifting his eyes, Kelly slides his mug to where I can reach it.

Carrying it to the pot, I say, "Weren't we going to cut everything away? Wasn't that the plan?"

"I need to sweat with those young men, Scott. They're fresh souls. Unwritten souls. They're standing where a world can find them, and that's where I need to be." Leo removes the reading glasses he's using and gestures them at me. "You should think about that yourself. What're you doing to prepare? How will you become naked?"

I dislike Kelly referring to practice with his team as a vehicle for becoming naked, especially since he's proven to be quite literal on the nakedness subject. Also I've diffused enough sweaty-naked-young-men-in-public situations for one morning. And why am I amping this man up with more coffee? Leaving his mug on the counter, I return to the table and sit on the edge of my chair with hands folded between my knees. Arranged this way, it's like I'm beseeching Leo to open his heart to the Lord and Savior Jesus Christ.

"If you want to practice," I say, softly, "I get that, Coach. God knows we need to do everything we can to deserve Michael and Audrey. I'll practice with you, you bet I will. I'm committed to this one thousand percent." I'm overcome with emotion, and though it's only frustration, my damp eyes and urgency hopefully convey warmth to Leo. "But you've been going all day, big guy. And night. And it's been one hell of a day and night. Why don't you get some sleep? Peter can take practice this morning. We'll round up the guys later on, or this weekend."

Kelly returns the reading glasses to his face, and reviews his notes. "Why would I put this off, Scott?"

I just *said* why you would put it off, motherfucker. "You'd put it off," I say, "because it's what's good for you. And Michael loves you and wants what's good for you."

Leo's eyes—what I notice now are yellowish, veined eyes—puzzle at me over the rims of his specs. "*Loves* me?" he says. "What on earth gives you the idea Michael loves me?"

I sit back in the chair, rubbing my nose. And wait, does Michael not love Leonard? Did I miss something? Maybe with all of this being totally fucking imaginary and stupid, I jumped the gun on the love thing. "Well," I manage to say. "He doesn't want you grinding yourself into dust. How about that? Till there's nothing left of you. Look, I won't pretend to understand more about this than I do, Coach. But Michael wants something with you, doesn't he? He needs it just like you do, and if it's going to happen, then you need to look after yourself. For his sake."

Licking his pen, Kelly scribbles at the bottom of one page and onto the next. "Michael may well want me to grind myself into dust, Darrow. For your information. And that's if he wants anything from me, which I'm starting to think he doesn't. So fuck love. I'm a curiosity to Michael, at most. And not a major one, by the looks of it."

"He cares about you, Leo. You should honor that."

"What happened to that coffee?"

"I'm not saying we can't practice," I say. "But let's get our feet underneath us, and—"

"We *are* practicing, Scott. In four hours. Now cut the shit and get my coffee."

17.

JEREMY WAS HONEST about my office light, it seems, since when Kelly at 7:00 sharp marches his guys and me with them across campus toward West Quad, I see it up there on the top floor of Coleman Hall: my virtuous office, shining out over the college as if an angel labored in there with holy tools. That should do the trick, I think. Though the community might suspect that I'm not truly in my office once they see me instead down on West Quad, neural purging with Leonard Kelly.

Leo shuffles ahead of us through the grass, his gimpy strides leaving something like ski tracks in the frost. I'm gimpy myself, with the glute, and also the backs of my hands have developed a hot rash, my knuckles throbbing with it. Reaching the trees surrounding campus, Kelly pivots and knifes his hands in both directions for the dozen of us to fan out. I glance up the hill at Main Building and the lighted courtyards, the parking lots. Nobody could spot us down here—it's too early and too dark—and if there are security cameras on this part of the quad, I don't see them. Still, I wish Leo would march us fully into the trees, where nobody could see us even after sunup. For that matter, it'd be nice if he marched us off campus altogether, down to The Cove or somewhere equally concealed. (Another nice thing that Leo could do would be to not march us period—to be a sane man instead of a batty one.)

Person by person, Kelly moves his stare down the line of us, from me at one end to Peter and Harvey at the other, stopping along the way at each yawning, booger-eyed college student in attendance. The kids wear unlaced sneakers this morning, and pajama bottoms, hoodies and beanies. From our conversations last week, Muraro had me expecting some of the team to have bought into Leo's voodoo and be raring to go this morning. To a soul, however, they seem pissed as fuck to be enduring the cold at 7:00 a.m. in their PJs. Odie in particular isn't having it. The kid stands with his arms drawn in from his sleeves, hugging his torso, his hoodie's collar lifted over his nose. Not that anyone's pain registers whatsoever with Kelly. His whistle in one fist and notepad in the other, he lowers his gaze to the earth at his feet. At a whisper, he says, "We'll take a minute now. We'll breathe this air. We'll dissolve."

It's difficult to tell, with Leo speaking so softly, but to my ear the man sounds short-winded. As his breath leaves his lungs, it seems to sieve through his voice, reducing his sentences to stray words and words to loose syllables. Kelly's exhausted, clearly, and who wouldn't be after the 48 hours I've put him through? But if Leo's mission today is to make a demented scene on campus, then he'd be advised not to broadcast his poor vitality, as I'll exploit it without hesitation and not feel shame about that, either. Scanning the quad for students or administrators, I happily see none. But there's blue creeping into the air, the gray frost turning white. It'll be daylight soon.

"Let's relinquish," Leo says, "the lie of the present moment, and surrender to deep time. Time underneath."

Up the line, Peter like a dipshit closes his eyes and surrenders to time underneath. It's what I expect from Muraro, who always blows with prevailing winds, aiming to please everyone (and thank Christ for it, since where would I be without a chump on Kelly's staff I could bulldoze around?). But Peter needs to wake up and realize that playing along with Leo's shit this morning means playing against me. If he doesn't realize that yet, then he will soon enough.

Past Muraro, his hands folded and eyes staring down the line at me staring at him, stands a man who certainly understands who's playing for which team today, and who on each team is the captain.

Since thirty minutes ago, when I walked into the locker room two steps behind Kelly and stood with him at the whiteboard, watching players shuffle in, Harvey in his windbreaker and pressed slacks hasn't blinked, hasn't smiled, hasn't sneezed or coughed and damn well hasn't taken his eyes off me. For the most part I've returned his stare, since the cat's out of the bag between us and fuck him. Leaving the Fieldhouse, Crowe snagged me by the arm and held me back a minute. "You could've told me you had him, Darrow," he said. "I'd have accepted that."

"Okay," I said. "I had him."

Harvey frowned. "Listen to me. You can't play fast and loose with somebody like Leo. He loses his true north. Goddamn it, you need to consult me about him."

A janitor came up the hall, his boots slapping the tile. Once he'd disappeared around the corner, I said, "I don't need to consult you, Harvey. I need Leo not fucking my life up. That's what I need."

Crowe rubbed his jaw. "That's one hell of a compassionate view, son. Jesus."

"I'm not a social worker, Harvey. I'm not a shrink or medium or whatever the fuck he needs."

Sticking a finger in my face, Crowe said, "You seem to forget, I can fuck this up for you all by myself. *All* by myself. You won't need Leo to do it."

And it was true, Harvey could. At any rate, he could boot Peter off the sideline. Leo'd be coaching again by this weekend. But Muraro running the team didn't matter if Toren gave me walking papers, and so I told Crowe: "If you're going to do something, do it. But Kelly's not fucking me up."

We watched each other in the dark hallway.

"Whatever you've got to do, Harvey." I patted his arm and left the Fieldhouse, catching up to the team. Now Harvey stares at me down the line of players and managers on West Quad, possibly wondering just what it is he'll need to do, and when I'll force him to do it.

Our surrendering complete, Kelly unravels the whistle from his fist, raises it to his lips, and will this man truly blow that thing, and snap open every snoozing eyelid for a mile? But Leo reverses the whistle, and aims its mouthpiece at the group of us. "You may have noticed," he says, "the days growing short. Dark and short. We travel," Kelly carves his whistle through the air, following it with his own droopy eyes, "farther and farther from the sun, leaving the light behind us. Until it's winter."

To my right, enormous Sam yawns extravagantly, pushing the beanie from his head and clawing his scalp, before tugging the hat on again. Noticing, Kelly flicks the whistle into his teeth and directs at Sam a ripping, pealing screech that I wouldn't have thought the man capable of, fatigued as he is. It causes several of the players to stumble backward out of formation, clamping their ears. A second later, the whistle's high note returns to us off the buildings across campus, in the vicinity of which, two inch-high figures—students, probably—halt on the sidewalk, peering our direction. I think: *Easy, Leo. Damn it, go easy.* Granted, some meathead coach blowing his whistle isn't in and of itself aberrant. Then again, what are we doing lurking way out under these trees, and what will bystanders think when it's not just whistles out here but cognitive masks, memory breathing and nakedness?

The students keep walking, thankfully. I let myself breathe.

Spitting his whistle, Kelly nods at Sam. "Because you think that's enough, I take it? You think a solstice clears away your year, so that you're a fresh little bunny come spring?"

Suffice it to say, Sam's upbringing in Vale, Oregon didn't prepare him to answer a question like that, not that any of us can field questions with no meaning in them but to the asker. The poor giant, all eighty inches of him, gums the air like a cod.

"Maybe for you it does," Leo says. "Maybe it does. You might be so clean of heart, and young." Moving his gaze up the line, Kelly's breath again eludes him. He heaves back his shoulders, struggling to fill his lungs. Still, he manages to say, "The sand sticks in the gears for all of us, though. Sooner or later, slag gets in the blood, and no December twenty-first clears it away. The sun follows us into the darkness and out the other side, and it's another year and we're the same bad meat we've always been."

What an upbeat, optimistic homily! Now let's adjourn indoors to contemplate what we've heard this morning, is my vote. Instead, hands at his back, Leo paces away from us and abruptly returns. "We need to shut it out," he says. "The light. All of it. Unless we sink entirely into darkness, no new light can find us. No next life will warm our skin."

It's a testament to how far from the falconer this team has strayed that a speech like Kelly's makes no impression whatsoever on his players. Next lives, light, skin, darkness, solstices— the kids chew their cuticles and peek at phones, having heard such trash out of Leo's mouth for three months running. It's fully dawn now, and across the quad a line of students like ants marches toward Everly Hall for what I remember is the last day of exams, or second-to-last. But Kelly for this batshit charade couldn't have waited two days, till campus was vacant? Closer by, other students trek across West Quad from the dorms on Oyster Hill, and I dislike that Leo fixes his gaze on them, watching them go.

Again addressing his team, smiling queerly, Kelly says, "It's not such a terrible place, is it? This sleepy school. These people you see out here. It's a fine place and they're fine people, and don't we like coming here each day to find life just as we left it?" A moment passes before Leo says, "Well. Let me share this with you unequivocally. This school you see before you ..." he points up the hill at Everly Hall and Main Building, his hand trembling noticeably, "... down to its last molecule, is the cage. *Familiarity* is the cage. It traps us in that old, poisonous light, and by God to be free, we'll smash our cage to pieces. We'll *destroy* familiarity, and when we open our eyes again, we'll see a world like this one but fresh to our senses."

I think: No, we're not doing that.

"It's a question," Kelly continues, and though he succeeds in projecting his voice he obviously strains to do so, forcing a tomatoey flush up his throat, "of disappearing. This place and our comfort here won't disappear on its own. But we'll disappear from it."

For once—concerning the value of disappearing from Fog Harbor Community College, in general, and from this exposed quad in particular—Leonard Kelly and I are in full agreement. Though of course by "disappear" he means something more fucked up and bizarre than just getting out of here. "Your caps,"

Kelly says, waggling his whistle at the team. "Those of you wearing caps, pull those over your faces. If you don't have one, shut your eyes like you're dead and stay dead."

Playing hide-and-go-seek or pin-the-tail-on-the-donkey or whatever wouldn't be so awful if we did it back by the trees, in the shadows, but Harvey marches up the line, jerking beanies over faces and barking orders at eyelids that don't close, and with everyone sightless, Leo again blows his whistle. "Now walk!" he croaks. "March into your fear!"

Nobody does anything. Some hooded faces swivel around as if conferring with other hooded faces.

"Put one foot," Kelly says, "ahead of the other. And then again. And again." Nobody moves, even though Leo shuffles aside to let his team stampede up the quad. He tells them: "Walk into this familiar place, this school. Feel yourself disconnected from it. Feel yourself as only a being in the dark—no more. You're an aliveness floating on its own, even as you're treading known ground."

The first asshole to stagger out of the gate, feet shambling as if manacled and hands groping empty air, obviously is Peter. He ventures into the darkness behind his eyelids with a gaping mouth, as if meaning to taste it, and I'd happily bust Peter's teeth for him or dig a hole in the quad for his ass to fall into, but Crowe starts marching behind the team, clapping and shouting, "Move it! Let's go!" and pretty soon I have ten horses to get back into the barn. They stumble up the hill, Kelly's blind zombies, leaving the shade and wandering out into broad daylight. And it's 8:00 a.m. and people are everywhere on the quad and I don't think so.

Dragging my glute, I hustle past the team and start clapping like Harvey, cheering everyone on while truthfully steering them back gently, toward the trees. "That's right!" I shout at the eyelids and beanies, nudging kids' shoulders and outstretched arms, urging them downhill. "Feel that darkness!" I yell. "Get disconnected!" I might as well be hollering *Hah! Hah!* and waving a Stetson, since this is how they haze beef on ranches in Montana, and since if I don't diffuse this freak show quickly, I'll need to get used to cowboying or some other menial profession.

My efforts pay off, or else the team lacking vision tends naturally downhill, like water. They're still spread out wildly, though. It looks like a nitwit field trip out on West Quad.

I'd prefer another approach, but with none at my disposal, I limp through the team dragging kids to a stop and yanking up hats. "Very good!" I say. "So good! Now let's open our eyes. Okay, good work with that. That'll do it. Get those eyes open."

Leo looks on, gnawing his whistle, while somewhere behind me, Crowe says, "Dr. Darrow, I don't believe we were finished with the—"

"I don't know about the *rest* of you," I shout, and they maybe can hear me across campus, but it won't matter: I'm about to fold this tent. "But that felt fucking perfect to me! That felt wonderful! Coach?" I point at Kelly over everyone's heads. "This young team felt alive in that darkness! They shut out the light! Thank you for that! Everybody, goddamn it, thank Coach for that experience!"

One thing about lazy kids: they'll stumble around with hats on their faces, they'll march straight into the ocean. A lazy kid will do anything in the world provided you command him to do it with more starch than he can muster against you. And I'm nothing today if not starchy.

"Thanks, Coach!" nearly the full team shouts. I see only two players who abstain, and that's the best and worst of them, Dajuan and Odie.

Making his way through the team, slipping between and around people, Harvey reaches for my elbow just as I skip and hop ahead of him, glute be damned. I swim through the pack to where Leo stands, arms folded. Pointing a finger at Kelly's head, pacing before the guys, I shout, "I don't know how many of you appreciate this, but this man leading your squad has been on a journey this year! A *painful* journey!"

Harvey catches up to me, but must recognize correctly that stopping me now would require violence past his capacities. Dropping his hands, he waits with everyone else to see where I'm taking this.

"And he comes here," I say of Leo, "every damn morning to help you men on your journeys. To cheer *you* on! You might say it's his job, but Coach doesn't need this. He does it for *love!* Coach *loves* this team! Now goddamn it, it's time we show Coach some love. Let's cheer *him* on! On *his* journey!"

With that, I snatch the beanie from Matty's head—Matty whose hands don't even flinch when I rip off his hat—and jerk the thing hard onto Kelly's melon, knocking the specs from his forehead. I tug the hat down to Leo's chin and he accepts this calmly, swaying with the yank of it. Confiscating his whistle and notebook, tossing those with the glasses, I shout into Kelly's hooded face: "Now damn it, Coach, it's your turn! *You* do it! The darkness is yours and we're with you every step of the way!"

"Scott ..." Peter says, somewhere behind me, and over the course of stating even my one-syllable name, he loses heart and mumbles.

Ignoring Muraro, I whisper to Leo, "Be a being in the dark, Coach. Be an aliveness."

I don't like any of this one bit, especially since Kelly's knees and hands tremble, his balance wavering. He shuffles forth into the quad just the same, though, advancing one sneaker and the other, holding nothing back. *You could learn from this mother-fucker,* I want to tell Peter and the others.

"Coach?" Crowe calls to Leo. "You don't need to do all this ..."

But oh he does, Harvey. He does. Kelly *craves* this, and even if he didn't, he committed himself to it the moment he made it his ass or mine. "Go," I breathe into Matty's hat, walking alongside Leo. "*Go!*" And he shuffles faster. Crowe jogs after us, but I shove him back. "If this is too much for you," I hiss at Kelly, "I understand. We'd all understand. Michael would understand."

Naturally that does it. If you can call it running, Kelly runs off into the quad, drifting not downhill but up, pumping his arms like some pathetic sprinter. Slowing almost immediately, he stumbles into the grass. He regains his feet and makes it several more strides before stumbling again, heavily, and pitching forward. And lying still. Harvey races past me shouting Leo's name, and scanning the panorama of campus I'm satisfied that nobody in particular seems to have taken an interest in this baloney.

Crowe sits his friend upright, tearing the beanie from his face. He kneels with Kelly in the grass. Returning to the team, I make an announcement: "Nobody worry about it, Coach is fine. He does this, he's one hell of a hard worker." Frankly, the kids don't seem concerned about it one way or the other. Back up the hill, Harvey gets Leo to his feet. After interrogating his senses, snapping fingers at Kelly's eyes and waving a pen past his nose, he helps the old gorilla across West Quad toward staff parking.

"Let's clear out," I say, fanning my arms behind the team. "Meet back at the Jub. Coach Muraro has some sets he wants to look at for Shoreline."

Wandering toward the Fieldhouse in pairs and threes, Sea Lanterns Men's Basketball looks blessedly like nothing anybody would whisper about. It's down to Peter and I standing in the grass—Peter who eyes me with a sidelong, disgusted look.

"Fuck you," I say. I collect Leo's specs, whistle and especially notebook, which I can't have some stranger discovering.

"What was all that?" Muraro says.

"Watch out for Harvey, okay? He probably won't try anything, but he might." Then I add, "Oh and you're welcome. You're welcome, Pete."

PART IV

PART IV

18.

WOULDN'T YOU KNOW IT that the clouds blanketing Fog Harbor turn charcoaly and gross as Friday wears on, and rain drifting in off the ocean dims everything to an early dusk, falling at lunchtime, as if dusk on its own weren't arriving practically at high noon anyway these days, rain or no. Out the window of 2F, the haze obscuring rooftops could be haze or could be exhaust from HVAC flues. Or: every building in Fog Harbor is burning to the ground. All I know is it makes sense for Goodwin to call today. It's end-of-week, for one thing, which is when business like hiring decisions gets handled, and also with this shitty weather it'd just feel correct to snuggle under an afghan by the window, shooting the breeze with Ed Goodwin about me leaving Fog Harbor forever. Moreover, with Crowe on high alert now, keeping Leo clothed in public won't be as simple going forward as it was this week. If you could call this week simple. If you could call Leo, this week, clothed. So yeah. Let's have Goodwin get his shit together and dial my number so we can lock this up. But 2:00 comes and goes—that being quitting time out east—and my phone only stares at me, displaying time and date. "Fuck this," I say. "Fuck you, Ed."

High up Terrace Street, an hour later, headlights shine in the downpour as I trot through the intersection at Seventh to creep along under Kelly's neighbor's shrubs, in my overcoat. Reaching the property line, I peek around into Leo's living room—or would be peeking into his living room were the blinds not down. But a band of yellow light shines from under the kitchen blinds, and a shadow crosses into that light and out again.

That should content me for now, since nobody would be in the house if it weren't Kelly or Harvey with Kelly, and if Leo is in his house then he's not out in town, fucking me up. But "in his house" only counts for so much when the man departs his house totally randomly to get into shit. I'd feel better about leaving Kelly here if I were confident he was still incapacitated from this morning, and from yesterday and the day before. Nobody on earth could be less welcome at Chez Leo right now than I am, if Crowe's around, but I march onto the porch anyway and ring the bell.

The glowing peephole goes black. "I don't think so, Darrow," Harvey bellows through the door.

"Come on, Harvey, open up. We're adults."

"You're an adult like shit you are. Get out of here."

Rain clatters in the gutter and downspout. "I've got to see him," I say. "Just let me see him, all right? I feel like shit. I'll say hello and I'll leave."

A moment passes, then Crowe opens the door and stands in the light falling out. Quickly, I take in the living room, kitchen and back hall. I don't see Kelly, but his sneakers and hoodie lie on the floor in a heap, near some Rite Aid bags. "Where is he?" I say.

"Why?" Harvey says.

"I want to talk to him."

"No—why do you feel like shit?"

The object in Crowe's palm is a thermos, not a club, but he holds it loosely at his side like you'd carry a club or sap, and with it being a week today since Odie clobbered me, I wonder: What is it with Fridays and people jonesing to kick my ass? Shrugging, or just showing Harvey my defenseless hands, I say, "I shouldn't have pulled that crap this morning. I feel like a dick."

"You're a dick all right," Crowe says. "And a jackass. We're in agreement thus far."

He stands firmly in the door.

"But ...?" I say.

"But I don't believe that you're sorry. Not for any of it. You're too selfish for feeling sorry."

"Just let me talk to Leo."

The corners of Harvey's mouth turn downward. "Not happening, son."

"It'll take two seconds."

"The answer is no. Now get the fuck out of here."

"Wait ..." I fumble in my coat pockets. "I have his glasses. Just let me give him these."

Plucking the specs from my hand, tucking them into his shirt, Crowe says, "I'll see that he gets them. Thanks for being such a good Samaritan, Scott."

"Harvey ..."

Crowe shuts the door in my face, leaving me out in the weather. Accurate though he is about my untroubled conscience concerning Leo, the man can't really believe he scared me off with a thermos, though, can he? Does Harvey believe that? Try the sap next time, you drawling prick. Wandering up the block, face lowered to the rain, I simply duck into the alley and let myself into Kelly's backyard through the gate. With the blinds all down, I needn't even be artful about this. Beelining through the grass to Leo's bedroom window, peering through the margin of the blinds, I make out in the dim room what for all intents and purposes is a cadaver. The bedside lamp doesn't do Kelly any favors, with its gloomy bulb, but with his hands composed on his chest, his face square to the ceiling and skin an asparagus color, I would believe Leo was dead except that he blinks—one thoughtful blink, then seconds later another. For all that a man in that condition could leave bed to journey through town on psychotic errands, he might as well be cuffed to the headboard. And I did it to him, and the way I should feel about that is heavy-hearted or contrite, whatever. I'm relieved clear down to my toenails, though. Stay in bed. Stay in bed, you vexing mother-fucker. The way I should feel about feeling *that* way is ashamed, but if I wouldn't change any of what I did, then shame isn't driving the bus.

I slip out of the yard, easing the gate closed and leaving shame where it belongs, discarded under Leo's fruit trees. On such a dreary afternoon, I doubt anyone in Western Washington feels as joyous as I do, with Kelly laid low and my Oxfords floating down Terrace as if to pedal me out into the sky over the harbor—even if waiting for me on campus is another freight of shame, or anyway embarrassment. Jeremy isn't at his desk when I step off the elevator, but then he appears from the staff lounge, pulls on his headset and scoots into his workstation without comment. I enter my office. Eventually Harrington carries in his laptop, shutting the door behind him.

I nod. "Jeremy."

"Scott."

Papers that I have no business with—papers I could not iden-tify—clutter my desk, and it could be embarrassment that causes me to fetch the papers into a stack, tap the corners and begin poring over them intently. It could be embarrassment that causes Harrington, standing across from me with the laptop on his arm, to frown gravely at his screen, hammering keys with his free hand. "Just a second," he mutters. "Got some things here for you."

"Yep." I hold two pages side by side, as if comparing them.

But I saw Jeremy buttfucking in the trees yesterday, and he saw me see him, and so we're far enough past embarrassment that I doubt that's what this is. Instead, I think we want to show each other work. I think we don't like what happened yesterday, he for his reasons and I for mine, and want to perform what getting past that could look like, if we get there.

If we get there. Harrington comes around the desk, sets his computer where I can see it, and what I want badly to tell Jeremy—some mix of *I feel like shit* and *I hope you know it's all right, nobody worthwhile cares about that*—presses so hard to get out of me that it's like my body swells and I'm physically crowding the kid. I should speak my mind—why not?—but we're past what happened, is why not. That's why we're in this office, showing each other work. So I won't say anything and Harrington won't, either. The kid's noticeably sweating, hunched at his laptop, and I want to tell him that that's fine, too, people sweat. But I manage only to nod at his computer. "Okay, so what is this? What am I looking at?"

"Two things." Jeremy indicates the screen, but I'm able to focus only on his trembling hand and not on what he's indicating. Seconds go by. I tap my lip, nodding.

"It's from Chancellor Toren," Harrington says.

"Hmm? Oh yeah." I quickly scan what Jeremy's showing me, an email that reads: *Pass on to Dr. Darrow—no news is good news, I appreciate his efforts.*

"Wonderful," I say. "Good. Thanks for showing me that." And it is good. It is wonderful.

"I don't know what he means, but I assume you do."

"He means the stars are in the heavens. Thank you."

"And then this." Jeremy flicks the mouse, minimizing one message and casting around for another. With his tremor, he can't lay the cursor where he wants it, though. It sails past the message, then overshoots the other way.

I shake my head. "These shitty laptops. They should buy you something good."

"I got it right here."

Harrington loads the message, this one paragraphs in length. To study it, I claim the laptop and roll away in my chair, giving Jeremy breathing room.

If lucid reading is like understanding through a straw, ingesting information in a concentrated stream, then I manage with this email only to tear off the lid and dump its contents on my face. I catch the gist of it, but then need to reread, and reread again. Returning the computer to where Harrington can reach it, I say, "When was this?"

"It came through this morning."

"And that's Tom Moses? TM?"

"I guess so?" Jeremy says. "I don't know."

Dragging the computer back to me, I reread the message a third time. "He's not very definite about it, is he?" I say. "What'd you tell him?"

"I didn't tell him anything. I wanted to check with you. Who's Tom Moses?"

The message reads:

Re: Leo Kelly
Attn: Athletic Department, Fog Harbor CC

Greetings—

Hoped to catch Coach Kelly directly but email bounced back. Does he have a rep or anybody? Exciting story with him starting at FH and hearing he's taking risks. New approach, using FH as proving ground, reinvention, etc. Don't think anybody's covering it and hoping to get the jump.

Thinking long form, multimodal, etc. HMU. Out east with bowl szn and Hawks but hoping to get that way in a week or two. Best wishes and thx.

TM

"He's a writer." I push the laptop back to Harrington. "Or blogger, that kind of shit. In Seattle."

"I've never heard of him."

"Well," I say. "Other people have."

We're silent awhile. Then Jeremy says, "Going out on a limb here. You're not excited about this, are you?"

I laugh, and immediately wish I hadn't laughed, since Jeremy clearly thinks I'm laughing at him: his back stiffens and face drains of expression. "No," I say. "No, you're right. I don't want anybody poking around here, if I can help it."

Harrington collects his computer. "So I'll tell him no?"

"Hang on a second." I contemplate my desk.

"Scott?"

"The important thing," I say, "is time."

"Excuse me?"

"Come on." I drag over a chair. "Have a seat, Jeremy."

He watches me. Then he sits.

I shouldn't share this stuff with Harrington. Nothing is more reckless, after all, than disclosing to others how deeply you understand your own tricks. But I don't want the kid going back to his desk just yet. "Time," I say. "Plain and simple. You give a hard no, then that closes the books. It's on to his next move."

Jeremy's confused. "Next move?"

I shrug. "Maybe he comes here on his own? Maybe he snoops around without asking and writes a takedown piece? Or he just tells people we said no and people wonder why." I nod at Harrington's computer. "Then everybody sends requests."

Jeremy rubs his chin.

"Even if Moses does nothing, we tipped our hand. You never tip your hand."

This last remark hangs between us, and I worry that Harrington hears in it an accusation regarding last night. If nothing else, the young man in that forest tipped his hand. But it's too late for all of that—for worrying about that. "Time," I say. "That's our whole play here. Moses isn't hurting us right now, is he?"

Harrington thinks this over. "No."

"So how do we keep right now going? How do we put him in a holding pattern?"

Easing back in his chair, Jeremy gazes out the window. Finally he says, "We tell him yes?"

Damned if I'm not proud of Jeremy Harrington. "There you go," I say, not masking my joy. "Exactly fucking right."

"But we tell him not right away. We stall him."

"Do we even have to, though?" I nod at the computer. "He didn't ask to come right away, Jeremy. That's not even what he wants. Let's wait through the weekend, then tell him yes flat out."

"What if we said after Christmas?"

I wag a finger at Harrington. "Yes. That's good. We tell him the sooner the better on our end, and we can't wait to meet him. We can't wait to show off Leonard Kelly's innovative basketball program. But probably it can't be before Christmas, with everyone's schedules."

"That's how I should tell him?" Jeremy's skeptical. "All enthusiastic like that?"

"We're telling him yes, aren't we? Let's make sure he hears yes."

"I guess so," Harrington says. "But what happens after Christmas?"

I smile at my assistant. Then I point at the laptop. "Jeremy, that motherfucker will not lay foot on this campus ever in his life. Not one foot. He's just going to think he will. And keep thinking it."

It feels good between Harrington and me, with our scheme hatched. Last night I humiliated the kid while he fucked his boyfriend in the trees, though, and now my office falls so silent that blood thuds audibly in my neck. "Well," I say, glancing around for something to glance at. Standing to leave, Jeremy pats his pockets. When I hear in one of them that lovely hollow *thwock* that I miss so badly, I think: Oh, but Scott, you wouldn't. You would not do that. You monster.

But then I say, "You mind parting with a few of those?"

"What?"

I tap two fingers at my lips. "It's a secret of mine, Harrington. Just every now and then."

"Oh." He digs out his pack. "Yeah, no worries."

I knock the American Spirits Jeremy gives me on the desk. "Between you and me, right? That's how we're doing this?"

Harrington eyes me. He doesn't speak.

"I'm pretty sure that's how we'll do this," I say. "With secrets and things. Let me know if you don't think so."

19.

THE BLUE FLOODLIGHT on the walkway fritzes in and out, lighting up my bedroom blinds with flashes like distant gunfire. If guerrilla warfare raged in the alleys of Fog Harbor, Washington, maybe it'd look this way at night—and maybe I'd like the place better for its desperate spirit. Nobody around here cares enough to fight, though. They don't care enough even to stand up when they grocery shop, preferring motorized scooters instead. Not that I don't get it. Tonight I get it. After just four hours' sleep in three days, and after spending those days dancing contretemps to Kelly's schizoid boogie, I understand and even endorse some sedentary behavior. Confine your haint-worshipping, asshat coach to bedrest, repair trust with closeted employee before extorting him for cigs, rub cortisone on hands, eat takeout, flop on mattress. These American Spirits aren't half bad. The smoke drifts toward my ceiling through the fritzing blue light, until the light quits entirely and it's dark in my room.

Not so clever, as an insomniac, to pair the first night in several available for sleep with the first nicotine I've used in weeks, and rather than lying lifeless for twelve hours on Benadryl and Heineken, 1:00 a.m. comes and goes and I'm taut as piano wire. If I just smoked and was done with it, I'd sleep fine, but I'm nipping what Jeremy gave me so frugally that it's like I'm thwarting rest on purpose, paying out my buzz till dawn. I smoke, snuff out the cherry and smoke more after a while.

Far short of dawn, however, I'm left with three chewed-up, speckled filters lying in the takeout box beside me, and assuming weight suddenly, hundreds of pounds by the second, my body plunges me into sleep. It's shallow, colorless sleep that leaks out through my pores and eyelids, or else the colorless room leaks into me. I awake believing that no time has passed, before awakening later with the sense weeks or months have passed, years. A phone rings out in the kitchen, and it's not my phone but a landline somehow, with the shrill jangling of an actual bell housed in its plastic. Gazing past my toes, through the open bedroom door, I of course see no phone like that anywhere in my kitchen. It's silent. When a fist pounds my front door, I climb out of bed, walk up the hall and open it. Running north-south through Hamilton, Montana, dividing west Bitterroot Valley from east, was the old Northern Pacific railbed with powerlines swooping along it, and standing in the doorway of 2F—the doorway itself now freestanding on the tracks—this railway and the town hugging it and the wall of mountains flanking the town confront me, on an August afternoon. Maybe it's September. Late September, seen through the frame of a doorway. I don't have time for this. I need to bank serious sleep, since once Leo is up and moving, I'll need to be up and moving with him. But my feet straddle a creosote tie, gravel digging into my socks, and if a train is coming, I don't hear one. I hear wind stirring the ditch-grass and rattling leaves farther off. I hear birds. There's the sense of school letting out, of red lights flashing on a yellow bus, though no bus appears anywhere in the streets—and actually no vehicles at all appear, and no people. It is a vacant fall day in the town where I lived, with clouds traveling over the peaks, and if anything fills the air besides light slanting down, it's just the suspicion that Hamilton is mute to me, its hands concealed. It came all this way to find me in bed tonight, from the mountains to the sea, and school is finished and something else is more finally finished, though the town won't say what it is. A train approaches after all, the knowledge of it surrounding me, even if the silence is unbroken and there's nothing to see up or down the tracks.

"Not yet," rings in my ears as I wake up, and I'm convinced someone in 2F has spoken to me. I glance around for who it is. But I'm alone in the condo and just playing tricks on myself, talking in my sleep.

I should keep off my feet till noon at least, when Fog Harbor tips off against Shoreline—needing as I do to store up strength for whatever happens next—but I shower and go into the office to shuffle papers around, even if nobody is there at 8:00 a.m. on a Saturday. Someone happening by in the courtyard would already have believed I was in my office slaving away, with the lights all shining, but now if someone climbs the maple tree in the court-yard and peeps through my office window, they'll see me in here working. So there you have it. I needed to come into work today in case someone climbed a tree to spy on me.

My coffee stash is used up, and what they brew in the staff lounge tastes like Copenhagen spit (and not in a good way). Coastal Washington masquerades as the Vatican of java, but stray two miles out of Seattle and it's basically Folgers Classic Roast as far as the eye can see. Unbelievably, I'll be drinking Greta's Blend this morning. I pick it up after leaving the office. Therese mans the counter, womans it, whatever. "Did you like your sandwich?" she says.

"What? Oh, from yesterday. Yeah."

Handing my cup over the register, she says, "You must think we've got pirate's treasure buried back in here, all the times you walk through that door."

Therese is a kind person, who with her shouldery build and deep eyes, her dyed curls, stares out at me not from a lunch counter but from an era lost to memory. "Okay," I say. "Have a nice morning."

"Don't go and get your hopes up," Therese says, "about that treasure."

With time to spare before tipoff, I make my way up Terrace Street through a rain that's hardly rain, that's just a nuisance about the eyes, like I could bat it away. I toss the coffee in a trashcan. Things are dead at Kelly's place—just as, looking out over the misty rooftops and harbor, they're dead everywhere in town, with Christmas approaching and soon a new year. Freighters appear way out in the fog, patrolling the zone where sea mingles with sky. Settling onto the retaining wall across from Leo's yard, hands in my pockets, I wait for something to happen at the house or else to ensure that nothing happens, whichever. The blinds are down, furnace smoke rising from the chimney. One of the blinds stirs, then I decide it didn't stir, I made it up. Crossing the street, I ring the doorbell. I ring again without success. Circling around to the backyard, I find the lamp off in Kelly's bedroom, keeping me from seeing in. Doubling back to the porch, however, ringing a third time, I hear floorboards complain under someone's heels. That's something, even if nobody answers the door.

Stepping off the porch, I notice out past the harbor that one of the freighters has vanished, having sailed for Korea or wherever—maybe for Sendai, Japan. The ship was a blot of gray. Where it vanished is now regular gray with no blot. Rain speckles my clothes, and what keeps leaning into my thoughts is Hamilton,

Montana on its dry September day, leaves whirling past its mail-
boxes. Nobody walked the streets, nothing at all happened, but
the town held something behind its back.

"No," I said in my sleep. "Not yet."

20.

I KNOW GYMS. The year I played for Kent State and all the years I played in high school, I would enter this gym or that one and understand at a glance, from the balanced lighting and acoustics, from the floor's sheeny cure, from rims tilting courtward graciously, bowing—or else understand from a less articulable harmony of light, sound, floor, rim, ball and moment—that I and everyone associated with me would triumph in that atmosphere. We would win. Some nights, my foreknowledge of victory was so total that playing the game itself struck me as moot and even boring. Other nights, entering other gyms, I would understand just as totally that we were fucked. The lighting was grease drippings, the rims eleven feet high, dangling nets like arrogant nutsacks. Those nights, too, I didn't see the use in playing the game.

I know gyms, and for all my disgust with Fog Harbor as a place and college, I applaud what Jubinsky Fieldhouse offers as a home venue. I like the color scheme, maroon being a rich tone that brings objects—maroon-padded backboards, for instance—closer within reach, somehow. Maroon also is a blunt tone that flattens shadows, sharpening goals into relief despite hazy arena air. The floor at Jubinsky imparts bounce to sneakers with clean, bird-like chirps. Our basketballs are that muddy leather that sponges in your hands, which sounds disgusting but actually is sexy. It is a sympathetic gym, and getting comfortable in the press box, watching Dajuan, Odie, Matty, James and the others trot onto the court for warmups, I would expect to feel optimistic about our chances against Shoreline.

I don't.

Whatever is hanging in this gym today—call it a pall or heaviness—it carries the stink of defeat. And weakness. Blame another shitty night's sleep for this, maybe, and the aftershadow of my dream—and blame December, with its grayness and night and Christmas and rain and bullshit. But none of that is real. That's mental static, whereas what is real and not static—and what truly I blame for this ill feeling regarding Shoreline—is the bunny rabbit of a coach striding onto the court as I speak to you. There he is, Peter Muraro, wearing his—what is that, Joseph A. Bank?—Joseph A. Bank blazer and fifth grader's brocade tie.

"Jesus," I say to the press box window. "Is that your tie, Pete? *That?*"

Suffice it to say, I've never tremendously believed in Muraro. Oh, he's a nice little motherfucker, sure. If my tire exploded on the highway, Peter would be there in five minutes with a jack and spare. But fuck the jack and spare since he would botch changing my tire and I'd need to call a professional to do it or else change the bitch myself. As for Sea Lanterns Men's Basketball, it certainly did blow a tire this year. And I understand it had to be Muraro I called, since who else was there? I'll even say that Peter stepped in admirably for being twenty-four and stupid. He flung himself into the storm and went .500 over two weeks, which is punching above his weight.

But picking off one home game against Yakima Valley isn't an achievement, especially since the team would have won that game anyhow, energized as they were to be playing true basketball again after three months of Leoball. No, one game is nothing. It is sustaining a team's energy week upon week, with magnetism and authority, that determines a coach's worth. And Muraro today wore a brocade tie.

Anybody could see that he's a pitiful person, even from up in a press box. With the last seconds ticking off warmups, Peter doesn't hook fingers into his mouth, whistle like a general and get his guys organized. Instead, he moseys down the sideline to greet Shoreline's coach, shaking the man's hand and sharing laughs. Excuse me, Peter, but is this donut hour after Mass? Will you and Johnny Shoreline fish together for crappie later, sipping two beers apiece? Or is a game tipping off that will be played just once in history, and that you'll win if you cut throats and lose if you suck ass?

The horn sounds, and joining Fog Harbor's huddle, Peter without Leo or Harvey down there looks castrated, just castrated. I can't believe the sight of Kelly and his valet would comfort me now, but I need killers on that sideline—even a senile killer would do. Briefly, I consider calling Crowe and begging him to rush Leo over. We could prop up his sick body in a wheelchair somewhere just to lend gravity to the proceedings. But the horn sounds again. The refs break up the huddles. Muraro is doing this alone.

The game tips off, Fog Harbor's maroon and Shoreline's green spilling over the court like holiday confetti. Sitting forward, elbows on my knees, I say through the glass, "Show me something, Pete. Goddamn it, do something. *Do* something."

It must feel like a holiday atmosphere to Muraro, too, though— a real fucking pageant—since the little elf is all smiles from go, following his own clapping hands up and down the sideline. And hey: I like smiling. Everybody, let's smile! But get your mitts on something to smile about first—like a lead in this game—and we don't have that, we don't even have a tie. Except a brocade one from Joseph A. Bank. Eight minutes into the half, we trail Shoreline by three, and that's nothing to go cheesing through the gym about. Jam your foot into somebody's ass, Peter. Matty Martin gets fancy on the wing, scissoring the ball between his knees before losing the handle, coughing up two points at the other end? For Christ's sake, sit his ass on the bench. Get your face two inches from his and scream holes into his eardrums. But the next dead ball, still clapping, Muraro only steps onto the court to pat Matty's tush, his improvement over Kelly in this instance being just that he waited for a halt in play before invading the floor. Two minutes later, the bald ref dicks us on a blocking call and Peter applauds even this, nodding like a bobble-head. He pursues baldy up the sideline, holding his applause out to the man. *Here, sir. Take these claps I made for you. Please, feel joy.*

"Is he serious with this shit?" I say. When a WET FLOOR sign in the press box doesn't answer me, I kick it into the wall.

Before the game even tipped off, I could have told you that Odie's focus and drive would be an issue. Campus is deserted, it's the last game before Christmas. Moody kids—and Odie's that if nothing else—don't shine when the barometer falls and their environments lose definition. I might have warned Muraro about this, but when Odie with six minutes left in the half bricks an open dunk because he cocked it to his shoulder blades and tried to ram it through like God, instead of *transmitting the ball through the hoop like a practical human being*, and when the miss so flummoxes the kid that he swipes an arm at empty air and stares off into the seats, in lieu of hustling back on defense, Peter offers no correction whatsoever except to shake his head good-naturedly—shake his head and even *laugh*—and if that's how fucking Muraro addresses dereliction from a player, then it's hard to imagine what warning him (about Odie or about anything else) would've accomplished.

"*Get*," I scream through the glass, "*mad*, Peter!"

We're down four at the half, but four feels like forty when you shouldn't be down at all, and wouldn't be down if one dimwitted coach woke his ass up. And I don't know what I'm doing up in this press box. If Muraro won't push the needle then goddamn it someone has to, and skidding my chair across the floor, I make my way back along the iron catwalk and down the ladder. When Shoreline inbounds for the second half, I'm seated courtside, Ferragamo tie smoothed down my chest, Tag Heuer peeking from under my cuff, Allen Edmonds aimed like spears at the Fog Harbor bench. (If Peter won't show this team dignified attire, then I guess that falls to me, too.)

The question is: Who wants some? Two minutes into the half, Shoreline reverses court to right in front of me, on the wing, their ball handler a pit bullish guard à la Dajuan. The Sea Lantern who lunges to cover him isn't Dajuan but rather our very own Austin, though—albino, praying mantis Austin. He reins his weight, waving his arms spastically as if begging the Shoreline kid not to drive. *Don't! Don't! Don't!* he's obviously pleading. The result is a here-nor-there species of defense that's too slow to harass the jumper yet too klutzy to stop penetration, leaving the ball handler to proceed as he wishes. The kid elects to drive, side-stepping Austin like dog shit and laying it in for two points—two points plus a free throw, since Sam, bungling the rotation, also hacks the kid's arm.

The ref's whistle signaling foul acts on me like a hypnotist's *snap*; instantaneously, I'm everything Peter Muraro fails to be.

Rocketing up the sideline (retweaking my glute in the process, but fuck it), screaming, stamping feet, I stab a finger at Austin's freckled nose and another at the chubby pumpkin of Sam's face. Spittle flies from my mouth, my voice rolling up and down Jubinsky's tiers of vacant seating. Players from both squads along with all three refs halt in their tracks, trading glances, till the nearest ref jogs over and touches my elbow.

Taking my seat, I glare across the court at Peter on the far sideline, my face saying: *Like that, you miserable shit. Like* that! Muraro returns my look, but unreadably.

Minutes later, I fly up the sideline again, Dajuan having sold out heroically for backside help only to have Odie ignore Dajuan's man, who hits a three. "Will you tap your fucking helmet?" I growl at Odie, charging after him up the court. And should the refs boot me for these outbursts, so be it. But they don't. And they won't. After the initial elbow-touch, not one ref lifts hand nor whistle against me. And do you know why? Do you know why, Peter? Because I'm *blazing* is why. If you're blazing—with something, with anything—nobody on earth short of law enforcement will stop you. With ten minutes remaining, James floats a limp pass into the lane that Shoreline intercepts, and I react about as you'd expect. Later, when Matty rifles his own mindless pass straight out of bounds, I shout at the kid's skull: "Will you amount to anything in your life, Matthieu? Jesus, you're a human fucking turnover!"

Through it all, Muraro keeps mingling at his Christmas soirée, grinning, applauding. Matty's errant pass lands in Peter's hands, and after stepping onto the court to surrender the ball to an official, Muraro pats Martin's fanny again. "No worries," he says, wandering back to the bench. "We're good. We're good."

—

Unless "good" means letting games slip through your grasp without objection—unless good means 1-7—then we are not good, Peter. That is what bad is. We're bad.

After the handshake line, with Shoreline making for their bus in possession of twelve Fog Harbor souls, I lead Muraro by his hip toward the locker room. "We need to chat, Pete," I say.

Unperturbed—whether by my request, by the loss, by any of what's happening—Peter says, "You bet, Scott. Always happy to chat."

"Finish with the guys and come find me."

It's 4:00 p.m. when I open the door to Greta's, ushering Muraro in and out of the rain. The loss today doesn't torpedo me with Leighton, necessarily—it slims my margin, certainly, but I don't think I'm fucked. Just the same, Fog Harbor Athletics isn't giving off groovy vibes right now. When Therese comes around the counter, smiling and straightening the corners of menus, I cut her off before she even speaks. "Yeah, I get it. I'm always here. Give us that back booth."

Her face goes solemn.

"Listen," I say. "I'm not in a playful mood. Can we just have your back booth?"

I walk ahead of them to the table, Peter behind me whispering to Therese, "He's been grumpy lately. I'm sorry." We situate ourselves, Therese pouring water then wandering off.

I say: "Grumpy? I've been grumpy?"

Muraro stares at me, hands folded before him. "Yeah," he says finally, and his nerve is refreshing. "You've been grumpy, Scott."

"Good for you standing up to me, Pete. Goddamn." I clap my hands boisterously, some other diners glancing our direction.

Muraro looks away.

"No, I mean it. You're such a pussy on the sidelines, I wouldn't have expected any spine from you. Not even this little bit. You're more of a pat-my-ass type of guy."

"Calm down," Peter says.

"Now I do expect that from you. Calming down. Telling everybody to calm down and not do their jobs."

"Scott ..."

"You can knock that shit off right now. Don't Scott me."

"It's one game," he says.

"It's seven games, Pete. *Seven*." I flash him five fingers on one hand and two on the other. "But this isn't about the game. Fuck the game."

"Oh," Muraro says. "Yeah, you definitely didn't care about the game, did you? Going off on everybody? Losing your *mind?*"

"I don't care about it. How can I?" I point out at the street. "You threw the game out the window, my friend. Game's gone."

"I threw it out the ... wait, *I* did? You think today was *my* fault?" Peter's disgusted. "Why don't you just tell me what this is about, Scott. So I can go home."

Therese marches toward us, and with her still halfway across the diner, I shout, "We don't want anything! Just charge me for something! It doesn't matter!" She swats the air disdainfully, and walks back to the register. Peter and I watch each other while darkness falls on First Street and the shore.

"This is about culture," I say.

"Well. I agree with you there."

"I don't like you dicking around and not doing anything with this team. And making nothing happen. Being ho-hum. Knowing that that's what you're up to, Pete ... Christ, it makes me nauseous."

"That's what you think I'm doing?" Muraro says. "Nothing?"

"Worse than nauseous. It's like you're nailing me into my coffin. And look, we lose a game here and there? Fine. Teams lose games. But if you're going to work for me, Pete, I need to know you have a pulse."

Muraro eases back in the booth, withdrawing his hands. "If I'm going to work for you," he says.

"Just do us both a favor. Get a pulse."

"You know," Peter says. "I'll put this out there. You've fared all right with me working for you."

"Oh," I say. "Winning one game. It's been glorious, Peter."

"Actually, I was referring to having a spy on the team. And me telling you everything and doing what you want." Muraro shrugs. "But whatever."

"What I want is some fight."

"Yeah," he says. "Okay."

I stare at Peter awhile, then nod. "Well, I'm glad we understand each other." I push a menu across the table. "Order something if you want. We're here."

"I quit," Muraro says.

"What? No you don't. Shut up, Pete."

"I quit. You don't need me being a pussy on the sidelines anymore, and I definitely don't need you talking to me like this." Peter collects his jacket.

"What are you doing? Sit down."

"Thanks for the opportunity, Scott."

"You *quit*?" I say. "You *quit*?"

Muraro starts for the door. I grab his arm. "Sit down, Peter. Just take a breath."

He says, "I want to hear you say that you appreciate what I do. You need me, too, Scott. We both know you do. But I want to hear you say thanks."

"Let me get this straight," I say. "Because I can't wrap my mind around this. You don't know anything. You have zero experience and zero connections. But I give you a college team to coach and you want to quit?"

"I didn't say I wanted to. And I know things. Why would you say that?"

"Sit down."

Muraro stands there, turning his gloves in his hands.

"What?" I say. "What is it? Say it."

Eventually Peter says, "I think it's my turn to make some demands, Scott. How's that sound?"

I lean away from Muraro. "My, my. Look at you."

"I'll keep coaching your team," he says. "But it's my team from here on out, okay? And stop belittling me. And no more taking me to Greta's like this to work me over. This is B.S. I don't want you talking to my guys, I don't want you coming to games. And all that crap between you and Coach? Leave me out of it. Like you said, this is a culture thing. I don't want you poisoning my team's culture anymore. If you can live with that, then we're good."

"Fuck you, Peter."

He watches me, squeezing his gloves.

And then I say—because what can I say?—"Yeah, fine. Whatever. We're good."

21.

IT WON'T MATTER. By the time Fog Harbor travels to Lower Columbia College in twelve days for Peter to fritter away another game—his third squandered game in four—Leighton will have officially come through for me or else failed to, and what Muraro does with his squad won't weigh in the scales. That's what I'm going with, anyway. So when Peter walks up the hill into the drizzly night after our spat at Greta's, I wish him Godspeed. I should chase after him, rub his shoulders and coo venom into his ear, since I know that simple turd can still be had. But Godspeed, Pete. I watch him pass under streetlight after streetlight exactly in the manner that Kelly left me in the rain two weeks ago—left me on this very patch of sidewalk, in fact.

It's Saturday in Pacific County—Saturday at 4:30 p.m. and already Saturday night—and with the semester finished and town vacant, and with sporadic doorways along Bay Avenue and First Street winking Christmas lights, I feel a dose of those blahs that caused Odie today to flub a dunk, wallow in self-pity and not get back on D. Surf crashes behind me, under the wharf, but no other direction, left, right, or straight, distinguishes itself meaningfully. All of it is flat, like I've blindfolded myself with a poster of this shitty place, or like the town is painted on the inside of my head. It's like you said, Jade. Just like it. And if I visit tonight, will you pour spiced wine, harvest miner's lettuce and bread clams for us? Will you stoke the fire and at a sleepy moment stroll through the house in pajamas, dimming lights? I should go to her, but my feet carry me up Terrace Street instead, past old people in dead living rooms watching cathode-ray TVs.

It's a familiar story by now. I ring Kelly's bell and peep in windows and ring again, calling Leo's and Harvey's names. A light glows in the house, behind its blinds, but the place is otherwise lifeless. They've gone somewhere, damn it. I brainstorm as to where and how to get there and what to say when I find Kelly to get him back indoors. Kicking the doorjamb, I wander off the porch. I'm nearly to the street when Crowe exits the house and shuts the door behind him. We stand together in the silent dark, Harvey on Leo's top step and me in the yard. Then I climb the porch, unbutton my jacket and sit with the old prick on some mismatched deck chairs Kelly has.

"Can I get you anything?" Crowe says.

"Some time with Leo would be nice." I reach behind me, knuckling the house. "Is he up and around?"

"How about a drink instead?"

The silence descends on us. Harvey rubs his jaw, and nods out at the dark yard and street. "Looked like a nail-biter up there today," he says. "Six points? Eight? Nearly pulled it off."

"I didn't know you followed Sea Lanterns Basketball, Harvey. Despite coaching them."

Crowe shakes his head. "I don't. I'm patronizing you, Darrow."

I laugh at this. "Okay."

"I do bet they turn it around, though. You watch. Peter's no generational coaching talent, but he cares."

"Let's not talk about Peter," I say.

After a while, Harvey says, "You sure about that drink?"

"I'm not staying. I just wanted to check in on Leo, if I could get past his maid."

"There you go, son." Crowe grins. "Now you're getting and giving it."

When Harvey has nothing to add, I pat my thighs. "Well. I'll see you around."

"You know, Darrow, you seem damn confident that you're going about this the right way. You got that look to you. Like you don't see a thing but what you see."

"That's too abstract for me, Crowe." I hike a thumb at the house. "You should save that for Mr. Miyagi in there."

Harvey lifts his hands, then settles them onto his armrests. "Not that I don't appreciate the combative approach. You bet I do. But I could've been of use to you, Scott. We could've worked together on your next thing. Whatever thing you're dreaming up that's got you climbing over backs and stuffing laundry into closets. Leo could've helped, too. Man knows people in this business."

"You could've helped," I say, "by doing your jobs."

"Well. Our jobs are like yours, aren't they? Get what we need and fuck all else? It's the virus principle. Speaking of which, if you've read that news coming out of China—"

I stand up. "Goodnight, Harvey."

"Sometimes Mother Nature," Crowe says, "when she needs to show us something, will paint a portrait. A portrait of what we are."

"You betcha," I say.

I'm halfway across the yard when Harvey shouts after me, "How much have you even thought about him, anyhow?"

"What?"

"Leo. You think about him at all, or is the man just a chess piece to you?"

"He's a chess piece."

"Come on up here," Crowe says.

"No."

"Get back here, son. I want to talk to you."

I stay put, but also I don't leave and Harvey comes out into the grass. With the porch light behind him, his eyes and wrinkles deepen. "What about the way this might end for him?" he says, standing close. "You given that any thought?"

"Not particularly."

Crowe stares at me. "That's a sad thing to hear you say."

I glance around at the yard, and at the mist under streetlights on Terrace. "Well, what thought has he given to me, Harvey? How this could end for me?"

"He's thought about it," Crowe says. "Sure he has."

"He needs to think harder about it."

"He likes you, Darrow. He trusts your energy. He told me so just earlier today."

Patting Harvey's elbow, I say, "That's amazing to hear. You let Leo know I'm touched."

"Not that it matters what he thinks about you," Crowe says. "Or whether he does."

"No?"

"No. Because you're not an ill person, Scott. What's so hard to understand about that? You're not suffering like he is. Look at it this way: what Leo's been chasing all these months—all these years, if you want to know the truth of it—do you think that's out there waiting for him?"

"Is that a serious question?" I say.

"I can't think of one that's more serious."

"Then no? My answer is no?"

"So what happens," Harvey says, "when somebody needs something like Leo does, and it's not out there? How does that go?"

I leave the yard, shutting the gate behind me.

"You think that folks in that position stick around very long? Just needing?"

I start down the street. "Goodnight, Crowe."

"You should be kind to him!" Harvey shouts down the block. "He's not young like you! It gets harder to believe!"

22.

"DID YOU PAINT this place when you bought it?" I say. "Or land-scape it or something? What'd you do?"

Jade carries the whiskeys out from her kitchen and sits with me on the sofa, on her folded leg, licking her thumb where some Bulleit sloshed over the side. A fire burns in the stove, its iron ticking with heat, and throughout Jade's living room little stair-cases of paperbacks lead up into lampshades. "You asked me that last time, Hoots. I didn't do anything. I bought it." Wearing a loose flannel shirt, Jade shoots her wrists from the sleeves before handing me a mug, again spilling some. "Oh and neglect it. I've neglected it, if that counts as doing something."

"You did something to the front. It looked different when I walked up."

"I mean, there's a wreath on the door?"

I wag my finger at Jade. "I saw the wreath. I didn't like that. But there was something else."

"Something you did like."

"Yeah."

Jade sips her whiskey. "Something that didn't piss you off. Like a holiday wreath does."

"I think you cleared out some trees. Does that ring a bell? I don't know, the house was *there* when I came up. It looked prominent."

"It called to you in the night," Jade says. "But actually, no. I know what it is."

"Is it the trees? You cut down trees?"

"It has to do with trees. You're going to hate what it is when I show you."

"Fuck. Then forget about it."

"I'll show you in a bit," she says. "When you're ready."

Balancing my mug on the armrest, I bring my face close to Jade's, where the fact of her lips hovers an inch beyond them, midair. We kiss, and it's a thing of its own aliveness folding us into it, drawing my hands along Jade's sides and raising hers to my face, orchestrating its knot of us until the thing moves on, leaving behind two shadows.

"You're so affectionate," Jade says, "when you're tired."

Retrieving my drink, I stretch out down the sofa with my head on Jade's lap. She works her fingernails into my scalp.

"You think I'm tired?" I say.

Digging around in the sofa cushions, Jade retrieves her phone and holds it over my face, mirroring. On its screen, I see not just a fading shiner's sick-yellow residue but the more general wreckage of dark sockets and used skin that my eyes stare out of. Tapping the button, I capture this mugshot for posterity.

"Plus you're here, right?" Jade discards her phone. "You must be tired."

"What?" I say.

She laughs. "Come on. It's no mystery, Scott. You come here when you're spent. If I hear hooting out in the trees, it means you used yourself up again."

"That's not true."

Jade pats my chest. "Sure it is. Not that I blame you. I came here when I was used up."

I tip some bourbon over my lip, letting it coat my mouth.

"Though I stay here," Jade says. "Whereas you jump back in the frying pan. Maybe I blame you for that."

"Be careful what you say, Jadey. You'll never get rid of me."

"Ooh." She gnaws her cheek. "Good point."

"I'll show up here with my suitcases. You'll never be happy again."

"Okay. Let's see." Jade thinks awhile. "Well, how about this? I have that pump shed in the yard, back by the compost out there. That can be yours, Hoots. Your private temple. Just like the house is my private temple, with the furniture and plumbing and stuff."

I nod. "I'm listening."

"Mi pump shed es su pump shed, you know? For no rent at all, either. I mean, it'll seem like no rent. I have to charge you something, don't I? But then you can come inside for dinner and drinks and things, once I'm done being happy for the day."

I sip my whiskey. "Tell me more about the 'and things' part of that."

"Oh that?" Jade waves me off. "That's just the hard fucking."

"I see."

"Yeah. Over in the bedroom there, if you want to see what I mean?"

Forget exhaustion—I feel airborne in Jade's bedroom, and uninjured, though when I stand from the bed afterward to fetch us oranges from Jade's fridge, I lug my glute to the door like an infantry vet. Returning, I toss Jade her orange and climb under the quilts with her. She prises the peel with a fingernail. "Hoots," she says. "Why are you wounded every time you show up here? I don't mean tired now. Wounded."

I hold my knuckles to the light falling in from Jade's living room. "You noticed my rash?"

"Your rash, your eye, your leg ..."

We chew our fruit.

"Well?" Jade says.

"I run interference a lot," I say. "At work. It bruises me up."

"Interference? What, are you a fullback now? I thought you had a PhD, Hoots."

"You have a PhD," I say. "It didn't save that tooth."

Jade stops chewing. Then she resumes.

I shrug. "It could've been worse than what you're seeing. This guy from work wanted to brain me with his thermos yesterday. This old dude."

"It's an old dude now?"

"Hmm?"

Jade touches my cheek. "You said a kid did this one. A basketball kid. Now it's some elderly person."

"I don't know what to say. Everybody hates me, Jade. Therese hates me."

Jade laughs. "*Therese*? From the *diner*?"

"We had a work thing spill over there. She got involved. And there's this other guy, Pete. He hates me."

We finish our oranges, Jade wiping her fingers on the sheet. I stack our peels on the nightstand.

"Does all of this," Jade says, "really strike you as worth it, Scott?"

From where we sit, our backs against the wall, I try to make out in the window the shore and surf, but see only the two of us here, naked. *Five thousand miles* comes to mind, strangely. *No islands, nothing.*

"It's a job," Jade says. "You can get any job. Or no job. Half the people in town don't work."

"What about the deposit," I say, "on my pump shed?"

Jade laughs, but I know she's expecting an answer.

"It's worth it," I say. "It's getting me where I'm going."

Jade hovers a finger over my knee, as if debating whether to touch it. "Let's hope that that's a good place, then." She touches it. "With what it's costing you."

Weather wheezes against the cabin, pushing a draft in from the living room. Eventually, Jade throws off the quilts. "Let's go look at that thing," she says. "The house thing."

"That thing? You said I wouldn't like that."

"Put on some socks or something. Let's go."

Outside, wearing blankets like capes, we walk off the deck into a storm blowing ashore, its gusts whipping our hair and tossing whitecaps out in the dark.

"It's not a big deal!" Jade shouts over her shoulder. "It's just a thing!"

"What am I looking at?" I say.

She crosses the yard to an outlet box mounted on a post near the beach. Kneeling, managing her hair with one hand while rummaging her other in the grass, Jade recovers a cord and shoves it into the socket. Near her driveway, a massive drift log as imposing and white as a whale jaw rests against a tree; suddenly, scythes of red, pink, green and blue swoop out from the log, bathing me and the cabin and winging up into the forest and sky. The bulbs lashed to the log wag in the wind. It's like standing inside a disco ball inside a tornado.

"Hah!" Jade points at me. "What did I tell you? You hate it!"

She comes to stand with me, and observing it all, shaking my head, I say, "Motherfucking Christmas."

"Motherfucking Christmas." Jade kisses me and leads us inside, and though her bedroom is at the far end of the cabin, opposite the lights, we fall asleep to colorful ghosts dancing out in the woods, their shadows slinking in through the windows, climbing the walls.

I'm confused, since when I open my eyes in the morning, it's not gray outside but fiery bright, and instead of rising in the east, the sun has reversed course overnight to break over the western horizon, in Jade's window: it's framed blindingly between the north and south capes of Fog Harbor. Morning shouldn't look this way until time loses steam and unravels through the universe, pages flying back onto calendars. Maybe that's what's happened, but then the shower punches off in the bathroom, and Jade wanders in rooting a towel in her ear. And what I've taken to be the sunrise is just ten million glaring flickers in the pools and slicks left behind at low tide. They riffle in breezes, relaying an easterly sun.

Jade inspects her towel, then roots more. "I practically had to hold a mirror under your nostrils," she says, "a minute ago. You looked dead."

"I feel like it."

"Dead?"

Stretching out under the quilts, stiffening my body then falling limp, I watch the glare wisp around on Jade's ceiling. Discarding her towel, Jade crawls across the bed to lay her cheek on my shoulder. She lifts a quill of her hair, and writes wet calligraphy on my skin.

"Dead but in a good way," I say.

"What are you doing today?" she asks. "What's your plan?"

Today? Today I'm cracking Harvey's skull to seize control of Leo. I'm cracking Peter's skull to seize control of the team. But I say, "Nothing. I'm not doing anything today."

Jade smiles. "There you go."

"Can I stay awhile?" I say.

After eggs and tea, and after more tea on Jade's deck, under the trees, we cross the lawn and pick our way down onto the beach and flats, where ooze, puddles and birds stretch away for miles. The sun is high now, knifing off every surface. Shielding my eyes, I say, "What is this shit? This shiny shit in the sky? This isn't Pacific County."

I left my shades at Jade's house, but somehow she brought extras. She hands them to me, a pair of ladylike Revos, and we stroll together out from shore, her hands at her back like a scholar.

"You look like Cobain in those," Jade says. "With that white pair he had."

I kick at the sand, my brogue coming away with a plug of muck. "I don't think Kurt wore Oxfords, Jade."

"Maybe not. But maybe you don't either, deep down."

We walk awhile.

"You know he grew up here, right?" Jade says. "In Aberdeen?"

"Cobain did? I thought he was pure Seattle."

She shakes her head. "Aberdeen."

"That's hard to picture," I say.

"Oh, it makes perfect sense."

"I don't mean hard to picture him in Aberdeen. I mean hard to picture him growing up, that he was ever a kid." Off in the distance, a thin line separates blue tide from blue sky. "That'd be some bridge to cross, wouldn't it?"

"What do you mean?" Jade says.

"Being a kid here then being Kurt Cobain. How does that happen?"

"Maybe he was always … Kurt Cobain."

"Are his parents still up there?" I say. "In Aberdeen?"

Jade gazes around at the harbor. "Who knows?"

Some gulls land ahead of us, strutting around and stabbing their faces at things. We walk up and they fly away. "That was already so long ago, huh?" I say.

"Cobain? Yeah, he died ..." Jade thinks it over, "... a quarter century ago. This year."

"Maybe they're still there," I say. "His parents."

Some flat boulders come into view, and we walk over to them and sit. The gulls swoop toward us, interested in our hands. One lands and approaches, its face sideways. This far from shore, we can see around the point to the radio towers and wharf downtown, and up the hill to the college. A delivery truck inches along First Street, glinting in the sun. We stretch out with our shoulders on the rocks, their earthly chill seeping through my jacket. "I don't know if it is," I say. "Actually."

"What?" Jade says.

"A good place. Where I'm going."

Jade looks at me. I watch her, too, and then we face the sky again. Reaching from her rock to mine, Jade pats my hip.

"You said it was a job," I say. "God, it feels like more than that."

"Maybe it is," Jade says.

I watch some clouds sail over.

"If that's what you believe," she says, "then case closed."

Time passes. We lay on the rocks under the sun for thirty minutes, forty-five—for hours, until the purling sounds of an incoming tide start competing with the bird sounds, and wind. My cheeks feel puffy and raw.

"Let's not drown out here," Jade says.

Walking in, we follow our own tracks while the rising harbor erases them behind us. Inside, my eyes adjusting to the dimness, we eat sandwiches and chips and nap and fuck and nap and breathe and fuck and talk. It's late afternoon, the day ending properly in the west, when Jade carries my phone to where I lie on the sofa, making a gunsight of my toes to aim at the dying sun. "You're ringing," she says.

"What?"

Getting the phone to my ear, I hear Ed Goodwin say, "Dr. Darrow, forgive the weekend intrusion. Could I bother you a moment?"

PART V

PART V

23.

TUESDAY EVENING, twelve hours before my flight to Albany—where I'll glad-hand, flirt and secure what I can by way of actionable promises from Goodwin—the doorbell at 2F of Sea Breeze Court buzzes for the first time in my year of occupancy. It's a harsh buzz, like the battle cry of insects, and if this is the first time my ears hear it, it might also be the last.

Jade walks past me up the hall in her olive slicker, seeking in the dining area a table on which to set the package she's carrying, which looks heavy. But there's only boxes in the dining area, one of which I've opened to retrieve the garment bag I'll use for my trip (and all of which, hopefully, I'll slap Albany addresses onto in a few weeks, covering up the Sea Breeze Court addresses I slapped on them this time last year). Giving up, Jade thuds her package on the kitchen counter and peels off her coat.

"I'll take that," I say. And once I'm holding Jade's slicker, I face the puzzle of where to set something down as well. Reclaiming her jacket, Jade lays it on the counter with her package.

We stand awkwardly in my home, she rubbing her thighs and rocking onto and off her toes. Finally, Jade's gaze settles on my boxes. "Got to admire your confidence," she says. "Packing your shit before you even interview."

"These are actually—"

Then Jade gets it. "Oh ..." she says. She thinks this over and seems to dislike what she's thinking.

"I'm just lazy," I say.

Jade chews her lip. "Okay," she says.

After a while, Jade crosses to the window and peers out over Fog Harbor's dark rooftops and alleys. Then she pivots and takes in 2F all over again. "Well, it's kind of beautiful," she says. "I'll hand it to you, Scott. You don't need much to get by."

"Not much stuff, anyway." Offering Jade the kitchen chair (my lone furnishing in 2F, unless you count my bed and the Washington State mug on my windowsill, where I ash Camels), I claim a box for myself, and we sit. An ambulance passes down in the streets, its lights vaulting through my window unaccompanied by a siren. The red strobe of them plays over one wall, then another, then vanishes. "So," Jade says. "Nearly go-time, Hoots. You excited?"

The cardboard sags underneath me. I opt for the floor instead, using the box as an armrest. "Yeah," I say. "It's a big deal for me."

"I know it is," Jade says.

"I want to see Albany, too. I've never been."

"I have," she says.

"Really? Albany, N-Y?"

Jade crosses her legs, wrapping half of her sweater over the other half. "You should know this by now, Hoots. I've been anywhere there's dirt."

I should grab Jade's ankle—it's right in front of me, above her sock and below her jeans—and climb up her leg to the heavens. But also Jade's ankle is out of reach, somehow. "That's probably most places, then," I say.

"We had a project in Massachusetts but we stayed in Albany. At the Beverly or something, some old hotel."

"The Beverwyck?"

Jade smiles. "That's it. Is that where you're staying?"

"I think that's what they called it, the Beverwyck. Yeah, they've got me there."

"You'll like it," she says. "It's downtown and everything, near the stuff. You'll like Albany, too, Hoots. It's not Paris, but it's not Fog Harbor, either."

"As long as it's not Paris."

Jade and I eye each other, and we nearly laugh but don't.

"Let's drink something," I say. "You want something?"

"What have you got?"

"Tap water."

Now Jade laughs—one barking, brilliant laugh.

"Out of your cupped hands," I say. "Or you can stick your head under the faucet. But it's hot or cold, all the gourmet temperatures."

"Can I use this?" Plucking the Wazzu mug from my windowsill, Jade spies the gross butts in it and replaces it swiftly. We laugh.

"I haven't mastered the hospitality thing yet, have I?" I say.

"No, you haven't. You haven't." Jade prods my arm. "But you do it for me, Hoots. Did you know that? You found my heart."

If it looks to Jade like I'm greedy, waiting for her to say more, it's only because I like so much what she said, and if I'm silent now, her words could reach my ears a second time echoing off the bare walls.

"Can I show you something?" Jade says. "I brought you something."

"I hope it's furniture," I say. "Or cups."

Crossing the room, Jade returns lugging her package. I lift away my arm so she can unload the thing on the box beside me—she does, the weight of the package splitting the cardboard underneath it. On its top, Jade's package reads DANNER BOOTS over a silhouetted forest, but unless Danner sells a pair made out of lead, this is something else. Jade hands me the penknife on her keychain, and sits cross-legged across from me as I slit away the tape.

"It's for New York," she says.

Lifting the lid, I find in the package what I could mistake for a homemade bomb. But it's a bulk quantity of batteries is all, six-volt. Any one of these monsters (and there are a dozen here, easily) could obliterate a car's windshield. "I don't ..." I frown at Jade. "Am I missing something?"

Slapping the package closed, heaving it aside, Jade says: "It's a joke. I don't want you out east with dead batteries, Scott."

I rest my head against the wall. "Oh," I say. "I like that, Jade. That's good."

We sit together, Jade squeezing my calf. But then she squeezes harder, and with fingernails. "Okay," she says. "Fine, it's not a joke. It's not. Listen, Scott, if you go out there—I mean if you *go*-go—you need to keep up your charge, okay? Don't fuck yourself up."

"I won't."

"No," she says. "You will. You will because you're you. But *when* you do, I want you to call me, all right? I'll come see you, Hoots."

"Jade ..."

"No no no. Listen to me." Jade spreads her arms. "What do I have going on? Huh? I'll come to the Empire State and take you for walks. They have clams out there. We'll fry clams. And if it takes more than that ..." Jade stares at me hard. "Then I'll come for more than that."

"Jade, come on. You have your life going on. That's what you have going on."

Gripping my feet, Jade leans back almost horizontal to the floor before using my feet to haul herself upright again. "*Hoots!*" she yells. "I can't believe how much about myself I need to explain to you over and over again."

"What?"

"I've got my life going on. Yeah, *finally*, I've got my life going on. Now if it's all the same to you, I'd rather my life not box me in. Do you get it? Listen, I don't need to come with you—I'm not some hot mess—I'm just saying: if going out there starts to make sense, I'm doing it. Nothing's stopping me except whether I do it."

I think this over. Then I say, "They do probably have better tea there."

"In Albany? Of course they do. Or I'll grow some on your windowsill. Or I'll open a shop for it. Or fuck tea and I'll smoke weed. Or fuck weed." Jade shows me her empty hands, then drops them in her lap. "Everything's an or, Hoots. *Or.* That's what you need to understand."

We're silent awhile, until I shake my head. "But Jade, Jesus. You're so happy here."

"No, I'm not," she says. "You're being stupid again, Hoots. I'm *happy*. There's no here about it. I'm happy."

I already failed once to take hold of Jade's ankle. I won't fail again. But my hand doesn't reach her before the doorbell at 2F— for the second time this year—buzzes.

"What the fuck?" I say. "Is that mine?" Leaving Jade on the floor, I move up the hall toward what I see, behind my sidelight's pebbled glass, is a figure on the walkway. And this can't be who I know damn well it is. It cannot be him. When I prowled through Leo's yard this morning to peek in his window—just ten hours ago, that was—he plainly remained out of commission, laid flat on his back with his toes in the air, as if waiting to be shoved out to sea.

But when I open the door, Kelly stands before me in his windbreaker and jeans, some rain starting behind him over Bay Avenue. He hasn't shaved, and looks in this state to be just a yellow slicker shy of gracing boxes of fish sticks. And I'm practically tapping syrup from New York maples and strolling with Jade in tartan scarves under covered bridges at this point: this motherfucker isn't taking that from me.

"There you are, Darrow," he says. "I've been looking for you."

I say, "Coach, great to see you. Great to see you. Though Christ, it's arctic out there. What are you doing?"

Leo wipes a palm down his face and jaw. His eyes are sunken, on top of the white beard, and just generally he looks like shit. He looks how he looked in his bedroom earlier, except vertical—verticality being the worst part about him.

"You know what I'm doing," he says.

I glance down the walkway. "Where's Harvey?"

Kelly flicks a hand. "Harvey's gone. Fuck Harvey."

"What?"

"I fired his ass, Darrow. He's gone. Man had no belief in him. Wanted to stay indoors and comfortable his whole life."

"There's something to be said," I say, "for indoor time, Coach. Isn't there? And it's the right season for that. It's Christmas."

"That's it exactly, Scott. You said the word. It's Christmas." Leo glances around, straightening his posture and sucking air into his chest. "You can smell it out here that it's Christmas. And by God, he loves the holidays." Kelly nods. "He'll be out there tonight, you mark my words."

"There's no doubt about that, Coach. Michael's out there. We know that."

"I'm glad you see it that way. Harvey could learn something from you." Kelly shuffles down the walkway, then glances back at me. "Well, you coming or not, Darrow? Time's a-wastin'."

Stepping out of 2F, some rain blowing over the railing into my eyes, I say, "You bet that I want to, Leo. I'm on board with this. You know I am."

He keeps walking. "Then let's go."

Raising my voice, I say, "Well, but let's make a plan, Coach! How does that sound? We've gotten this wrong too many times. We've missed too many times." Kelly reaches the stairs and looks back at me. A curtain stirs in one of my neighbor's windows, and I come down the walkway to speak quietly to Leo. "Let's think this over and be meticulous and get it right. *This time* let's get it right."

Studying me, Kelly totters slightly on his feet. The upward pitch of his eyebrows actually appears to be all that holds him erect, like he's hanging from a hook in his forehead.

"Let's go." I beckon him toward the condo.

"He's out there, Scott."

"I know that he is. We won't let him be alone, either. We'll find him."

I haven't said anything to change Leo's mind. But just the saying, the pressing, the urging is enough. It's a stiff headwind to fight against, and rather than fight it, Kelly draws one difficult, deep breath and succumbs. Putting the wind at his back, he limps past me toward 2F.

I shut the door behind us. And following Kelly up the hall, I wonder just where this shit will go. Clearly, I don't have much for Leo, as I'm boarding a plane in ten hours. But this motherfucker isn't waving lanterns around tonight, nor tomorrow nor Thursday while I'm gone. That will not come to pass. Though like I said, I'm curious to know what I'll do to stop him.

We walk into the living room. "Jade," I say, "this is Leo Kelly. Leo, meet Jade."

Jade glances at Kelly from her vantage on the floor, then climbs to her feet.

"I didn't know we'd have company," Leo says.

"You'll be glad she's here," I promise, wondering what I could mean by that. "She knows her stuff."

They shake hands as Kelly steps past Jade to the window. Behind him, she eyes me strangely. *Knows her stuff?* she mouths.

It's fine, I mouth back.

Turning from the window, appraising the bare walls and jangling change in his pockets, Leo says, "Well, Darrow, let's hear it. What's our plan?"

Putting that off, I say, "Jade, Leo and I work together. He's our basketball coach."

"Oh." Jade wags a finger at Kelly. "*Leonard* Kelly. I've heard of you."

"We're not here about basketball," Leo says.

Jade laughs at this. Kelly doesn't. Crossing to Leo, I squeeze his shoulder and say, "Coach and I have something we're working on, Jade. Not basketball-related. It's a side project."

Kelly shrugs away my hand. "A side project? Is that what you think this is, Darrow? Jesus Christ, do you have something in mind for us or not?"

Patting the air like a dipshit, I say, "Not a side project. Not that. It's definitely the main project. On the side of *basketball*, is all I mean. But this is bigger than hoops. Far bigger. Come on, Coach, you know how I feel about this."

"I'm waiting, Darrow."

I open my mouth to say more, but nothing comes. Dragging over the chair, I gesture for Leo to sit. He ignores this, and walks past me and past Jade, up the hall.

"Coach!" I trot after Kelly, and return him to the living room by his elbow. "Now what did we say? We'll get this right and we'll get it right tonight. But let's be patient. Let's talk this through." I indicate the chair and Leo sits in it, smoothing an eyebrow with his finger.

Fetching her jacket from the counter, Jade nods up the hall. "I'll head out, Scott."

And probably Jade should head out. That's likely best. She should head out, and I'll catch up with her later after stuffing Kelly down a hole somewhere. But exiting 2F with Jade would be a ... I don't know what it'd be. A something. Definitely if she left the condo right now, some *value* would exit with her, and I don't want that value—don't want Jade, I mean—going where I can't reach it. Where I can't reach her, is what I'm saying. "No," I say. "Stay. Can you stay?"

"You've got some ..." Jade gestures her coat, "... stuff going on. It's cool, Scott."

"Well," I say. "Why don't you help us out, Jade? We could use you."

She winces. "I don't think so. Call me later, okay?"

Crossing the condo, I nip the jacket from Jade's hands and toss it onto the counter. "Come on," I say. And I think: *Darrow, you fucking snake. Darrow, what're you doing?* Leading Jade back into the living room, I toe aside the battery package for us to sit at Leo's feet. "You'll want to hear about this," I say. "It's powerful stuff."

Like cub scouts with their den leader, Jade and I arrange ourselves on the floor near Kelly's shoes. Hands in his lap, Leo stares out the window. I nudge Jade. *It's not powerful stuff,* I mouth.

What? she says.

Just ... I pat the air.

Kelly turns his gaze on us finally, observing our faces as if through fog.

"So," I say. "Coach." I shift around on the floor. "I won't lie—I didn't expect you tonight. You knocked me for a loop there. But listen to this." I touch Jade's arm. "She's smart. And she has a sense about things. She'll help us out." I bet Kelly believes this when I say it, since hearing the words exit my throat, feeling the strength in Jade's lean arm, I myself believe it absolutely. This is true even though I don't know where exactly I'm taking this. It's true even though I distrust where I'm taking this. I say, "Believe me, Leo, she's a resource. We're lucky she's here."

Studying Jade, Kelly says, "Fine. So what do you know about them? What have you got for us?"

"What have I ...?" Jade glances at me. "I don't really ..."

"Mysteries," Leo says. "*Mysteries*. What lives behind the living. What do you know about them?"

I say, "Coach, wait a second. Jade doesn't know about this stuff specifically. She's a soils person. She's a scientist."

"A *what?* Darrow, what the hell?"

I start to see it then. Ugly as it is, there's an angle here. I say, "She knows this place, Leo. Do you understand? She knows the land. She knows these forests."

Kelly stares at me.

"Let's put it this way. She knows where things are *found*, Coach. In all of those forests out there. She knows."

"Hang on." Jade touches her forehead. "What is this? What are we talking about?"

"Is that true?" Leo says.

"I don't know," Jade says, "what's going on."

"It'll make sense," I say. "It's confusing at first, but we're looking for something out there. That's all this is."

"Out where?"

"In those woods by Azalea Street," I say. "Or out north of town. We're not sure."

"I am so lost," Jade says.

"Well, but you're not lost in the woods, right? That's where you can help us, Jade. What did you tell me the other day? I wouldn't believe what you know about the woods?"

"About dirt," she says.

"Dirt's in the woods, though. You know what I mean. And you're no slouch out there. Coach, ask Jade how much time she's spent in the woods."

Jade studies me then. It's like she's never seen me before tonight, and maybe she hasn't. I give her a look that says: *Go with it.*

"Well?" Leo says.

Jade flops her hands. "I've been in the woods. Sure."

"How much?" Kelly says.

"Lots. Lots and lots."

"And she's committed," I say. "Look at her tooth."

"What?" they both say.

I laugh. "Sorry, Jade. But you busted your tooth out there, didn't you? Tell Coach how it happened. Or I'll tell him. She was climbing a mountain, Leo. She was working in the woods. And Jade, did you turn back?"

She touches her lip where the incisor is missing.

"When your tooth got knocked out of your head," I say, "did you turn back?"

"No," Jade says.

"I don't know if you two see this," I say. "But it's right in front of us. All the pieces. Leo, what keeps going wrong? When we go out there, what happens?"

"We don't find him," Kelly says.

"Exactly. We don't."

"Him?" Jade says. "Who's him?"

"Now why is that? *Why* don't we find him? Because I think I know, Leo. We don't find him because we keep running out there like dipshits in the middle of the night, zooming all over the place. You see what I mean? Maybe that doesn't work."

Leo's silent. Jade's eyebrows perch high on her forehead.

"But now," I squeeze Jade's knee, "we have a scientist with us. You understand? She'll help us, Coach. She'll give us what we need and that's *method*. Let's get precise about this. Let's map it out. Grid it out." I smack the knuckles of one hand into the palm of the other. "Until it works, Leo. Until we find him."

"We're going now," Kelly says. "Tonight."

"No," I say. "We're not. Because we always do that and we fuck it up. We're going tomorrow, first thing."

"Tomorrow?" Jade says. "Scott, you're going—"

"This comes first," I say. "This first."

Leo mops a hand down his face. He stares out the window.

"We'll take you home, Coach," I say. "Jade and I. You work on this tonight. You pray and get close to him. And you rest. We'll need your ears tomorrow, so you can hear what he says. In the meantime, I'll bring Jade up to speed."

"Goddamn it," Leo says.

"If it hurts," I say, "that's a good sign. You're earning it."

In the car, Kelly rides silently in the backseat, his face floating in my rearview with streetlights and shadows swimming over it. Jade watches Terrace Street go by. After we drop Leo at his place, I say: "We're not doing any of that shit, by the way. Don't worry."

Jade peers at me. "What?"

I lift a hand off the wheel. "Leo's nuts. Which I'm sure was obvious. I had to get him home and get him to sleep, that's all. I'll call him from the airport and tell him it's off."

"Wait." Jade frowns in the dark. "So all that stuff at your place. That was bullshit?"

"It wasn't bullshit. It's what I had to tell him."

"What you had to tell him," Jade says.

Fog Harbor goes by.

"Anyway," I say. "You're off the hook. That's the point."

"No I'm not," Jade says.

"What?"

"I'm not off any hooks. I said I'd be there."

"Yeah, but he's not right, Jade. The rules are different with someone like him. You're fine."

We drive in silence, First Street floating by, and the wharf. North of town, thick forest closes over us. As I pull into Jade's driveway, the glowing log in her yard blobs my windshield with color.

"I can't believe this," she says.

"You don't have to do it, Jade. Come on."

"What's it all even about? He's looking for something? Then he's looking for some guy?"

"Leo's insane. It's about nothing."

"Well," Jade says. "I'll find out, won't I?"

"Jade..."

"It's cool. What do I have going on?"

After a while, I say, "Listen to me. If you do this, he'll expect you to keep doing it. For a few days, at least. Okay? And you'll feel obligated, since he's a sad old fuck. Just forget about it. I'll take care of it."

"I can do it for a few days," Jade says. "Who cares? You're gone anyway."

The engine hums, then subsides again. "Also," I say, "if you do it, you have to make sure he doesn't get around other people. I know that's stupid, but he can't. He can't go to campus, either. Even if that's his job."

Jade watches me in the dark car, rain tapping the roof.

"I'm sorry about all this," I say. "I feel like shit." And I do.

"You know," Jade says. "This whole thing works out okay for Hoots Darrow, though, doesn't it?"

"What?"

She laughs. "But you didn't plan it that way. A guy like you? No way."

We sit together, Jade patting her thighs. Then her hands stop. "Couldn't you have asked me instead, Scott? Would it have killed you to ask? This is me. I'm your friend."

"Jade…"

She unbuckles. "Forget it. I'll take care of your guy for you. Good luck in New York."

Jade moves through the rain to her house. The door closes behind her and the porchlight goes dark.

24.

DR. GOODWIN and his pod of lesser suits, which fins along in his wake, leaping and splashing and chirping and frolicking, feasting on the scad Goodwin churns up, want to sit me at a conference table in Founders Hall, snow racing past the windows' gray trees, reading down my vitae while every few items, hands in my lap, I supply tidy nods. And I'm happy to sit here for this.

"PhD," one suit says, "Leadership and Administration. Ohio State University."

I nod.

"Assistant Athletic Director, Kenyon College. Associate Athletic Director for Compliance, Washington State University."

"That's correct."

"Member-at-large, Pac-12 Competition Committee. Member-at-large, Pac-12 Governance Committee. Committee for Institutional Integrity, Washington State University."

Down the table, a suit with explosive curly hair brings her copy of my vitae to her face. "And I'm seeing here ..." She clutches the paper to her breast, as if scandalized. "Leonard Kelly. Appointed Head Basketball Coach, Fog Harbor Community College. That's *the* Leo Kelly? From Iowa?"

"I don't always believe it myself."

"Incredible. Landing Leo Kelly at a junior college." The suit glances around at her colleagues, then casts away the vitae. "Incredible."

I say, "He's lost some games. But I've never seen anything like the culture he's building."

"It must be something."

"It," I say, "is something."

"Student-Athlete Engagement Committee, Washington State University," another suit says, tapping his chin.

Preliminaries exhausted, Goodwin at the far end of the table raises his wrists into view, adjusting his cufflinks. "So," he says. "Dr. Darrow. How far is this for you, anyhow?" The man's spectacles like his person generally are efficient; at this distance, they practically vanish from his face, reappearing now and then as stabs of glare.

"To get here, you mean?"

"It's a mighty journey, Seattle to Albany. And unless I'm mistaken, you're not quite in Seattle?"

"It would make more sense," I say, "as a one-way ticket. If that's what you're asking." The laughs around the room, small laughs, are like playing cards I've knocked on the table and dealt to these mannequins. Dealing one lastly to myself, the group shares a moment so airy and fine that it could be miles, miles away from us. It feels miles away.

"Very good," Goodwin says. "Quite good." He straightens the corners of some papers, then folds his hands on the table. "Well, Scott, you can expect a relaxed few days here. We'll have you in meetings. We'll have you in meals. It won't be anything you haven't been through before, though I do hope our institution makes an impression on you."

"And likewise," I offer another tidy nod, "likewise. I'm grateful to be here."

"Now you haven't visited our campus before, unless I'm mistaken? I believe you said you'd never traveled to this part of the country."

"I went skiing once," I say. "At Killington."

"Well." Pushing back from the table, Goodwin gestures for everyone to stand. "You'll have to forgive us if this echoes that experience. Your skiing experience." Pulling on his wool coat, Goodwin nods at the blizzardy windows. "But let's show you our humble grounds."

Without exception, the dozen of us wear black overcoats out into the storm, where gray dormitories float past on the ghostly, blowing quad like a memory of dorms. Sculptures, trees and hibernating fountains vanish in the whiteout just as abruptly as they appear, and I'm aware that even with Fog Harbor, Washington as a reference point, one could not call Albany any Shangri-La of weather. Trotting ahead of us, skidding slightly, one of the suits begins backpedaling and pointing shit out to me, shouting over the wind. Hearing zero of what he says, I nevertheless furnish nods, less tidy now than engrossed, impressed. The group halts to rewrap its scarves, and down the hill, past Leighton's chapel spires, I glimpse what could be Albany's downtown, or else is just some accidental geometry aligning in the murky sky. Or else is both. Farther out, I catch sight of the Hudson until sheets of snowfall curtain it off. No—no Shangri-La by any means. But interviewing candidates in December like this, Goodwin risks alienating a chunk of his talent pool, and once the search concludes and the milk-livered have scattered, you can rightly guess who will remain, standing thigh-deep in New York drifts, carving up the air with his nodding chin.

Again walking, my docent shouts, "It's not always like this, Dr. Darrow! We do get sun!"

"How bad are your winters?" I yell, and the laughs race out of their mouths like birds.

—

After dinner, and after the one cocktail I nurse with my hosts, using the occasion to massage into our banter the first name of every suit around the table (one's own name being to any ear the sexiest utterance on earth), I Lyft back to the Beverwyck to try Jade on her phone, wherever her escapades with Kelly have taken her. It's 5:00 p.m. in Washington, but already it'd be dark there and the forecast for Fog Harbor, when I check it, is nasty: ice and wind overnight, snow tomorrow. Shitty weather is what you want when babysitting Leonard Kelly, unless he's feeling indomitable about the conditions (which he reliably does), in which case shitty weather is everything you don't want. More importantly, Jade by now could want or not want other things that I need badly to hear about, even if they scare me. The call rings forever then reaches her voicemail. I toss away my phone and chew a pen cap, my heels on the Beverwyck desk.

Outside, I notice that Albany's blizzard has quit, and the city platted out five stories below could be an arrangement of glass, for all its glinting and stillness and evident fragility. Across the street, in a park, the snow under bare trees snaps green, yellow, red and green with the cycling of a traffic signal. A pedestrian steps into the street, gazes around at everything, then continues to the far curb. My phone in ten minutes hasn't chirped, buzzed or glowed, and spitting away the pen cap, I pace through the room, chewing my lip instead. Dropping back in the chair, I spend a moment appraising these accommodations that Leighton

U has arranged, which are fine, just fine, though which truthfully are far shabbier than one would expect from "the best hotel in New York State not in New York City," per one of the suits' impassioned reviews of it. My eye follows, along the baseboards, a blotchy eczema of chipped paint; it vanishes behind the dresser then resumes on the other side. The undersides of my socks, in the mirror over the desk, are sooty with the grime they've scuffed up from Beverwyck carpets. From the wall's analog thermostat to the egg-colored phone with its Jolly Rancher of a message light to the appalling duvet Peter Muraro himself might have stitched together from a sampling of his best ties, Ye Olde Hotel they've put me in amounts basically to a holdover from 1990 that the present century soon will purge. Raising a heel, I kick the desk phone idly, though it goes nowhere on its felt pads. My own phone, lying on the bed, isn't cooperating either. "Jade, Jade Jade Jade," I say, with no ear around to hear me. Then I lurch from the chair, yank on my coat and shoes and head out.

I could loiter downtown, gulping bourbon with coarser manners than I nibbled that cocktail with earlier. I could puff twenty cigs. The Knicks are playing, and seeking out a brotherhood of Albanians, I could scream and bitch at a TV, pounding the bar top for bourbons three, four and five (unless this is a Celtics town, which it could be, who knows?). Instead, my Lyft arrives at the curb and I sail up the hill again, toward Leighton, cruising through intersection after intersection that could be two streets meeting in any city in America but a lovely one.

The driver taps his screen. "Fairlawn and Western?"

It's this address or another; I've dropped a pin indiscriminately in the neighborhoods near campus, where I've decided I'll buy a home soon.

"That the address?" the guy says.

Leighton floats by, its chapel underlighted spookily, like a face. I watch it until I can't anymore. "Yeah," I say. "Sure."

There's no music playing, but the heat blowing from the vents, the buzzing tires and swish of my driver's jacket as he fidgets in his seat roar in my ears compared to the brittle silence of walking alone up Fairlawn Street, three minutes later, the asphalt and parked cars glittering under streetlamps and the crunch of ice underfoot more probing the silence than breaking it. Gold-lighted living rooms in Fairlawn's colonials, federals, whatever they are, drift by like a train I don't hold a ticket for. Except you'd better believe I hold a ticket. Goodwin in his armband and visor is punching it now, clipping it to my seat, and pretty soon some other poor fuck will be lurking out in the cold, peeping in at my life.

It's on another street, off Fairlawn, that I come eventually to a steep barn roof overhanging a deep porch, like a forehead, every window of which porch shines with flawless, edged light. Behind its windows, the house contains nearly nothing besides this light, and what it does contain likewise is flawless, edged, sheer: the knifeish contour of a low sofa, a foyer table on match-stick legs, above which hangs a canvas with three or four licks of paint, nothing more. Over the concrete hearth, a vast TV's physical reality dissolves purely into swarming color—a hockey game. "This," I hear myself say. Watching the house, I discover that even the gentleman who carries his drink out from the kitchen to watch hockey is edged and clean, in a mellow sweater. Benefitting as this man does from his home's godly light, it's doubtful I'll escape his attention should I walk up his driveway and ascend the porch, yet here I come.

Softly, I creep along the porch to the first window, the light falling from which practically exhales cool breath, like a waterfall. This homeowner who isn't Scott Darrow but soon will be stands at a slanting view through the glass, his slipper propped on the hearth, and what the fuck am I after here, anyhow? Is there no better use of my time? When I take another step, a security light snaps on at my movement and that is quite enough: skipping off the porch, skidding down the icy driveway, I start up the street.

"Hey!" the man shouts from his open door. I walk faster. At the end of the block, glancing back, I see the guy watching me from his mailbox, roughing his arms in that sweater. And that'll do it for fucking skulking around tonight, since Ed Goodwin himself probably lives around here, along with the rest of Leighton's brass. "Christ, Scott," I mutter, rounding the corner and digging out my phone to get a Lyft. Of all people, I should understand how unsympathetic college administrators are to dickheads pestering the locals.

—

I try Jade from my room later, with midnight in Albany diffusing whitely through the curtains and a salt truck down in the streets grinding gears up the hill. *This is Jade's phone. I'm busy, but if you ...* Trying again, I reach her immediately. "Scott," she answers. "It's fine. I'm handling it. Stop calling."

"Jade," I say.

"Go back to sleep. What time is it there?"

"I'm not calling about Leo. How are you doing?"

The line's quiet until Jade says, "Not calling about Leo. So you get to say that, but also you get to sneaky check on Leo, huh? Since if something was wrong, I'd have to tell you about it."

"Listen. Don't tell me shit about that guy. I want to hear how you're doing."

"Fine," Jade says. "I'm pissed. Other than that, I'm having fun."

"You're what?" I say.

"I am, I'm pissed off. You used me."

"You're having *fun?*"

"Are you trying to weasel again, Hoots? You're trying to get me to say something about Leo."

"No," I say. "No no no. Forget it."

"He's not crazy," Jade says. "I'll tell you that much. He's sad and he's weird, but he's not crazy."

"Okay."

"And yeah, I'm having fun. He's a gentle old horse, Scott. We hiked around today. He didn't even ask where you were. I dropped him at his house a few minutes ago."

Which actually is everything I needed to know regarding Kelly. "Well," I say. "Let's stop talking about him. I'm calling because I fucked up, Jade. Okay? I don't expect you to believe it, and it doesn't matter, but I didn't mean to push this off on you."

"How's the interview going, Hoots?"

"Jade ..."

"Okay," she says. "Fine. You didn't mean to."

Grabbing one of the pillows, I press it on my face and speak to Jade from the darkness underneath it. "Like I said, it doesn't matter. And I wouldn't believe it, either, in your shoes. But I just—Jade, I do this shit. I don't know why. I always do it."

Jade laughs. "You don't know why? You don't have any idea?"

I lob the pillow across the room.

"You can't be peaceful, Scott. That's why."

"I'm sorry. That's all I want to say. I'm sorry."

"Thank you," Jade says.

The salt truck grinds through Albany, its yellow lights licking at the curtains.

"I'm seeing him again tomorrow," Jade says, "if the weather holds off. Then you're back Friday."

"Yeah."

"So we'll see, Scott. Does that work for you? We'll see."

"I wish this hadn't happened."

Jade's silent awhile. Then she says, "There's a lot of that going around."

—

It's late Thursday, standing outside a chophouse in snow blowing off the Hudson, after meetings and lunch and meetings and meetings and dinner—a day of hurtling through Albany—that Goodwin grips my palm, pumping it thoughtfully, and says, "I'll hand it to you, Dr. Darrow, I really will. You knocked our socks off."

"It was a special trip," I say.

A courtesy vehicle idles at the curb, its driver muttering into his Bluetooth; opening the back door, Goodwin offers me the chariot gallantly. I say, "Though, Ed. If you'll forgive a blunt question—"

He nods. "Fifty-fifty. It's a coin flip, Scott."

"Fifty-fifty."

Goodwin surveys the snowy street, rubbing his chin. He twirls his hand. "We're interviewing four. Two are serious. You're one of those."

"I'm comfortable with that," I say.

"You should be. And you should feel confident. You checked every box, Scott."

"Though if it had to be," I say, "sixty or forty. Are we talking more like sixty?"

Goodwin chuckles at this. We both do, but I don't withdraw the question.

"I'd say it's about at that fifty number." Goodwin winks. "Maybe fifty-five. You'll hear from us soon."

"I enjoyed this, Dr. Goodwin." We shake again. Gathering my jacket, stepping into the car, I think: *You cagey son of a bitch.*

I didn't see it coming, but for the first time in weeks, twenty-four hours now stretches ahead of me with nothing hanging over it. Leo is seen to, there aren't meetings left to negotiate nor hands left to squeeze. No more nodding. Goodwin will call, and probably sooner rather than later, but I can't do any more to shape the nature of that call, and anyhow he won't ring before my flight leaves Albany tomorrow. I haven't heard from Harrington. That means Rod Toren is happy or else dead of old age—either is cool—and means as well that Tom Moses probably is on ice till after Christmas. Peter Muraro and his twelve apostles don't play till the twenty-seventh. What else?

Well, I know what else.

Certainly, I know what else. But she said, "We'll see, Scott," and now I should keep my hands off my phone, since beyond *I'm sorry, I'm sorry,* there's nothing else I can tell Jade. Or there is. There's always more that Scott Darrow can tell a person, plenty more, and it's for this reason I'll keep my hands off my phone tonight, and just munch this can of Pringles at the Beverwyck Hotel, guzzling beer and watching Bergeron and Marchand fly over the ice. Maybe I'll step out for cigs, though more likely I'll think better of that, since a Leighton suit could spot me at the register. I'll relax here, staining this Beverwyck duvet with Pringles grease, and I won't call Jade. Because, hearing her voice, I can't trust myself to say words that are simply dependable words, and not a bouquet of one thing concealing thorns of another.

The TV fritzes, it being a dinosaur Hitachi that Beverwyck management, thirty years ago, likely ordered from the same

Montgomery Ward catalog where they found: *Panasonic speed-dial phone plus answering machine function.* Bergeron divides into three Bergerons, carving ice like synchronized triplets, before tightening back into himself. "Fucking thing," I say, chucking a Pringle at the screen. No sooner does the chip fall to the carpet than the phone I just mentioned, on the desk, bursts into shrill, mean ringing, its red light flashing in duplicate: once on the console itself and once in the mirror behind it. And I can't move. The ringing and flashing quit and still I can't move, since this exactly was the ringing in 2F last week, that night I wasn't asleep, yet was—that night that a landline wasn't out in my kitchen, yet was.

The phone rings again, then quits. The light flashes and quits. Leaving my beer, crossing the room, I stand over the desk with my hand ready. On the next ring, I snatch the receiver to my ear. "What? What is it?"

"Sir? Mr. Darrow?"

"Who is this?"

"Mr. Darrow, I have you listed for checkout tomorrow morning, December twenty-first. This is a hospitality call to verify that—"

I drop the receiver into its cradle. And nobody else calls and the TV is fine and ultimately the Bruins top the Senators 4-2. I finish the chips and beer, and with the phone not ringing, the console light doesn't flash, either. Still, the atmosphere of a message chokes the room. Something like this was bound to happen, wasn't it? Sooner or later, in Washington State or New York, or in another state or another, I was going to find myself in a tired room, and the old things in that room would speak to me. So it's not startling—really this is fair and even overdue— when my own phone, later, buzzes with a number that I don't recognize. A Florida number. And it was always going to be Florida, or else Hawaii.

"This is Scott," I say.

With no affect, a voice says, "I'm trying to reach a Mr. Scott Darrow. Son of Becky Hodges."

"You can say it," I say. "Go ahead. Say it."

25.

WHEN IT CAME, the call about my mom should have come from her husband, Doug, who would be grief-stricken and blubbering and to whom I'd have no clue what to say, since the woman he'd be mourning would be a person I hadn't known in my life—a Doug-wife, which my mom became only after putting behind her the years we'd spent together, in Colorado, Montana and Cleveland. Losing Mom would be terrible, but who would this Becky Hodges be? I don't know any Hodges, and never visited anyone in Clearwater, Florida. Even calls with my mom became scarce after the invitation she mailed for hers and Doug's wedding (which contained the only photo I ever saw of my stepdad, actually) went onto my windowsill in Gambier, Ohio, where I worked at Kenyon, before going deep in the trashcan instead, and going unanswered. No doubt about it: Doug's call about my mom would wreck me. But it would embarrass me, too, like eavesdropping on a stranger's call to a stranger's surviving son.

But Doug didn't call about Mom. It was a hospital counselor who called. And when the counselor transferred me to Records, they confirmed the information the counselor had: no Douglas Hodges listed anywhere in Becky Hodges' paperwork. No Doug, no *D* initial. Their file for Becky dated back just two years, but in all that time, she'd marked her forms *single*. The only contact she'd listed was a Scott A. Darrow of Pullman, Washington. "Her son, it looks like," the clerk said.

"Got it," I said.

She transferred me back to the counselor, who after some grieftalk worked his way up to saying: "So. Mr. Darrow."

"What?"

"It's the last thing you want to think about, I appreciate that. But we need to know how to proceed."

—

By the time I land at Tampa International, after driving to LaGuardia for a redeye, they've moved Mom to the home I found online, whose reviews checked out and who also answered the phone when I called at midnight—though such places, I suppose, always expect a call. Beyond the home, I also found online, while waiting at the gate in New York, a small item in the Pinellas County archives: REBECCA L. HODGES V. DOUGLAS T. HODGES, DIV. GRANTED FEBRUARY 2017. Which doesn't say much, but says it all.

In the rental car, I navigate among Florida's nail salons, bungalows and drainage ditches, with a silky morning collecting up in the palms, until I arrive at a yellow cinderblock building with ironwork over its windows. One car waits in the lot, predictably a Lincoln. Because what but a Lincoln accompanies architecture like this, and out of what but a huge Lincoln steps the sort of man who handles bodies in Florida?

Though Ted is younger than he sounded on the phone—my age, maybe. In a collar and tie, his hands composed, he waits near his car till I exit mine, then steps forward to greet me. "Scott, I take it? Becky's son? This is a difficult time." Following the man inside, I glance up at the whitish sky and think how strange it is that here another day breaks over Florida, and though my mom saw all the days on this earth since 1952, this one won't find her.

Ted leads us through his lobby and up the hall, lights flickering on. In rooms left and right, I notice without wishing to the galleried urns, casket corners and plush linings. More rooms wait farther back.

In Ted's office, I suppress my judgments about his basic, dull furniture, outmoded color schemes, chintzy picture frames and lone window obstructed by iron filigree. The only way through this place is straight through it, without lingering on details.

Once we're settled, Ted says, "You made it here quickly, Scott. I'm touched by that. Your mother would be touched."

"Right," I say.

"A son's love. Though I can't tell you how many…" Ted winces. "Well, this is Florida. You understand."

"Excuse me?"

"Oh, it's just … a lot of elderly folks here. And their children—their adult children—don't always come running."

A door slams somewhere in the building. Voices drift past Ted's office, and whoever the voices belong to, they jangle keys and open another door up the hall. I don't care at all, not at all, to imagine what waits for them behind that door, when they flick on the lights.

Perhaps following my thoughts (I'm not the first bereaved son to sit in this chair), Ted quickly says, "So what questions do you have, Scott? That's mostly what this is today. We'll have items to discuss, but what are your questions?"

I shift in the chair. "They already told me what happened," I say. "Basically."

Ted says, "Do you have questions about the circumstances? I'll answer what I can."

I don't know whether I have questions like that or not. Nobody has explained anything to me, but besides the principal thing, what is there to discuss? "They said a neighbor found her?" I say.

Ted nods, closing his eyes. "That's my understanding. They had a time they met, a regular time. Becky didn't arrive and the neighbor checked in on her."

"They said a medical event. That's all they said."

"That's the information that I have, too. A physician's chart usually offers more details, if you wish to obtain that. I can help with the process."

"Medical event is fine." I chew my lip. Ted contemplates me.

"So she's here?" I say. "You brought her here?"

"We did. Last night."

I think about the lights and tables and hands in that next room. I think about surgical masks, tubes, pans and drains. "So am I supposed to ... I mean, is there ...? I've never done this before. Is there something I need to ... with her?"

"You're asking about identification?"

"Is that what I need to do?" I say.

Ted shakes his head. "That's not necessary. You do have the opportunity, if you like, to provide clothes for a viewing. And we welcome input about preparation. But none of this is obligatory. We'll take care of anything you'd rather not. Or aren't able to."

"Just tell me," I say, "what I need to do."

"Pardon?"

"What's the first thing that I need to do here?"

By mid-morning, I've answered Ted's questions, paid a deposit and left the man to his duties—the man and those people in the back room. Not bothering with breakfast, I go to my mom's house to dispense with affairs there. I'm to collect clothes and makeup, and also sort through her files, though I wouldn't know which documents were the needed ones if I held them in my hands. Not that I can even access Mom's house, lacking a key. Fuck it. I'll figure it out.

It's driving to Mom's house that I call my dad in Hilo for the first time this year, with the year nearly finished. It's 5:00 a.m. Hawaii Time, and if Gerald Darrow is anything at seventy like he was at forty-five, he's as likely to be awake still as awake already. But he's asleep when I reach him.

"Scotty," he mumbles. "What's happening, bud?"

"Did anybody call you yet, Dad? Did the hospital call?"

"Hospital? What's going on?"

"Dad—"

"What are you talking about, hospital? What happened?"

"She died, okay? Mom died. In Florida."

He's silent awhile. Then he says, "Goddamn."

"I didn't know if anybody would call you. But you should know about it."

"Where are you at, Scotty? Christ, that's hard news. Becky. Where are you?"

"I'm in Tampa."

"Was she sick, or did she ...? We didn't keep in touch."

"She wasn't sick, she just died. Listen, I don't have much to say about it. You just needed to know."

"Okay," Dad says. "Okay."

"If there's anything you can think of, if you have any ..." I squeeze my eyes, "... I don't know. Wishes or something. Let me know."

"What do you mean, wishes?"

"I don't know what I mean. Forget it."

"Scotty, I don't know that having wishes—for your mom, I mean—is my place anymore."

"Yeah, I didn't know it was my place, either. Okay, Dad."

"How are you holding up, bud? I remember losing my mom. Those were hard days."

"I've got a lot to do here, Dad."

"Okay," he says, "okay."

"I'll see you."

"Don't be a stranger, Scotty," he says.

—

It's a shotgun house off Drew Street, with a Mazda in the drive and dwarf palm in the yard, and nothing about the place advertises at all that my mom died here yesterday. Traffic drifts by. The flowerboxes are weeded. Even Mom's sprinklers kick on as I work my way around the property, jiggling doors and peering in windows. It's not lost on me, at this queer moment, that my life lately and perhaps going forward and perhaps all along could be summarized as a succession of homes to which I'm denied entry.

I try hoisting a rear window, and am making headway when a woman in gardening pants strolls over from the next yard, plucking gloves from her fingers. She's an old woman, bony and papery. Sidestepping the sprinklers, she says, "My, my. It's been an eventful few days over here."

I release the window, leaving it wedged in the jambs.

"You're Becky's boy," the woman says. "Or else you're a posh burglar."

I gesture at the house. "I don't have a key."

"No, I expect you wouldn't. What would've been the use in that? You need something from inside?"

In this suit I wore yesterday and last night on the plane, and in this muggy air, lacking sleep, food or coffee, I'm not explosive enough to send this granny packing and simply kick in the window, though I'd like to. So I say, "Just a few things."

Tossing her gloves in the grass, the woman digs keys from her pocket. "Let's go," she says. "I wanted to poke in later anyway."

—

In the front room, daylight spills across Mom's Saltillo tile floor, around the edges of which stands rattan furniture, a potted plant and bookshelves. A ceiling fan turns. If not messy, Mom's house isn't neat, either, with a cushion dangling somewhat off the sofa, a crumb-dusted plate on the table and shoes littered around. The closet where I'll find Mom's dresses and things, along with the medicine cabinet where I'll find cosmetics (my plan with the makeup being to sweep every tube, cream, compact and brush into a plastic bag, which I'll present to Ted like a shot rabbit for him to skin), waits for me up the hall, probably. Any file cabinets should be back there, too. But a minute passes and I'm right where I started, in the foyer.

"Quite understandable," Mom's neighbor says. "Very much so. It's not easy."

I start toward the hall. "I'll just be a minute."

But she touches my arm. "Don't do that. This all just happened. Don't rush yourself."

I linger there. "I should get started," I say.

"Do you want to hear something?" The woman lifts her chin at me, her eyebrows raised. "If you'd have told Becky—yesterday, I mean—that her son would be here tomorrow, she'd have been the happiest gal in Florida."

I stand in the foyer.

"You could have mentioned the dying part, even. She'd have preferred that happen *second*, I'm sure. But otherwise, it'd have struck her as a fair deal. I'm certain of it."

"Okay," I say.

"Scott. It's Scott, isn't it? I'm just talking about your mom. I'll miss her."

"Do you know where she kept her files?"

Taking my wrist, the woman leads me into the living room. "Let's forget," she says, "about files for now."

"I've got to get started."

"No. You've got to sit on this sofa with me." Straightening the cushions, adjusting pillows, the woman indicates where I should sit. I don't. But eventually I do, and arranging herself beside me, smoothing her trousers, the woman gazes around at Mom's bright, silent room and turning fan. "Isn't that better?" she says.

A moment passes. Then the woman nudges my leg like she knows me. "She's closer now. Becky is, when we sit like this."

That's a stretch. But the sofa is comfy and sleep could be closer, with this fan chopping lazily and breezes floating through the door.

"She hated this house, you know," Mom's neighbor says.

My head is as heavy as a watermelon. "What?"

"It was like jail to her. I don't know why. She kept the place perfect, all her books and things. But get some wine in Becky and she stared daggers into these walls. She wanted to burn the place down."

It's not the question I've come to Florida to ask, but I hear myself asking it anyway. "How was she?" I say.

"Hmm?"

"My mom. Was she okay?"

The woman thinks about it. "Your mom," she says, "was okay. Yes."

"You can tell me."

"I am telling you."

"You don't need to make it into some nice thing," I say.

The woman sets her hand on the sofa between us, like an item. "I don't know what you want me to say. Was your mom clicking her heels in the streets?" She scoffs at this. "Who do you see doing that?"

I imagine her then, my mom who was Becky Hodges, tilting a watering can over this fern in her house. Running a fingertip down the spines of novels. Night falling in her windows. The phone on her wall.

"Everything considered," Mom's neighbor says, "she carried it off beautifully. You've never seen a woman so proud of a house she hated. And always put together. Becky would iron her gloves just to weed the—"

My phone buzzes, and lacking the stamina for excuses, I just walk out of the house and into the yard to answer it. "Jade," I say.

"Hoots. Am I interrupting?"

"I'm just traveling."

"Okay. Well, this isn't me asking permission—don't think that. But Leo wants to hit up Portland today to see his kid. So we're going."

The sprinklers finished, Mom's yard shimmers with bright globs. Across the street, other sprinklers snap rainbows into the sun. "His kid," I say.

"Yeah, his son. He lives in Portland."

"His kid."

Eventually, Jade says, "Scott?"

I watch the sprinklers across the street. I watch the sky, where palms, powerlines and cell towers jumble together. "What does he want with him?" I say.

"What?"

"He wants to see his kid. What does he want with him?"

"I think," Jade says, "he wants … to see him? What are you asking?"

Mom's neighbor steps onto the porch. I walk farther into the yard.

"Scott?" Jade says.

And I did, Mom. If you can believe me, I did, at least for a morning, have something for you. You never had me, but I flew down here and for a few hours, I stayed. You'll know this song, though, won't you? You'll know the words to this one: a phone rings, and it turns out Scott's life is elsewhere. I couldn't break news to you that's less startling than that: your son's life is elsewhere.

"Scott?" Mom's neighbor calls after me.

Climbing into the car, pulling into the street, I say: "That's terrific, Jade. About Leo's son, I mean. Like you said, Coach is a sad guy. This is great news for him."

Jade says, "I wasn't sure you'd feel that way."

I say, "Hold off just a day. One day. I'll be back tonight, and we can ..."

26.

So long as I'm Athletic Director at Fog Harbor Community College, Leonard Kelly will not travel to Portland to visit any human being—son, uncle, cousin, whatever. He doesn't visit people, because Leo with people fucks me up. As for Michael? Michael will be in Portland after I'm gone (or as in Portland as he ever was, since this latest "illumination" from Kelly likely strays no nearer to reality than anything else the man has said). Once I'm gone, Leo can cruise to the Rose City to say, do, catalyze as he pleases. It won't be my carnival anymore.

But as of today, it's still my carnival.

Easing the Buick into Jade's driveway late Friday night, I find lights on in the house and see through the window the back of Kelly's head where he sits on Jade's sofa. And Jade O'Neil, she knows what this is from the moment she steps onto the stoop, closes the door behind her and walks into my headlights. She knows that I'm here to shut everything down, even if she's giving me a chance to be better than that—better than I am. But Jade, this is a chance to be who I am. That's all this is. It could be all anything is. Hugging her arms, she watches me exit the car with the engine running.

"We're not going to Portland, are we?" she says.

"Can you go get him, please?" I say.

Eventually, glancing around at the forest, Jade walks inside. While I'm waiting, I decide that I heard something on the drive here from SeaTac. Off in those woods along 111 with my windows down, I heard something about nakedness, or mystery. I heard something about prayer. Anyway, Portland is definitely where we're going. We are headed to Portland. But maybe let's check out this other thing first. Or something else, or something else.

—

Christmas night, after Harvey turns up again, shooing me off Leo with some fiddle-faddle about infirmity, compassion, et cetera, I skip the Reuben I've planned to order at Greta's and go instead to Long Pier Saloon. Fog Harbor's worst await me there, despite the holy day, hunched in their denim and caps and Neanderthal beards and perms. And I get bonkers drunk. I slap shoulders and shout stories and laugh, even if I'm wearing my Tag Heuer and an argyle scarf, and even if these salts of the earth would as soon be left to it, staring into drafts and heaps of pull-tabs. Soon enough, these will be Albany salts of the earth cutting me mean looks. I walk outside into gusts blowing off the harbor, and soon enough these freezing winds will be the Hudson's.

I keep an eye on them, Kelly and Harvey, holed up together on Terrace Street. Though I'm prepared at any moment to give chase, harrying these assholes back indoors like the freaks they are, days pass and they don't leave. From my perch across the street, on the neighbor's retaining wall, I see shadows behind Leo's blinds.

The night of the twenty-seventh, loading a livestream in my office, I watch Peter's Sea Lanterns blow a double-digit lead at Lower Columbia College in Longview. A smart piece of advice: don't give a bad team a lead any more than you would give fools money. It depresses them, and they can think only of squandering, squandering, squandering it, until they feel like themselves again. A bad team leading is a fool with money is a Dale Clark working his Power Five job. *Oh,* they all think. *No thanks. Not for me. Please take it away.*

As you would expect, Dajuan Simms exempts himself from this. His demeanor in the first half, while amassing their lead, deviates not at all once the lead is obtained and further doesn't deviate as his chicken-brained, dipshit teammates piss everything away. Dajuan just plays, and watching him from my office, I know for this kid that it's simply a matter of time. Any barrier could present itself; Dajuan would fall to it with a hammer and chisel, *tink, tink, tink*-ing until the thing crumbled and he moved right through it. I wonder what that young man will be.

You could as well argue that Odie's demeanor doesn't change, but that's only to say that he's careless about good basketball, needing as he does to broadcast how everything is elementary to him (the kid practically blows on his nail polish after sinking a bucket or swatting a lay-in into the stands), then is *extremely* careless about shitty basketball, needing to prove that it doesn't affect him. But I don't wonder what Odie will be. He's a worthless juco player. He'll be an ex-worthless juco player. His life will be various configurations of what I see now on my iPad: an LCC player strips the ball from him and bolts downcourt to score; Odie watches the play recede from him almost nostalgically, before strolling after it, scratching his ear.

"Good hustle, pal," I say.

This is facetious. But the whistle blows and who but Muraro vaults off the bench, trotting out to Odie with applause, nods and encouragement, none of it facetious in the least. It's a timeout, and Peter spends half the time with his arm ringing Odie's waist, speaking what I assume is self-help literature into the kid's ear. I say, "Pete, fuck you."

There is a world where I need Fog Harbor to win this game. Possibly I don't—who knows, until Goodwin calls?—but I would certainly breathe easier if they pulled it out. So, Peter, let's set aside your tender heart just for tonight. How does that sound? Your soaring humanity, high ideals and equally high horse—let's table all that. Be Mahatma Gandhi tomorrow. Because Pete. Peter. We know what's real, don't we? Between you and me, we know it. We know what's substance and what isn't, we know what works and what doesn't, and so for the next few minutes— just the next five minutes—how's about you retire your silly shit, fuck these kids up and win the game?

During a free throw, Muraro steps off the bench to rub Matty Martin's shoulders. I feel like I need an asthma inhaler. When an LCC kid drives the lane and Sam lumbers up to greet him like a fat St. Bernard, giving up the backdoor lob, Peter charges down the bench smacking high-fives, then charges back up the bench pumping his fist. "Great help, great help!" he shouts, and I tap down the iPad's volume.

"Get those handshakes ready," I tell the screen. "Time to be graceful losers."

Against the odds, and more through LCC's dereliction than Fog Harbor's resilience (two sorry teams like this will hot potato a lead, both frantic to rid themselves of it), we're down just two points with six seconds left. James snatches a rebound and calls timeout.

It won't matter. I might as well close the browser window. In the Fog Harbor huddle, I see despite the pixelated feed Peter's big grin swinging left and right like a tray of candies. Everybody take one. Take two! Everybody love me!, he's begging. And you don't win like that, Pete. Goddamn. Nothing good ever came from needing to feel good. What kind of child are you not to know that? Leaving the huddle, Muraro walks some distance onto the court, his arm again encircling Odie. Coddling Odie with love. And definitely nothing good ever came from doing that.

It's not a fancy play Peter's drawn up—his mind can't generate fancy. Odie simply trots to the top of the key, his hand aloft as if to receive the inbounds pass, before tucking neatly into a flare screen. Matty brushes off the screen, receives the inbounds pass and nails a three, game over. Easy as that. The shot was basic for a good shooter, however, and the inbounds pass wasn't hard; what won the game was a sound screen, a flare screen, and when the ball splashes through the net, the backboard zapping orange, Odie marches toward Fog Harbor's bench with his finger extended like a bayonet. Peter marches toward him from the other direction, his own finger extended, until they swat away each other's hands and hug and wrestle and laugh.

I toss aside the iPad, my office silent and still. And I'm glad we won. I am. Finding yourself on the winning end of things—what beats that?

—

Fuck Tom Moses, since the phone rang this morning and I accepted the Leighton job. The numbers were right, everything was right. So Moses can be my guest. Come to Fog Harbor today if he likes. Ride along with Leonard Kelly to Portland for an afternoon of ghost hunting—naked, urban ghost hunting. Send Rod Toren the photos.

But Moses isn't coming, I learn. I'm leaving my office in Coleman Hall, shutting the door for what could be the last time (what from that office would I take with me? A mug?), when

Jeremy rises from his desk, his hands relaxed at his sides like a damn professional.

"What?" I say, pulling on my gloves.

Harrington stares at me, fighting off a grin.

"What?"

"I told him," he says, "that we liked it so much, his multimodal idea—"

"Told who?" I laugh. "What the hell are you talking about, Jeremy?"

He fidgets, readjusting his stance. "Moses. Tom Moses. When he called earlier, I told him that we liked his idea so much—his multimodal idea—that we wanted to do a movie with him. A documentary."

"You told him *what?*" I say.

"I know. I know, I know, I know. Hear me out."

"You definitely have my attention."

Harrington pats the air, soothing me. "It's all good. I told him we wanted to do a movie, and that he should look into production plans. A crew and everything. Studio stuff."

I study Jeremy.

"To which *Moses* says: I can't do that. I've got to stick to streamlined work. And I tell him, Cool. That's totally cool. But we're going movie-scale with Coach Kelly, so if he's not interested then we'll need to rain check with him. Exclusivity and all. We don't want to rain check—we're Tom Moses people over here—but that's where things stand."

Speaking of movies, Jeremy poses before me now with such dignity, such posture and gleam, that he could be an Oscar statuette.

"Well," I say. "Goddamn. Jeremy Harrington."

He laughs, only now breaking composure, slipping his hands into his pockets.

"Where did you learn to fuck with people like that?" I say. "Good for you." I start toward the elevator, adding another, "Good for you," over my shoulder.

Punching the button, I wait awhile in the hallway, adjusting my gloves. The elevator opens then closes again, dinging. I study myself in the brushed steel reflection. Then I walk back up the hall to Jeremy's desk.

The smile drains from his face. "What?" he says.

"What are you doing here, Jeremy?"

He shakes his head. "I don't—"

"You know what I mean. Fog Harbor. Why haven't you left?"

Harrington scratches his eyebrow.

I say, "Jeremy, a place like this, people like this, they'll—"

"My family's here," he says.

We're silent.

"I don't know what you want me to do. They're here, Scott. All of them."

After a while, he says, "Scott?"

I walk down the hallway to the elevator.

—

The extension cord lies in the grass, running from the outlet box to the driftwood, but she didn't wait long after Christmas to unravel her lights from the log and box them away. The unadorned wood looks accidental now, just something stranded by the tides. As I walk her yard, a balmy wind cruises off the harbor, months ahead of season, lipping waves and blowing ashore into the grass and trees. It's not a storm, but the house appears battened down anyhow. Every blind is lowered, the deck furniture gone. I don't even find joint leavings in the dirt near Jade's stoop. After trying the doorbell, I wander out onto the beach to view the house in its entirety. Today's wind, I decide, is carrying off Jade's flue smoke. That's why I don't see it. But I don't smell anything and the wind dies and there's no smoke rising from the flue. She went away somewhere. And the wind stirs again.

—

SeaTac allows tobacco in one area that I know of, down at the end of Departures. These should be good Camels tonight, with the weather fair and nobody around to give a shit. Hanging my garment bag from the NO PARKING sign, I tap one out and spark up. A raft of idiots happens along, wearing conical hats and blowing kazoos. They brought smokes of their own, certainly, but I toss them mine anyway, plus my lighter. If I still owned the Buick, I would toss them the keys to that. If they asked for a condo, I would sign over 2F.

The idiots break out vodka and mini champagnes. We toast and visit.

I fall asleep on my flight, curled under my suit jacket, then awake when some kids in another row start smacking their window, climbing over each other to peer down at Manitoba or wherever, at Michigan. There's nothing down there, but then I spot the fireworks they're jazzed about, little neon poofs inching westward on the black ground. "There's one!" one of the kids screams, attacking the plexiglass as if to break through it. His mom rests her chin on his shoulder.

A new year. And don't get me wrong, I'm relieved that midnight has passed, and now opening before me, over the eastern half of North America, is that vast, pure year—a wide valley of clean time. January first, two thousand something or other. Nearly my fortieth of these. Soon enough, dawn will break over Albany, and I'll fill up that city like the sun does, every corner of it. I'll fill up a house. I'll fill a campus. A new year, with last year in its grave.

"There!" the kid screams. "*There!*"

Deep in its grave. Though how confident are we, when bells clang at midnight, that those aren't the bells over that grave already tinkling? Memories wake up, after all. Count on that if you count on nothing else. They sneak ahead of us, far ahead, until we stumble at last into a sad town, or a forest without light in the sky. We haven't come this way before, and yet there's a knowing here, a shadow. More likely than not, we even could speak that shadow's name.

Until it goes again. Until it's gone. And off we go after it, chasing that name on our blistered feet. Such effort it took to outrun all those people. Then finally they outrun us.

ACKNOWLEDGEMENTS

A book starts with every feeling in the world and ends with just one of them: gratitude. Somehow, somehow, the world retreated to a respectful distance while I imagined not real people doing not real things. There's no accounting for luck like that. There's only gratitude.

So: Amy, thank you. Brady and Danny, thank you. Taxpayers of Kansas, thank you.

Not only did I get to write this book—Vine Leaves Press made it into a thing that strangers can hold in their hands. For that, thank you to Jessica, Amie, Melissa, JJ, and Alana.

The characters in this book run from love even while they're chasing it. For the most part, I haven't had to do that. Mom, Dad, and Joe, that's fundamentally because of you. Thank you.

I see trees outside my window today, and mountains and sky. There's something else out there, too, even if I don't know what to call it. But it has given me better years than anybody has any right to expect. What do you do with luck like that?

You bow your head. You say thanks.

VINE LEAVES PRESS

Enjoyed this book?
Go to *vineleavespress.com* to find more.
Subscribe to our newsletter: